PRAISE FOR MELISSA ESKUE OUSLEY'S
PITCHER PLANT

"A fun read that combines a classic haunted house story with romance and a very creepy serial killer."
—Hester Young, author of *The Gates of Evangeline* and
The Shimmering Road

"Melissa Eskue Ousley draws you into a drafty, old fixer-upper on the turbulent Oregon Coast with the perfect mix of creaking floors, creepy dolls, and mysterious footprints in the unfinished basement. She's crafted a suspenseful page turner that harkens back to childhood ghost stories with a touch of paranormal that will keep you guessing!"
—Kate Dyer-Seeley, author of *Scene of the Climb*

"Eskue Ousley skillfully weaves a tightly plotted tale with a memorable cast of characters, including an old house with secrets that won't stay buried--a riveting read that will keep you up at night!"
—Marian McMahon Stanley, author of *The Immaculate*,
a Rosaria O'Reilly mystery

"Seaside setting, haunted house (or is it?), creepy dolls—all the makings of a bewitching tale. Toss in a bit of romance and prepare to be up way too late, turning pages."
—Deb Vanasse, author of *Cold Spell* and *Out of the Wilderness*

PITCHER PLANT
A Pacific Northwest Suspense

Melissa Eskue Ousley

Filles Vertes Publishing, LLC

COEUR D'ALENE, ID

Melissa Eskue Ousley/Filles Vertes Publishing, LLC
Post Office Box 1075
Coeur d'Alene, ID 83816
www.fillesvertespublishing.com

Publisher's Note: This is a work of fiction. Names, characters, places, and incidents are a product of the author's imagination. Locales and public names are sometimes used for atmospheric purposes. Any resemblance to actual people, living or dead, or to businesses, companies, events, institutions, or locales is completely coincidental.

Pitcher Plant/ Melissa Eskue Ousley. -- 1st ed.
ISBN 978-1-946802-00-2
eBook ISBN 978-1-946802-01-9

For Chris, Aiden, and Elliot.
Always.

Chapter One

M y first thought after spotting the house was it had potential. The second was Mark was never going to go for it. If I'd known about the house's dark history, I wouldn't have wanted it either.

The online advertisement called the weathered gray house a "fixer-upper." That alone was enough to scare my husband off, but I hoped the price might appeal to him. After moving to the Oregon coast and beginning our search for a house, we soon learned our savings wouldn't go far in a real estate market located near the beach. Any halfway decent house seemed to be far beyond our means, and any house within our price range was sure to be tiny. With two small children and a dog, a one-bedroom beach shack wasn't going to cut it.

We found a three-bedroom ranch to rent. It had zero style, and the rent was high, but we decided we'd make it work until we found that elusive perfect house. Mark had a good job, and if I could just find a teaching position, we could save up for the down payment we needed. Unfortunately, that plan didn't come to fruition. As I was applying for a teaching job, both the local college and high school laid off faculty due to budget cuts. My not working was a problem long-term, but Mark and I were confident our savings could keep us afloat until I found a job or we found a place with lower rent.

That's where the fixer-upper came in. Priced well below market value, I discovered we had enough for a down payment, and the cost of our monthly mortgage would be less than the fortune we paid in rent. That revelation got Mark's attention. When I informed him the house was in our school district and two blocks from the beach, he agreed to call the owner to set up a showing.

Bob Peterson, the owner, said he'd bought the place a few years back in a government auction, and always meant to fix it up, but never got around to it. Mark asked him what needed repairs, and Mr. Peterson gave him a list—the roof leaked, the wiring needed upgrading, and the windows needed replacing. Mr. Peterson sheathed all the windows in plastic to keep moisture from seeping in during the coast's frequent winter storms. He was selling the house as it was, and that was why he set the price so low.

"The place was built in 1909," he told Mark, "and nothing's been done to it since. Gonna take a lot of work to bring the old girl into the twenty-first century."

When Mark relayed Mr. Peterson's message, I figured he'd cancel the showing. I was no expert on house repairs, but I knew enough to understand the repairs mentioned were pricey, and probably only the beginning of what would actually need to be renovated. But Mark was intrigued by the possibility of getting the house for cheap and selling it for much more later. The land alone was worth the price Mr. Peterson asked.

As we pulled up to the house, Mark got a call on his cell. He listened for a bit, nodding, and then pantomimed for me to hand him something to write with. I dug around in the glove box of the SUV for a pen, and Mark wrote a series of numbers on his hand.

After he hung up, I asked, "What was that all about?"

"Peterson," he replied. "He's stuck in Portland, so he can't drive down to meet us, Tawny."

"Oh," I said, disappointed. I'd been excited about getting a look at the inside of the house, but our adventure seemed ill-fated. "Did you reschedule?" I peered at his hand, trying to see if he'd written a date or a time.

Mark shook his head. "He said to go on in. There's a lock on the back door. He gave me the combination." He held up his hand, revealing the numbers 24-6-20.

I smiled at him. "Maybe it's better this way. We can check out the house without somebody breathing down our necks."

Mark nodded. "It'll be easier to make an honest assessment of it—see what really needs to be done to fix it up." He squinted at the house, his mouth set in a hard line. "I got the impression Peterson was glossing over things."

Although my DIY skills were limited, Mark's dad made his living renovating old houses. Mark would know if the repairs would be too much for us to handle. I had a feeling if the inside was okay, my husband might just be game for buying the house. But if he decided it was a no-go, there'd be nothing to convince him otherwise. Excited and anxious, I pulled my curly blond hair into a ponytail, grabbed my camera, and hopped out of the car. "Let's go—we've got two hours until the girls get home from school."

Climbing up the back steps of the house, we faced our first sign the house required more fixing than Mr. Peterson indicated. The back porch looked like it had once been enclosed, but was now a shell of two-by-fours containing the battered remains of a powder room. The exposed toilet was covered in rust stains and mold, and a spider web stretched over the bowl of the sink. Large black flies hovered around the bottom of the toilet stool and crawled through a crack between the floorboards.

"Guess we can add bathroom to the list of repairs," I said, frowning as I snapped a photo.

"Deadbolt and doorknob too," Mark muttered.

I glanced over to see him dialing in the combination. Sure enough, there was a round hole where the doorknob should've been, and the deadbolt mechanism was missing. Mark slid the combination lock into his pocket and wrenched the door open with both hands. It squealed on rusted hinges, which looked as though they might crack in two at any moment. The wood on the door looked warped. "Maybe a new door as well," I added.

Mark scowled at it and then stepped inside the house. The crease between his eyebrows deepened as he took in the kitchen.

In a word, it was a nightmare. Like the back porch, some of the cabinets were hollow shells, with broken shelves and no doors. One of the upper cabinets listed so badly I was convinced it might fall. I turned in a slow circle, taking photos to document what would need to be repaired. The countertop was splintered plywood. There was a stove, and surprisingly, a dishwasher, but no refrigerator. The floor looked like it'd once been tiled but someone chipped it away, leaving only curving lines of dark mortar. I chanced a look at the sink and immediately wished I hadn't. The skeletal remains of some rodent lay on the dirty porcelain bottom, surrounded by a halo of wiry brown hair and chunks of decaying flesh. I started to retch and covered my nose and mouth.

"What?" Mark asked. He'd peeked at the electrical outlets behind the stove, directing the beam from his Maglite between the appliance and the wall.

"Rat," I managed, and pointed at the sink. I backed away and gulped in air that didn't hold the stench of death.

Mark crossed the kitchen. "Lovely." He looked as disgusted as I felt.

"One would think, if you were selling a house, you might at least clean it up," I said, eyeing the sink from a safe distance.

"One would think," he agreed. He sauntered over to what looked to be a pantry or broom closet and yanked open the door. It came off in his hands, leaving him holding the knob and struggling to brace the door before it slipped from his grip. He clucked his tongue and carefully leaned the door against the wall beside the tiny closet. Judging by the look on his face, this house wasn't winning him over.

It was a look I knew well—he'd give me the same expression of disapproval whenever I suggested we break from our routine and do something novel, like try the new pizzeria in town or drive down to Cannon Beach to check out a new art gallery. Mark wasn't a fan of change. I thrived on it. I told myself it was just one of those things between people who'd been married a long time. One partner wants to try something new, the other doesn't understand why things can't stay the same way they've always been. I'd learned long ago when Mark got that look on his face, the best thing to do was to give him space, let him stew a while. He'd come around.

Leaving the kitchen, I stepped into a large room that seemed to be a combined living room and dining area, and took more photos. Beautiful windows were set into walls paneled in Douglas fir. I remembered the description of the paneling from Mr. Peterson's ad—he'd described it as a rare feature, and said it added to the beauty of the house. He was right. The paneling gave the room a warm, welcoming feel, which was a nice change from the horrors

I'd encountered in the kitchen. I imagined the ramshackle house, not as it was, but as it could be—a vintage beach cottage with airy furnishings and maybe even an outdoor shower to wash the sand from our feet.

Along one of the living room walls, it looked like there'd once been a fireplace—what if we restored it? I envisioned a hearth made of river rock and smiled. Maybe the place had potential. The kitchen was a mess, but we could gut it and turn it into exactly what we wanted. It was a blank slate.

I glanced toward the kitchen, where Mark inspected the pipes under the sink. They were rusty and he looked annoyed, muttering under his breath. I sighed. I couldn't fall in love with this house yet. Not before my husband rendered judgment.

That was another problem with us. I was a glass-half-full kind of girl, and he was a perpetual skeptic. He thought I got too swept up by romantic notions, and I wished he'd live a little, and not be so maddeningly practical all the time. Still, he was here, playing along at least. Perhaps this time we'd meet each other halfway. I could stand to be a little more reserved, and maybe he'd get inspired by the house's potential—maybe.

I returned my gaze to the large living-slash-dining room—the great room, as I'd started calling it in my head. The light fixture was missing, and scary-looking wires poked willy-nilly from the ceiling. The electrical system in the house definitely seemed to have issues, as Mr. Peterson had mentioned.

I took a photo of the wires and then crossed the room to look through a set of French doors. That room was empty, but beside it was an arched door that caught my eye. Peering through its dirty glass panels, I could make out a hallway on the other side. Next to the arched door was a smaller one. I opened it.

It was a closet under the stairs, the bottom of the risers draped with cobwebs. *Gross.* The floor of the closet was worse though. It was covered in junk—trash, discarded clothes, toys, and even a collapsed umbrella stroller for a toddler. I wondered who lived here before, and why Mr. Peterson hadn't taken the time to throw out this stuff before putting the house up for sale.

A thump startled me. I scanned the trash on the closet floor and spotted droppings. There was probably another rat, a live one this time. Shuddering, I shut the closet door. There was another thump—too heavy to be a rodent. The thumps continued, and I realized they sounded like footsteps.

We weren't alone in the house.

Holding in a squeal of fright, I rushed across the room, back to the kitchen. "Mark!" I whispered.

He stopped messing with the faucet and turned to me. His eyes grew wide at the fear written on my face. "What?"

"I think there's someone else in the house. I heard footsteps."

Mark gripped the long black handle of his heavy-duty flashlight with both hands, wielding it like a weapon. "Squatters," he muttered as he crossed the great room and studied the French doors. "Doesn't look like anyone is in there," he whispered, peering through the glass of the doors. Looking back at me, he asked, "Where did you hear them?"

I pointed to the paneled door next to the closet. "In the hallway, I think."

Mark nodded, his jaw set. "Stay here, Tawny."

I shook my head. "Alone? No way."

He scowled. "Then stay close." He eased open the paneled door to the hallway. A beautiful, curving staircase bordered it. I would've been impressed, had I not been terrified we were about to be jumped by a crazed meth addict.

Mark eyed the top of the stairs and then looked at the open doorway at the foot of the steps. He peered through for a moment and then stepped back with a frown on his face.

"What is it?" I whispered.

"Stairs to the basement," he answered, his voice hushed. "A very dark basement. Let's save that for last and check out the upstairs first."

I peeked through the doorway. The room appeared to be an oversized coat closet with shelves and a rack with wire hangers on it. Stairs descended below the floorboards, disappearing into blackness. A chill crawled up my spine, and I looked at Mark. "Good call."

He nodded and started up the stairs. I followed close behind, my hand gripping the back of his shirt. My other hand was clenched around the camera, which was completely useless as a weapon. I felt vulnerable, but it was better than feeling exposed while Mark disappeared into the bowels of this house.

Mr. Peterson described the house as having three bedrooms, but based on the first-floor layout alone, the house was much larger than the one we rented. As a potential buyer, I should've thought about the size as an asset for resale. Instead, I found myself fixated on the number of shadowy places a squatter could hide, waiting to ambush us.

The top of the stairs opened to a common space on the second story. There appeared to be two bedrooms on one side and a larger bedroom on the other. In between was what I assumed to be a bathroom.

Mark paused a moment on the stairs, listening, before heading toward the smaller bedrooms. Cautiously, he peeked into each one. Finding no one, he ducked his head into the bathroom and then checked the master bedroom.

I planted myself in the middle of the common area, listening intently, poised to run back down the stairs if someone other than Mark came out of the bedroom. I had no idea what I'd do if I saw someone coming *up* the stairs. Try not to pass out, I guess. Mark was the brave one—not me.

"There's no one up here," he said, rejoining me. "Why don't you take photos before we head back down?"

I nodded and retraced his steps while he stood guard at the stairs. The first bedroom was clear except for an old rug, rolled up and placed near the window. The glass was heavy with condensation, and dirty water had dropped onto the rug, leaving mildew stains. I snapped a photo of the leaky window and moved on to the next room.

The second bedroom had belonged to a little girl, by the looks of it. Tacked to the wall was a drawing of a squatty purple horse and a scribbled rainbow. Printed carefully in crayon, the note read, *"To: Mom. From: Tara. I love you."*

The *v* in love was curved like a *u*, and the *e* was backwards. A few other drawings littered the floor, next to the open closet. In the closet was a pile of dirty clothes, including a pink t-shirt and a pair of girl's underpants.

What kind of people lived here?

Whoever had lived in the house seemed to have moved in a hurry, leaving things behind.

"Tawny?" Mark called.

It surprised me he wasn't whispering, but he seemed less on edge now that he'd made sure the second story wasn't occupied. Knowing Mark, he probably thought me paranoid. Admittedly, it wasn't the first time I'd made him chase after odd noises. Maybe it really was just a rat.

"Yeah?" I snapped a photo of the drawings and hurried out to Mark.

"Can you take a photo of the bathroom window? There's a huge crack in it." He stood at the bathroom door, arms crossed over his chest.

"Yep—I'm on it." I squeezed past him and raised the camera to photograph the broken window. "Did you see the drawings in the little girl's room?"

Mark's voice grew fainter as he resumed his post at the top of the stairs. "Mm-hmm. Kind of sad, isn't it?"

"Why do you say that?" I asked.

"The wiring is shot, and I don't think there's any heat in this place. It'd be hard living without electricity and warmth."

It was chilly in the house, especially in the bathroom, where the plastic covering the window flapped in the breeze outside. The window wasn't just cracked, it was missing an entire pane. Similar to the window in the first bedroom, water had dripped down the wall. The toilet had rust stains—at least, I hoped those were rust stains, and the mirror above the grimy sink was webbed with cracks. The claw foot tub was ringed with grime. I thought about the little girl who had lived here—had she bathed in *that*? Surely not. I couldn't fathom my own children having to use such a filthy bathroom. Mark was right. It *was* sad.

I stepped out of the bathroom and headed toward the last bedroom. "I'm just going to check out the master, okay?"

Mark busied himself inspecting the broken light fixture over the stairs, and waved me on. "Yeah."

The master bedroom was messier than the first two. A pair of sleeping bags lay side-by-side on the floor. I thought about the possibility of squatters living here and felt a mixture of fear and sadness. This was no way to live. Around the sleeping bags was an array of garbage—used paper plates, cans encrusted with food, dirty plastic glasses, an empty potato chip bag, crumpled pieces of newspaper, and partially crushed pink pills. There had been rats up here too. Rodent droppings were spread across the floor and the material of the sleeping bags. There was a pile of dirty clothing as well, and more of the little girl's drawings…and a photograph.

I was hesitant to touch anything because of the droppings, but couldn't resist picking up the picture. With an abstract blue background, it appeared to be a school photo. The little girl's nose was dotted with freckles, she was missing her two front teeth, and her light brown hair was woven into two long braids. She didn't look all that different from my own daughters.

I turned the photograph over. Scrawled in black ink were the words, *Tara, 2nd grade.* No date. Reverently, I placed the photo back on the floor where I'd found it. The photograph was of a real person who had a name, and it made the room feel less like a squatter's camp and more like a shrine. It felt wrong to disturb it more than I already had. Based on the drawings, a mother and daughter had lived here. Depressing as it was, they'd had happy times too—the little girl's drawings revealed that much. I snapped a few photos and backed out of the room.

Mark sat on the top step of the stairs, absently shining his flashlight at the ceiling, waiting for me. "We still need to see that other room downstairs, and the basement."

The basement. I'd forgotten about that. Dread crept into my veins. "Have you heard any other noises? Footsteps?" I forced a smile and tried to laugh off my fear. "Rats?"

Mark shook his head. "Nope. Nada." He rose and started down

the stairs, his hand running along the banister. I took a last look around and followed.

When my husband reached the bottom step, he held up his hand, signaling me to stop. I arched my eyebrows in question, and he raised a finger as if to say, *Give me a moment.* I waited silently as he looked up and down the hall and then peeked into the coat closet which led to the basement.

"Did you hear something?" I whispered.

"Just...being cautious," he said. I studied his face, suspicious he was keeping something from me. He continued down the hallway, past the coat closet. It ended at the front entry. The door was barred from the inside. "That's weird," he said.

I eyed the boards nailing the door shut. "Why would someone do that?"

He shrugged. "The door was probably broken, and the person who did it was looking for a temporary way to secure it. Seems like there's been a lot of quick fixes in this house. That's why it's in such bad shape. No one's cared for it for a long time." I frowned, and he smiled. "Better add that to your list."

"Mm-hmm," I grumbled and took a photo of the barred door. "It's a *long* list."

It was a disheartening list. I'd had high hopes for this place, but it was a mess. It wasn't a fixer-upper, it was a disaster zone.

Mark pushed past me and went around to the room with the French doors. The hinges squeaked when he opened them. "This isn't so bad."

Like the great room, it had nice windows. It was spacious, with a built-on sunroom facing the south. Warm sunlight flooded the space, even with the windows sheathed in opaque plastic. The same wood paneling continued, adding to the warm, cozy atmosphere. Overhead was a vintage light fixture that appeared to be one of the few things not broken in the house.

"What would you do with this room?" Mark asked.

I looked over at him, surprised. Was my skeptic of a husband actually being positive? I was supposed to be the optimist, but suddenly he seemed more appreciative of the house than I felt.

Maybe he was just trying to pacify me, to ease the sting that I'd been so wrong about the house.

"I'm not sure," I admitted. "It could be a guest room. Maybe if there was a bathroom downstairs—other than that wreck on the back porch."

"A guest room," Mark mused, running his hand along the paneling. "Like a visiting mother-in-law kind of guest room, or a bed and breakfast guest room?"

I stole a glance at him as I snapped a few photos. "What're you thinking?" I asked cautiously. I was scared to get my hopes up, the few I still had.

He gave me a small smile. "I don't know. About possibilities, I guess."

I gasped, holding my hand to my heart, overly dramatic. "*You? Possibilities? I'm stunned.*"

He chuckled and swatted at my arm playfully. "Don't make fun. I can dream just as much as you can."

Mark, a dreamer. *That* was out of character. I liked it. I lowered my camera and grinned. "Who are you, and what have you done with my husband? You know, the frugal one."

He raised his eyebrows. "What—you have more than one husband? A frugal one *and* a big spender?"

I laughed. "Yes, big spender. What're you thinking?" Was he interested in buying the house? Even with all its flaws? I thought about my vision for the great room and started to feel hopeful.

"I'm thinking this house has a lot wrong with it." Seeing the disappointment on my face, he raised his finger to keep me from interrupting. "But, it also has a lot of character and more space than we need. I know you haven't found a job yet, and you like being around for the girls, so...I guess I'm thinking about how we could get out of the rental and make this work for us. Like, maybe fixing it could be your job, and then we could rent out part of the house for income. It's close to the beach. We could make a lot of money from summer tourists."

I nodded, considering the idea. "We could...but what about the wiring and heating? I can paint and tile, but electrical scares me. And you're so busy with work—you wouldn't have time."

"We'd have to bring someone in to do the big repairs," he said. "But we'd have to do that even if I did have time. I'm not about to touch those wires."

"Maybe," I answered. "But we've yet to see what horrors the basement holds. That could be a deal-breaker."

He chuckled and held out his hand. "Let's take a look, shall we?"

Mark made me stay at the top of the stairs as he navigated the steps to the basement, avoiding a broken riser. At the bottom, he paused, shining the beam of his Maglite into the darkness. He looked up at me. "Be right back."

The blackness beyond the doorway seemed to swallow him as he turned a corner and took the light with him. I waited, shifting my feet, toying with my camera. I was reviewing the photos I'd taken when a motor roared to life. It sounded like a power tool.

I froze, my ears pricked. Where was the noise coming from? It sounded far away and close at the same time—loud, but oddly muffled so I couldn't pinpoint the location. A horrifying thought occurred to me. What if the sound was coming from *inside* the house?

My fingers clenched the camera. I turned it off and stuffed it in my pocket as I scanned the room, looking for something I could use to defend myself. There was nothing—just a rusty-looking coat hanger on a hook—nothing that would stand a chance against someone who had an actual weapon. I held my breath, trying to listen, my imagination running wild. What if I'd been right about hearing the footsteps? What if someone had been in the house? My mind flashed to every horror movie I'd ever seen, conjuring up the image of a hulking stranger wielding a chainsaw, murdering my husband in a pitch-black basement.

Mark hadn't cried out, but what if he'd been taken by surprise, and hadn't had time to scream? I stood rigid with fear, trying to decide whether to rescue my husband or run, when Mark resurfaced from the black hole that was the basement doorway. The motor continued to roar, and he seemed completely unconcerned about it. No crazed killer then—just my imagination. Again.

"Do you hear that?" I asked.

Mark started up the stairs. "The lawn mower?"

"Yeah." Of course that's what it was—that made more sense than a psycho with a chainsaw. I tried to cover my embarrassment with a laugh. "Funny thing—it started up right after you disappeared. I thought maybe someone was murdering you down there."

"And you didn't come to save me?" he asked.

"I thought about it."

He chuckled, and the tension left my body. "There's not much to see down there, but go take a look," he said.

I took the flashlight from him and headed down the rickety steps, avoiding the broken riser.

"There's a hallway as you go through the door," Mark called after me. I turned and looked up at him, surprised he hadn't followed me back down. "Just keep moving forward and the room opens up from that little corridor there."

"Okay." I clicked on the light and stepped over the threshold, into darkness. Floating dust motes filled the air, dancing in the flashlight's beam. The basement floor wasn't finished; there were a few loosely connected boards near the basement door, and the rest was dirt. Mark's footprints were there, the dust stirred up just from him walking around. I took a few more steps down the narrow passage and reached the end of the hall.

The room before me was expansive, running the length and width of the house. On one end was a wooden stall for firewood, still stacked with logs. They'd come in handy if we restored the fireplace, though I didn't look forward to cleaning off the cobwebs covering them. The other end of the basement was stacked with junk and garbage, similar to what we'd encountered upstairs.

Everything was blanketed with a thick layer of dust. My nose was stuffy—all the dust triggering my allergies. I made a mental note to take an antihistamine when I got back to the car. Otherwise, I'd be paying for this excursion tonight when my sinuses were too clogged to let me sleep. I just hoped there wasn't any mold down here. I'd heard horror stories from my neighbor about getting mold removed from her home. The procedure had been costly, and if we got this house, it'd cost us enough as it was.

I ventured a little deeper into the basement, shining my flashlight on the pile of junk. I made out an old wooden trunk. Did that come with the house? Maybe I'd clean it up and use it for a coffee table.

The beam of my flashlight fell on a tattered ragdoll. The doll's fabric face and its light brown yarn hair looked dingy. Its flower print dress was dotted with rust colored stains and black flecks. The flecks looked like rodent feces.

There was a rustle to my right, and I startled, swinging my light toward the sound. I didn't want to see another rat, especially if this one was alive.

Suddenly the air was thick with flies. I clamped my mouth shut as they flew toward my face, waving my arms madly to keep them away. They crawled in my hair and buzzed in my ears, and I bit back a shriek. The beam of my flashlight flickered as I used it to swat the flies. I shuddered at the thought of it going out and having to find my way back to the stairs in the dark.

I stumbled back toward the corridor that led to the door of the basement, trying to see through squinted eyes, the cloud of flies, and the dying light of the Maglite. As I reached the passage, the buzzing sound eased, and the flies drifted back to whatever drew them to the basement.

I dared one last look, directing my beam to the offending corner of the basement. The dirt floor was carpeted with insects. Flies and other crawling things, though I was too far away to tell what they were. There seemed to be a small lump on the floor that attracted their interest. Another dead rat, most likely, but there was no way I was going back to find out. I shivered, brushed myself off, and headed out the door and up the stairs. On the way, I made another mental note. *If we get this house, Mark's on basement cleaning duty.* I'd volunteer for any other job, but I had no desire to go back down there if I didn't have to.

Mark must've seen something in my face, because he asked, "Are you okay?"

I scrunched up my nose in disgust. "I got attacked by flies." I handed him the flashlight and then shook out my hair, checking for stray insects.

"I thought I heard something, like a muffled scream, but I wasn't sure."

I narrowed my eyes at him. "And you didn't come to save me?"

"I thought about it," he shot back.

I laughed. "Touché." The horror of the flies crawling over my skin was fading, but I wouldn't be visiting that basement any time soon. I looked down at my jeans—they were powdered with dust, and the hem of my t-shirt had snagged a cobweb. I brushed it away. "I'm filthy. Let's go home. I want a warm shower."

"All right," he agreed. "I think we've seen enough, and we've got a lot to think about."

We left the house without another word, but as Mark secured the back door, I couldn't help but notice the flies hovering near the base of the old toilet sitting there, and think about that little lump on the basement floor, lying directly below us.

Chapter Two

Mark eyed the list of things wrong with the house. We sat at the kitchen table in our rental, getting ready to call Mr. Peterson and make an offer. Mark thought he could get Mr. Peterson to go for an even lower price on the property.

"See that?" he asked me, pointing to the third item I scribbled down when we were inspecting the house. "Wiring. That's a fire hazard. You've got to be careful about selling a house with bad wiring. He won't want to be held liable for anything that could happen."

I wasn't sure about that, but I nodded. The online ad said the house was being sold *as-is*, meaning Mr. Peterson had washed his hands of any liability. Still, if we were able to purchase the house for a lower price, it would mean more money for repairs.

Mark scanned the list, verbally checking off items. "We'll need a pump for that basement. It could flood with the winter storms. A new heating system, updated plumbing, a water heater. New roof, new windows."

I sucked in my breath. I'd written all this down, but hearing the needed repairs rattled off out loud like that…it was overwhelming.

"Tawny?" He looked at me over the list, adjusting his glasses.

"It's a lot to take in. Can we handle all this?" I remembered the mess of a kitchen and how the back door was shot. It'd taken Mark a while to secure it before we returned to the car—seemed like the combination lock was the only thing holding it in place. There'd been a lot of wind last night—I wondered if the door was still upright or if the rusty hinges finally snapped and it had fallen over, leaving the entry to the house exposed.

He smiled. "We can handle it. If we get the price a little lower, we'll be able to hire someone to help us. Plus, there's a chance we'll be able to refinance it at some point, and that will give us more money to play with."

"All right." I sighed. I was tired of paying rent, shelling out over a thousand dollars a month for what? Nothing. It was time to invest our money in something that would last. If Mark was right about the house and we turned the first-floor bedroom into a vacation rental, we'd actually bring in money, rather than give it away. "Call him."

"It's a good investment," Mark said, mirroring my thoughts. I smiled as he picked up the phone, punched in the number, and then put the phone on speaker.

Mr. Peterson picked up on the third ring. "Peterson here."

"Mr. Peterson, hello. This is Mark Ellis," Mark said. "I'm calling about the house."

"Ah, yes. I take it you had a chance to see it?"

"We did," Mark said, his voice guarded.

"Thanks for letting us take a look," I interjected. "It's a beautiful old house."

Mark gave me a dark look and shook his head. He grabbed a pen and scrawled something on the list, and then passed it over to me.

Let me do the talking.

Oops. Mark's first rule of haggling—don't offer compliments. He wanted to focus on the problems with the house so he could negotiate a lower price. *Sorry,* I mouthed.

"Still there?" Mr. Peterson asked. "Hello?"

Mark cleared his throat and took back the list. "Yes, we're still here. I was just looking over my notes."

"Notes?" Mr. Peterson asked.

"Yes. As I inspected the house, I took note of a number of repairs that will need to be made," Mark answered. "I'm sure you're aware that the house will need a new roof and windows." He checked items off his list as he mentioned them. "There's no heat, so that will be a priority, and I believe there are issues with the plumbing."

"Yes…well." Mr. Peterson sounded guarded now. "I did state in the ad that the house was a fixer-upper. Are you saying you're not interested?"

"No, we're interested," Mark said. "But we need to consider these repairs before making an offer. The wiring, in particular, concerns me. That could be hazardous. It needs to be addressed before my family moves in."

I cringed. Even though I understood what Mark was trying to accomplish, his tone was harsh, pompous even. I hoped Mr. Peterson didn't think he was rude, but I suspected he did, given his silence.

"You saw in the ad I'm selling it as-is, right?" Mr. Peterson finally asked.

"Yes," Mark replied.

Mr. Peterson's tone went from guarded to defensive. "I'm not interested in making repairs as part of the terms. Whoever buys it will need to make any repairs."

"I understand that," Mark said. He smiled slightly, circling the word *wiring* with his pen. "We certainly wouldn't expect you to make repairs. But given that the wiring presents a fire hazard, and will be expensive to repair, we'd like to make an offer of $125,000." His smile broadened, and I could tell he thought Mr. Peterson would take the offer.

"$125,000?" Mr. Peterson said in a harsh tone. "That's fifteen thousand less than I'm asking."

"I understand," Mark said, "but with the amount of work that needs to be done—"

"Look—I am well aware there are repairs needed on the house, but I've been forthcoming about that. I've priced it fair with that in mind. The land alone is worth it. And I've got two other buyers interested in looking at the house."

We blew it. There was no chance we'd get the house now. I opened my mouth, wanting to say something to soften things, but Mark shook his head and gave me a warning look. His second rule of haggling—let them stew. I shut my mouth and held my tongue, hands clenched together in my lap.

The silence stretched on, and then Mr. Peterson sighed as if he was relenting a little. "Thing is, I'm a two-hour drive from the coast, and since I bought the place in 2014, my job has become more demanding. I just don't have the time or resources to deal with the house. I need it sold. I'd be willing to meet you partway, to go down five grand, but that's all I can do." He paused a moment. "Like I said, there are other people interested, but I've held them off until I had a decision from you." Another pause. "Are you interested?"

Mark mulled it over, scratching the number on the page. "Five-thousand…we might be able to swing that with a twenty-percent down payment, but we'd need to refinance after two years. Any possibility of you carrying the loan until we can do that?"

"Two years?" Mr. Peterson asked.

"Two years. At most," Mark answered. "If we can't make it work, ownership would revert to you."

"Ah," Mr. Peterson said. "Well, that would reduce my financial risk, I suppose. All right. $135,000, twenty-percent down payment, and I'll carry the loan for two years until you refinance. Agreed, assuming all works out with the bank, of course."

"Of course," Mark said. "May we do one more walk-through? It's a big decision."

"Yeah. Sleep on it," Mr. Peterson answered. "But I need an answer by tomorrow."

Mark looked at me and smiled. "We understand. We'll call you tomorrow." He hung up the phone and checked to make sure the call disconnected before setting the receiver on the kitchen table. He clicked his pen and set it next to the phone.

"Did we just buy a house?" I asked. My fingers were still clenched, and my head spun from the stress of the call.

He grinned. "We just bought a house." I was both elated and worried. My anxiety increased as his smile faltered. "I was serious about that walk-through though. We weren't able to get as much shaved off the price as I hoped. I need to make sure we're not getting in over our heads."

Okay, I thought, watching him as he clicked his pen again and wrote down notes from the call. Mark could still change his mind—it wouldn't be the first time he'd backed out of something. I wouldn't start packing until we had a signed contract in hand.

**

We returned to the house that evening, flashlights in hand. Normally our neighbor, Mrs. Berger, would've been willing to watch the girls so they wouldn't be underfoot, but she'd gone to the evening service at her church. That was okay. I wanted to gauge the girls' reaction.

My seven-year-old, Sara, took to the house immediately. Once we got the back door open, hinges still intact, she ran into the kitchen to start exploring. I called out for her to be careful and stay close. The sun hadn't yet set, and the kitchen glowed with warm light streaming through the western windows. Still, it'd be getting dark soon. I didn't want her tumbling down the basement stairs or tripping over the junk left behind by the former residents. Sophie, the youngest, was more hesitant. She was only five, and it was her nature to be cautious. After she stepped over the threshold, she immediately wanted to be carried. I hoisted her up and set her on my hip.

I'd forgotten about the rat in the sink. How I forgot a thing like that, I don't know, but Sophie got one look, and her little arms tightened around my neck. I knew I wouldn't be putting her down anytime soon.

Sara, on the other hand, thought the rat bones were cool. She stood on her tiptoes to peer into the sink and gave me a grin. "Gross! But awesome, right?" Sara was fearless. Impetuous at times, but fearless. When one of her classmates brought a pet snake to school, she'd been the first to ask to hold it. Her teacher, impressed, allowed Sara to bring in bugs she'd found in our yard, so long as they were in a jar with a secure lid.

I managed a smile. "Yeah. Awesome and gross. But now we know what a rat's skeleton looks like, don't we, Soph?" Sophie buried her face in my neck.

"It's science," Mark said, trying to coax Sophie out by tickling the back of her neck. She giggled and turned her face to him, but wouldn't look at the sink.

"Science," Sara echoed, nodding her head sagely.

"Don't worry, Sophie, we'll clean out the rat before we move in," I assured her. "Who wants to see the rest of the house?"

"I do! Where's my room?" Sara asked.

"Upstairs," I said. She took off into the living room, and I called after her, "Wait for your dad!"

Mark caught up and took her hand. He let her open the door to the hallway, and they started toward the stairs.

At the base of the staircase, she stopped and peered into the coat closet. "What's that room?"

"It's a place to hang jackets," Mark told her, pointing to the lone wire hanger. He turned his flashlight on and directed the beam to the stairs descending below the floorboards. "Those are the stairs to the basement."

Sara looked at the stairs, the black hole of the door, and then up at him. "It's dark. I don't want to go down there."

"Good. I don't want you going down there," he replied. "There's a lot of old junk I don't want you getting into. You could get cut on something rusty."

"Plus, there might be another dead rat," I added. "When I was down there, I ran into a bunch of flies covering something dead. Super gross."

"Eeew," Sophie said, squeezing my neck tighter.

"Ew is right," I agreed.

"Are there any live rats?" Sara asked. "Will they come upstairs?" Sophie's eyes widened as she looked from her sister to me, and her face paled.

"No, honey," Mark said. "I'll make sure they're all gone before we move in. And I'll install a door for the basement." He smiled at Sophie. "No rats in this house, dead or alive."

"How about we go upstairs?" I asked, changing the subject.

"Yes, how about that," Mark said. He gave Sara the flashlight and took her hand, letting her lead.

I set Sophie on the steps. She squirmed and reached for me, but I shook my head. "I can't carry you up the stairs, sweetie. You're getting too big. Why don't you carry my flashlight?" I retrieved it from my pocket and clicked it on for her, showing her how to direct the light up the stairs. Pacified for the moment, she took it and started climbing.

I followed, watching Sophie dance the light off the walls of the stairwell, and listening to Sara's excited chatter. So far, so good. It wouldn't have been a deal-breaker if the girls didn't like the house, but I was glad they were gaining enthusiasm for our move.

Somewhere below me there was a thump, and I paused. *What was that?*

Sophie must've heard it too, because she stopped and stared at me with a question in her eyes.

I nudged her to keep going. "Go ahead, sweetie. Catch up to your dad. I'll be right back." Once she resumed climbing, I slipped back down the stairs and looked up and down the hallway.

Thump.

It sounded like the noise came from the basement. I poked my head into the coat closet again and listened for a moment—nothing.

Weird. Well, old houses do creak and groan, I reasoned and headed back up the stairs.

When I reached the top, Sara came running to greet me, holding something in her hands. Mark had picked up Sophie, and they were touring the bathroom.

"Look, Mom," Sara said, smiling. "Another girl used to live here." She held up the drawing of the purple horse. Her smile broadened. "And we have almost the same name! 'Cept hers is spelled with a 't'." On the paper, the name "Tara" was scrawled in crayon.

Sadness washed over me for the little girl who'd lived here, but I hid my feelings with a smile. "Yes, that must've been her room."

"That's the room I want," Sara said.

I hesitated, unsure, as I walked over to the room and peered in. Aside from the underpants lying on the floor of the closet, there was nothing visibly icky about the room. Dust motes floated in the last rays of the setting sun. We'd need to replace the windows at some point, and the walls could stand a fresh coat of paint, but the wood floors weren't bad—maybe a brightly colored rug to add some cheer…and furniture too.

Still, there was a sense of unease I couldn't shake. "I don't know, Sara."

I stepped back to peek into the other bedroom. It was in similar shape, though one of the windows leaked. We'd have to reseal it if we couldn't replace it right away. There was something peaceful about the room. No, not peaceful exactly—just an absence of whatever was disturbing about the other room. "What about this room? It's nice, and you could share it with Sophie."

"I don't want to share," Sara said.

"But you could sleep in here, and maybe we could turn that other room into a playroom," I said. "We could put your dollhouse in there. That could be fun."

"No," Sara said, determination in her eyes. "I don't want to share with Sophie, and I don't want a playroom. I want that room." She turned and went into the room she'd claimed.

I followed her and found her sitting crisscross on the floor, the drawing placed in front of her. With her finger, she traced the scribbled rainbow over the purple horse.

"Don't sit on the floor, Sara," I said. "It's covered in dust. You're getting dirty." She didn't answer—just kept tracing the drawing with her finger. She wasn't even listening. I sighed. "We haven't decided anything yet."

I looked over at Mark showing Sophie the master bedroom. That he was here and in good spirits about the house, meant he wanted it. Despite my reservations about the bedroom—Sara's bedroom—I wanted the house too. It was beautiful, or at least had the potential to be beautiful. I wondered if we could renovate the ground floor by summer, in time for the first wave of tourists, coming to enjoy the Oregon coast in Seaside. If we could move in by October, a month away, we'd have eight months to find out.

**

Our loan came through, and we managed to get out of our rental agreement a month early. Two weeks before moving, we got keys from Mr. Peterson and started cleaning, clearing away who knew how many years of dust and grime. We didn't bother tackling the basement—we decided to work on that later, once we were able to put a pump down there. Our priority was getting the house ready to move in furniture so we wouldn't have to rent a storage unit.

While I filled garbage bags from the first and second floors, Mark installed a new back door. Mark took vacation time from work, and Mrs. Berger was good enough to watch the girls after they got off the bus each day. She said she'd miss having us as neighbors, and we promised her a tour, once we got settled.

Donning gloves, I started by getting rid of the rat in the sink. Luckily, it had been dead long enough it no longer stank, but left a brown stain I had to scrub with bleach. After that, clearing away dust and cobwebs wasn't so bad. Even cleaning out the closet under the stairs was better than dealing with the dead rat.

I filled up several garbage bags, took them out to the container we rented for trash, and then swept out the closet. After washing the windows, the first floor actually looked livable. The kitchen was still a wreck—we couldn't use the upper cabinets, but the lower shelving would suffice for a few months. We didn't have updated wiring and plumbing either, but we'd be able to move our belongings in.

The second floor was a different story—not because it was filthier, but because of the photo of the little girl and her drawings. I couldn't bring myself to throw her things away—it felt wrong somehow. I set it to the side, eventually tucking everything away in a drawer in my living room side table. I bagged up the girl's leftover clothing and the rest of her belongings and took them down to the basement.

After navigating the steps, I directed my light to the corner of the basement where I'd been ambushed by flies. They were gone, and so was that odd little lump on the floor. It was almost as though I'd imagined the whole thing. I knew I hadn't though, because there were still plenty of flies hanging out by the back door upstairs.

I shuddered at the memory and crossed the room to place the plastic bag on top of the antique trunk. Maybe Mr. Peterson would know who the little girl was, and could pass along her things. I caught a glimpse of the doll sitting on the dusty floor and wondered if that had been Tara's as well. I wouldn't be doing her any favors by leaving it on the dirt floor. I picked up the doll and studied it. The doll's yarn hair was tangled, and her dress was stiff with brown stains of unknown origin. Good thing I was wearing gloves.

There was a noise behind me. *Mark*. I turned my head slightly, catching his figure in shadow out of the corner of my eye. "Do you think this belonged to that little girl too?" I asked, holding up the doll.

He didn't answer. I turned around fully, but there was no one there. I bounced the beam of my flashlight around the room, certain someone had been standing behind me. "Mark?"

There was no answer, but the hairs on the back of my neck stood up. With a shiver, I placed the doll atop the trunk and left the basement, forcing myself not to run.

Once I was at the top of the stairs, I realized Mark was banging on something in the kitchen. I remembered what I'd promised myself after the fly incident—I wasn't going into the basement again. I chuckled to myself. It was easy to laugh about my paranoia now that I wasn't alone in the dark.

I walked into the kitchen to find Mark lying on his back under the sink, working on a rusty pipe. "Hey," I called. "I finished hauling the trash from upstairs."

"Good. You have a new back door," he said.

"Hooray!" I crossed the room to take a look. We'd selected an arts and crafts style door to fit the architecture of the house. I swung it open and then closed it, testing the deadbolt. "Much better. Thank you."

He crawled out from under the sink and stood up. "I don't think either of us would've been able to sleep here without a real lock on the door."

"Yeah. How's the plumbing?"

"I think I've got a temporary fix, but we may have to do more later. Want to do the honors?" he asked, gesturing to the kitchen sink.

I smiled and turned on the faucet. It sputtered, and brown water flowed into the basin. My smile turned into a scowl. "Uh, that's not good."

"Give it a minute," Mark said. Together we watched the water slowly clear. "Lots of rust in the pipes, so we won't want to drink it. But it should be good enough for bathing."

I scoffed. "Not until I clean out the tub. You do recall the ring of grime waiting for us upstairs, don't you?"

He smirked. "Of course, love. That's why I bought you a present." He sauntered over to his tool bag, and, with a flourish, pulled out a pumice scouring stone.

I clasped my hands to my chest in a mock swoon. "For me? You sure do know how to make a girl feel special."

"I try." The corner of his mouth quirked up. "Scrub the sides of the tub with this. You might need to spray the tub with vinegar afterward. If you do, let it soak, but don't forget to rinse it out."

"Thank you *ever* so much, darling." I batted my eyelashes and trudged upstairs to do battle with the tub.

"Try the faucet in the bathroom," he called after me. "Tell me if it gives you trouble."

"Will do," I hollered back, my voice echoing in the hallway.

**

Pumice stone in hand, I turned on the faucet in the sink upstairs. The handle stuck. To call it vintage was kind—the neck and cross-type handles were ancient and covered with grime like everything else in the bathroom. I set the stone on the edge of the sink, to use both hands to exert pressure on the handle. The pipes groaned, and something dark dripped from the spout. Thick, watery rust plopped into the sink basin, splashing the sides. Something gave, and then the handle turned all the way. The water was brown, as it had been in the kitchen sink, so I let it run.

I glanced up at the mirror of the medicine cabinet, spidery cracks in the glass. My curly blond hair was a frizzy mess, springing free of my ponytail. I reached up to tuck a stray hair behind my ear, and caught movement behind me, a dark shadow in the tub. Startled, I whirled around, knocking the stone off the edge of the sink. It clattered to the floor, doing nothing to calm the rapid beating of my heart. I stared at the bathtub—there was no one there.

A breeze stirred the air in the room, making the plastic covering the window flap and cast shadows on the walls. That explained it— just a little wind. Geez, I was jumpy. I thought back to my earlier trip to the basement, how I'd felt unsettled.

Pull it together, Tawny, I thought. *If you're gonna go around, jumping at shadows, what's the point of living in a place like this?*

I took another look at myself in the mirror—my eyes wild and a little bloodshot. A lot of early mornings and late nights, trying to get the house cleaned and our stuff at the rental packed up so we could move in.

I turned off the water at the sink and tried the faucet on the tub. The handles turned more easily, and soon, dark water pooled at the bottom. I knelt down, retrieved the pumice stone, and started scrubbing the sides—rust and filth flaking off and circling the drain. My thoughts drifted back to the dark basement, to the shadowy figure. Had I imagined it, or actually seen something, a presence of some kind?

We didn't know much about the house. According to Mr. Peterson, the house was built in 1909, but he couldn't tell us anything about the history. He'd only purchased it a few years ago, in an auction for foreclosures. The house was over a century old. There was no telling who lived and died here. Wasn't it possible something remained of the house's former occupants?

I didn't know whether or not I believed in ghosts. My mother did, but she believed in a lot of things. Crazy things, Mark would've said. How many times had he snickered behind her back when she'd said something off the wall? Whenever she lost something—her keys, a sock—she'd blame it on brownies, for goodness sakes. She was joking, of course, but I think some part of her really believed it was possible such things existed. I'd never experienced anything supernatural, but growing up with Mom, I was open to the idea some things in life couldn't be explained rationally.

Mark disagreed—he believed everything had a scientific explanation and was completely closed off to speculation. Part of the reason we didn't live close to my mother was the conflict between her and him. He seemed perpetually offended by her—that she was mentally ill and living with my overbearing older sister didn't help. I think, subconsciously at least, he worried my mother's illness would rub off on me or our daughters. That's why he didn't take kindly to my bouts of paranoia. In his mind, insanity was a short step beyond me letting my imagination run wild.

If there was a ghost in the house, it would take a full-on apparition to convince Mark. Even then, he wouldn't leave, not with the amount of money we were investing. The question was, if the house was haunted, could I live here? Could I raise my daughters here? Mark would think it was crazy to even entertain these questions.

I thought about my first impressions of the house, dead rat in the kitchen sink notwithstanding. The house had been a mess, but it had potential—potential to be beautiful, and more than that, a home for my family. Still, from the moment I stepped over the threshold, there was a part of me that knew something was wrong with this house. But it was just a feeling, a passing thought at the back of my mind, something I'd never speak aloud, especially not to my skeptic of a husband. A silly notion, easily dismissed.

I rocked back on my heels and stood up to examine my work with the tub. Streaks of soap scum and rust still marred the surface, but white porcelain peeked through. I rinsed out the tub and then resumed scrubbing. Maybe there was something amiss with the house, some sadness in its history. But we could re-write history, couldn't we? Scrub away all the bad and fill the house with good.

I thought about the photo of Tara, the little girl who lived in the house as a squatter with her mother. It was easy to see from her drawings she'd been happy here, and clearly, they'd been roughing it. Even in the sadness of their impoverished situation, they'd found something good about this house, enough for them to stay for a while. They were probably forced to vacate when Mr. Peterson put the house up for sale. I made a mental note to ask him, to see if he knew where they'd gone. If the doll I'd found was that little girl's, I wanted to make sure she got it back.

I decided it didn't matter if the house was haunted or not. If ghosts did exist, that didn't mean they were a danger to us. What could they do, besides scare us a little? I laughed, thinking about Mark's idea of renting out the first-floor bedroom. Maybe the ghosts would be doing us a favor by sticking around, helping us attract summer tourists—a haunted bed and breakfast. Doubtful Mark would take to the idea, but worth a shot if we stumbled onto any convincing evidence.

Smiling to myself, I went downstairs to see if we had any vinegar on hand to finish cleaning out the tub.

Chapter Three

We moved the second week of October, with the coming of the autumn rains. The nights grew cold, so Mark planned to use space heaters until we got a heating system installed. I worried about burning the house down, but he assured me we'd be all right.

In the two weeks since signing the contract and getting the deed transferred with Mr. Peterson, we'd managed to clean the first and second floors, and get the plumbing and electricity working well enough we'd survive until those things could be repaired by an expert. There was still a lot to do before the house was presentable for guests. The windows leaked, the roof needed to be replaced, and the kitchen remained a wreck. We bought a small refrigerator and microwave to get us through the first few months—nothing fancy.

"Just remember, it's only temporary," Mark reminded me. That became our mantra.

Moving in our furniture and boxes took all Saturday, and much of Sunday was spent unpacking our essentials and cleaning out the rental. We'd settled down to a quick meal of take-out pizza when someone knocked on the back door. I looked over at Mark, and he raised his eyebrows in question. We weren't expecting anyone. Maybe it was a neighbor, bringing us a casserole.

Mark peeked through the window of our new back door, and then answered it. "Mr. Peterson," he said. "Hello. Come in."

Bob Peterson poked his head in to find me and the girls gathered around the card table we'd placed in the kitchen. Although the house had a more formal dining area in the great room, we preferred eating in the kitchen. With two small children, it made clean-up easier, and the table gave me extra food preparation space since my plywood countertops needed to be replaced.

"Good evening. Nice to see you, Mark." He nodded in my direction. "Hello, Tawny and girls."

"Hi, Mr. Peterson. Would you like a slice?" I asked, pointing to the pizza box.

"Oh, no thank you. I was in town today and wanted to stop by before heading back to Portland. See how you're getting settled and all," he answered.

"So far, so good," I said.

"You like what we've done with the place?" Mark joked, gesturing to the towers of boxes surrounding our living room furniture.

Mr. Peterson chuckled. "I'd say it looks better than it did. It's clean at least, and it's nice to know your family will be restoring this old girl. I hated to see her wasting away, but I just didn't have the time to fix her up."

"I was wondering about the people who lived here before," I said. "When I was cleaning, I found some of their things, some toys that belonged to the daughter. You don't have a forwarding address, do you?"

Mr. Peterson shook his head. "Sorry to say, I don't. All that stuff was here when I bought the place. I'm afraid I don't know anything about those folks."

"What about the people who built the house?" I asked.

He frowned and shook his head again. "Like I said, I know when the house was built, but that's about it." He scratched his chin absently, and then added, "But you might check with the historical society. Surely there would be records. Maybe even photographs."

"Good idea," I agreed. "We've thought about turning the house into a bed and breakfast. It would be great to get copies of old photos to display."

"It surely would," Mr. Peterson said. "Well, Mark, you know where to find me if you have questions." He held out his hand.

Mark shook Bob Peterson's hand. "We've got your number and your email. Everything's set with the mortgage as well. Our next payment is due before the first."

"Oh, I'm not worried about that at all," Mr. Peterson said. "I know this old girl is in good hands." He gave me a smile. "Well, you folks have a nice evening then."

"You too," Mark said. "Drive safe." He closed the door and sat back down at the table, folding his hands in front of him. "Tawny, maybe we shouldn't tell everyone about the B & B until we know for sure this is going to work."

"But I didn't tell everyone. Just Mr. Peterson."

He looked at me. "I know, but I also know how you are—you get excited about new projects. That's fine, but I think we should exercise caution until we can get this thing off the ground, you know?"

I bristled, realizing what he was really saying. He didn't want me to talk to my mom and sister about the bed and breakfast idea. If I did, they'd call at all hours, wanting to know about our progress and when they could stay with us. I understood where he was coming from, but still, it stung. "Yeah. Fine."

"You don't have to get defensive—"

"I'm not being defensive." My voice was raised, nullifying what I'd just said. I ground my teeth in frustration. "Look, can we just eat?"

He got quiet, and his mouth hardened in a thin line. I knew he was seconds away from leaving the table and going upstairs to bed, leaving me to clean up the kitchen and get the girls to brush their teeth.

"I'm sorry. I'm tired. We both are," I said. I reached across the table and took his hand. "Let's eat, get the girls to bed, and crash. It's been a long day."

He squeezed my hand and gave me a tired smile. "Yeah. It's been a long day."

**

The electricity went out four days after we moved in. Gale force winds battered the coast that night, so when I woke up chilled sometime before dawn, the red digital numbers on my bedside clock dark, I figured the power had gone out in our neighborhood. It wasn't uncommon for storms that strong to fell trees and knock down power lines. I woke up Mark, and we brought the girls to our bed to keep them warm. Sophie had burrowed under her blankets, so she was still toasty, but Sara had kicked off her covers. Her skin was cool to the touch, and it scared me to think of her shivering in her room while I'd slept.

I also worried about our food spoiling. Not that we had much in our tiny refrigerator, but still, we couldn't afford to waste anything, not on our tight budget. That morning, I checked the refrigerator to make sure our food had stayed cold. "The ground beef is still cool. Do you think it'll be safe to eat if I wait until dinner to cook it?"

"It'll keep," Mark said. "Just don't keep opening the fridge."

"Maybe I should pick up ice at the store," I suggested.

"If you want, but after work, I'll pick up a generator at the hardware store." He put on his jacket and picked up his briefcase. "I've been meaning to buy one ever since the big storm last winter."

That storm left us without power for three days, and Highway 26 had been cut off by a fallen spruce. School was canceled, and the girls and I found ourselves at Mrs. Berger's, seeking warmth. A seasoned veteran of coastal storms, she kept the gas tank for her generator full, and her cupboards stocked. I wasn't nearly so prepared.

"We really do need one," I said, "but can we afford it?"

"We'll make do," Mark told me. "See you tonight." He kissed my cheek and headed out the door.

I sent the girls off to school and headed to Josephson's, our grocery store. I was determined not to be caught off guard by another storm. I bought ice, bottled water, and non-perishables.

"Getting ready for the next storm?" the cashier asked me. She wore the Josephson's signature forest green smock over her blouse, and her dyed auburn hair was pulled back in an artfully messy bun. Tendrils of a floral tattoo curved around her neck, from her spine to just below her ears. She also wore a large diamond ring and had long, manicured nails.

I nodded. "Doesn't hurt to be prepared."

"We're up for another one this weekend," she said. "High wind and record waves. Hope my roof stays on." I glanced at her nametag. *Keri.* Below the letters of her name was a typed label that read, *Ask me about my dog.*

"I hope our roof's okay too," I said. "So...tell me about your dog."

She looked at me, confused for a second, and then laughed, glancing down at her nametag. "Oh, that. Toby's a mutt. One of those big dogs that looks scary, but he's such a sweetheart. Can you believe management makes us wear these name tags?"

"So, you have to, what, list a hobby or something?"

"Yeah. I mean, who cares?" She scowled. She was pretty when she smiled, but her frown gave her face a harsh cast. "What I do after work is nobody's business."

I wasn't sure what to say to that. "I guess so." Maybe the nametag thing was her boss' idea of an icebreaker, to give cashiers something to talk about while customers waited. It wasn't a terrible idea—I never knew what to say to the person at the check-out, though I always felt obligated to make small talk.

"Okay, total's $79.47," Keri said, placing the last can of refried beans into a plastic bag. She put the bag in my cart while I slid my credit card through the card reader to pay. "My husband's a roofer."

I signed my name on the screen and looked up at her. "Sorry?"

"You said you were worried about your roof," she replied, handing me my receipt. "With the storm coming."

"Oh." I thought about the argument Mark and I had about how much I should talk about the house, and decided it was okay to share a little. "Yeah, we're fixing up this house, and the roof is pretty scary."

"Well, if you need someone to look at it, my husband can do it. After he looks at mine, that is." Keri laughed to herself like she doubted he would. "Anyway, if you need a handyman, he can help. He's bonded and everything."

"Uh, sure. Why don't you write his number down? Maybe I'll give him a call." I turned my receipt over and passed it back to her.

"All right. He keeps busy cleaning up after these storms though, so you'll want to call him soon." She jotted down a name and a phone number and handed the receipt back to me.

I stuffed it in my purse. "Thanks. I will."

"No problem," she said and turned to the customer behind me. I gave her a polite smile and took that as my cue to leave.

**

"I'm home," Mark called. "Are the girls asleep?"

I looked up from the box I was unpacking. "Yeah—I put them to bed thirty minutes ago. School night."

"Sorry I'm late." Mark set his briefcase on the kitchen counter and opened the fridge. "I'm starving—what's to eat?"

"I made burritos. There's one in there for you. Did you get the generator?"

I heard the refrigerator door shut, and Mark sheepishly poked his head out of the kitchen. "Sorry. I got tied up at work grading papers."

"Good thing I bought ice, then."

Mark glanced up at the overhead light in the kitchen. "Why? The power's back."

"It didn't come back on until late this afternoon," I told him. "And there's a big storm coming this weekend."

"Tomorrow, I promise," he said, putting his dinner on a plate to reheat it in the microwave. "We do need to start thinking about the electricity in this house though. Can you find an electrician, get a quote?"

"Um-hmm. I actually got the name of a handyman today—don't know if he does electrical work though." I went over to my purse and dug out my receipt. On the back, Keri had scrawled the name "Jesse Hayes," along with her husband's phone number.

Mark bit into his burrito and watched me as he chewed. "Okay," he said between bites, "but I'd really like at least three quotes, so we get the best deal."

I plucked my phone from my purse and started scrolling. "Three quotes," I murmured as I researched our options.

"Might as well find out about plumbing and the roof too," Mark said. "I've set aside $7,000 for electrical work, but I don't know how far it will get us. I want to save as much as we can so we have money for our other projects."

"But the wiring is the priority, right?"

Mark finished off his meal and put his plate in the sink. "Right. The plumbing is holding out for now, though we'll eventually need to replace some pipes."

"And the roof? Is it going to survive the storm?"

Mark wiped his hands with a dish towel. "I don't know, Tawny."

That wasn't a comforting answer. I sat down at the kitchen table. "What if it doesn't?" I imagined shingles scattered all over our yard, and us trying to stem the flow of rainwater upstairs with a legion of pots and pans.

"If it doesn't, I'll have to crawl up there and patch it."

"That's a scary thought." I envisioned Mark climbing a rickety ladder in the wind, trying to nail down shingles in the middle of a storm. A suicide mission, but he hated relying on other people. It became a matter of pride for him.

"I can do it," he replied, insulted. "I worked on roofs when I was putting myself through school, remember?"

I shook my head. "No, you misunderstand me—I know you can do it, but I worry about you up there without help. What if you fell? It's a long way down."

He gave me a wry smile. "You'll just have to help me then."

I scoffed. "That's another scary thought." He knew I wasn't fond of heights. "But I'll do it, just so you don't break your neck."

He leaned down and kissed my forehead. "See? That's why I married you."

Chapter Four

Getting quotes for repairs did not go well. The two electricians I called estimated I'd need between two and seven thousand dollars more than I budgeted. I asked the man at Coastal Electric if he'd consider a monthly payment plan for the $14,000 he wanted. He just laughed.

"Lady, if I did that, I'd never get paid," he said. "I'm sorry, but the best I could do would be half upfront and half upon completion of the job, which should take about two weeks. Think you could swing that?"

"I'll have to take another look at our finances," I answered. "Thanks for your time."

The electrician from Jay's Electric Co. recommended we take a vacation while the house was being rewired. It sounded like a nice idea, but we could hardly afford a trip somewhere. "We'll probably have to open up the walls and cut through the ceiling joists," he explained. "It can get messy."

"Is that really necessary?" I asked. "We have this beautiful fir paneling, and I'd like to preserve it."

"Depends on your foundation and if you have an attic," he said, his deep voice gruff, but not unkind. "Is the house sitting on a concrete slab?"

"No, we've got a basement with a dirt floor."

"In that case, we might be able to fish the wires through the walls between the basement and the attic," he replied. "I gotta warn you up front though, materials alone are going to cost you a pretty penny, with the price of copper nowadays. Probably three thousand for that, and with man hours, we're looking at a total of nine grand. At least."

I sighed. "Well, that's better than another quote I got."

"I'd have to come out to the house and look around to give you a firm number," he said. "Want to set something up?"

"Possibly," I said. "I need to talk it over with my husband first, but if we're interested, I'll give you a call."

"All right, ma'am," he said. "Good luck."

"Thanks." I hung up the phone and sank into the couch, ready to tear my hair out. How were we going to fix this place up if our savings were sucked dry right from the get go? There was a lot we could do on our own—painting, tiling, replacing cabinets in the kitchen... but wiring wasn't one of them. We couldn't put it off either. We could rough it with the plumbing, taking sponge baths if needed, and rent a port-a-potty. Heck, there were public showers and toilets down by the beach, if we really had to rough it.

I looked over at the space heater Mark purchased. It helped take the chill off the house, but it really was dangerous with the bad wiring. I didn't want to chance burning down the house. Even the lamps we plugged in had a tendency to flicker and go out. We were starting to rely on candles on a regular basis, which presented yet another fire hazard. Something had to be done.

I wanted to scream or cry, but couldn't decide which, so I curled up on the couch. We'd been here less than a month, and already we were in a hole. In my vision of buying this house, I never dreamed my family would be camping indoors. I gazed up at the ceiling, at the naked wires poking out from a hole, and how Mark had warned me against touching them after we'd gotten the electricity turned back on. There was a set of plastic wire nuts he'd meant to install over the wires, to keep us from getting electrocuted, but he never got to it. I made a mental note to remind him when I delivered the bad news about the quotes I'd gotten.

I thought about my mother—she would be petrified to see bald wires. Mark was partly right—it was best to keep some things from her. Still, I felt terrible I hadn't yet told her we'd moved. I thought about calling her, but I hated lying. She'd ask all kind of questions, and I'd be forced to lie, to paint a cheerful picture of the house. If she thought I was unhappy, she'd make my sister drive ten hours to see us. That would just make things worse, because she'd complain about the house and my sister would accuse Mark of putting me and the girls in a bad situation. Telling them that buying the house had been a joint decision would do nothing. Mark and I were in over our heads as it was. We didn't need drama from my family.

I sighed and picked up my phone. I needed at least one more quote. Maybe I'd finally get some good news. I was scrolling through a list of local electricians when a circle of light caught my eye. It bounced off the walls of the living room as though it were reflecting off something. I sat up and looked around, but couldn't see what might be causing it.

From the street outside the motor of a passing vehicle roared. I peered out the window and caught a metallic flash, sunlight reflecting off a chrome tool case in the back of a blue pickup truck. A surfboard and a ladder stuck out a few inches over the tailgate. The truck turned a corner, down the street bordering our property. Without knowing why, I went into the guestroom, tracking it, looking out the window to see the truck pull to a stop outside our neighbor's house.

A man got out, grabbed a red tool box from the cab of the truck, and went up the front walk. His ball cap hid his face, but he was trim and broad-shouldered. I glanced back at his truck, trying to make out the lettering on the driver's side door. *J. Hayes, Seaside Handyman.* The name was familiar, but considering the number of names I'd scrolled through, that wasn't surprising. I watched as he knocked on the door, and spoke with the man who answered. The homeowner stepped out of the house and then both men retreated down the walk to gaze up at the roof. They spoke for a few minutes, and then shook hands. The homeowner went back in the house, and the handyman strolled over to his truck to retrieve the ladder.

A connection clicked in my mind, and I grabbed my receipt from Joe's, looking at the number Keri had written, and then comparing it to the number on the truck. Jesse Hayes. Of course—that's why the name sounded familiar. I looked back out the window, watching the man work. He seemed pleasant enough. I wondered if he worked on wiring. Maybe if I talked to him in person, rather than on the phone, he'd be willing to give me a good price to work on our place.

Quickly, I ran upstairs to the bathroom and pulled my hair into a ponytail. I inspected myself in the cracked mirror. My clothes were fairly clean—a little sweaty from unpacking boxes, but I wasn't trying to impress anyone. I slipped on my shoes and headed out the door.

**

Standing in my neighbor's front yard, I looked up at the guy nailing shingles, his back to me. "Hello?" I called. He didn't seem to hear me, so I tried again, speaking louder. "Excuse me—hello?"

Slowly, the man turned his head. When he saw me, he stood and walked to the edge of the roof, looking completely fearless as he balanced. "Can I help you?"

"Yeah, I was wondering—"

He held up his hand. "Wait a sec," he said. "I'll come down." He climbed down the ladder, dropping the last few feet to land neatly in front of me. His face was tanned and the hair peeking out from his hat had blond highlights—I guessed that was from working outside and from surfing, assuming the board in the truck was his. "What were you saying?"

"Jesse Hayes?" I asked. He nodded, adjusting his ball cap, and I held out my hand. "Hi, I'm Tawny Ellis, from across the street."

He shook my hand, giving me a warm smile that put me at ease. "Hi. What can I do for you?"

"Well, we're fixing up our place," I said, nodding over my shoulder at my house. "I see that you do roofing, and I was wondering if you do wiring as well. I met Keri, your, uh, wife, at the grocery store, and she gave me a referral."

His easy smile froze. "Did she, now?" He glanced over at my house. "Your roof definitely needs work. I'm guessing your windows do too, since most of them have been covered with plastic."

"Yes. It's an old house. We've got a lot of work ahead." I hesitated, caught off guard by his reaction to me mentioning Keri. "So, do you do electrical work? We're going to have to rewire the whole thing."

"I do, but I'd need to take a look before I could give you a quote." He looked back at my neighbor's roof and then met my gaze. "I've got to finish the job here, but I could come by this afternoon, if you'll still be around."

"Yeah, that'd be great," I said. "I've gotten a couple of quotes from electricians, but I thought it would be good to get another opinion so my husband and I could consider our options." Then, not knowing why I said it, I blurted out, "Actually, with the quotes we've already gotten, I don't know if we can afford to rewire everything." There was something about his professional demeanor that felt safe, like I could tell him things I probably shouldn't.

He nodded and gave me a sympathetic look. "Electrical can get expensive. Maybe there's another option, and you won't have to rewire everything. I'll look and see what we can do to get it up to code and still get you a good deal."

That sounded more hopeful than my phone calls had been. "Okay. Thanks."

He smiled. "No problem." He glanced up at my neighbor's roof, and then back at me. "This should take me about two hours. I'll head over when I finish."

"All right." I returned his smile. "It was nice to meet you, Jesse. See you this afternoon."

"See you soon." He held my gaze, a twinkle in his light brown eyes. Then he grinned and headed back toward the ladder, swinging himself up on the second rung. "Tawny Ellis from across the street."
**

I managed to keep my own grin in check until I got back in the house and closed the door behind me. *What the hell, Tawny?* Flirting with the handyman? Geez. I was married. Even if I wasn't, he was. Jesse was cute though, and charming too. Mark would shoot us both if he thought I was interested in another man. Okay, he wouldn't actually murder us, but I wasn't about to invite my husband's wrath. I was smarter than that.

Anyway, it's not like we were *really* flirting. Just a friendly little exchange, and maybe I'd get a better deal on rewiring this house. I laughed to myself as I sat down on the couch again, looking around. So much work to do. Maybe Jesse could give me a quote on the roof too, and give me an idea about the heating and plumbing. I had no idea if I could afford him, but it sounded like he might be open to working with us, even with our limited budget. At least after talking with him, I'd have a better concept about where things stood financially, and I'd finally know if buying this house had been a terrible mistake.

I got up from the couch and started cleaning up the kitchen to pass the time.

**

Jesse zeroed in on the bald wiring in the living room right away. "This isn't good."

"I was afraid you'd say that."

He turned to me. "These really shouldn't be exposed like this. Let me run out to the truck. I've got something to cover those wires, make them safe."

I grabbed the box of plastic wire nuts next to the couch. "We've got these—they just haven't been installed."

"Oh. Yeah, that's what I've got in the truck." He took the box from me. "Mind if I shut off the electricity for a few minutes?"

I shook my head. "I think the fuse box is in the coat closet. Next to the stairs." I led him down the hallway to show him.

"Okay. This won't take long." He opened the box and cut the power. Then he went back to the living room and covered the wires. He finished the job within three minutes. "All right. All done."

"That's it?" I was surprised—Mark had acted like it was a huge ordeal.

"Yep—that's it. Now no one will kill themselves on those."

"Thank you. What do I owe you for that?"

He laughed and shook his head, waving me off. "Nothing. I haven't even looked at your house yet."

"Well, thanks. What do you want to see first?"

"I should probably start from the ground up. I think I saw stairs to a basement?"

**

I gave Jesse the full run of the house and tried to stay out of his way. Not that I had any desire to go in the basement anyway. As I kept myself busy folding laundry, he tromped up and down the stairs. He passed by the living room a few times, to check the wiring and outlets on the first floor. Each time he gave me a polite nod, professional and not overly familiar. I returned his nod with a smile, and let him go about his assessment.

I wondered what Mark would think of me being alone, in our

house, with a stranger. He probably would've cautioned me against it, with good reason. There was something warm and genuine about Jesse that put me at ease though, made me more trusting than I would've been with another man. Our big yellow lab, Dune, took to him right away, so that helped. I've always thought dogs and children were good judges of character. Of course, Dune was friendly with anyone who'd pay attention to her, so maybe her opinion couldn't be entirely trusted.

After about twenty minutes, Jesse came back down the hallway. I set the socks I was folding in the laundry basket and rose from the couch. "So, what's the verdict?"

"It's not bad," he said, brushing a stray cobweb from his shoulder. He had dust on his knees and a smudge of dirt on his face.

I gestured to the kitchen table and went to the cabinet. "Can I offer you a glass of water?"

"Yes, please." He sat down at the table and then coughed into his elbow. "Excuse me." He gave me a good-natured smile. "That basement of yours is a tad dusty."

I laughed. "Yeah, I try to stay out of there." I filled the glass with water from the fridge and handed it to him.

"Thanks." He took a long swig and wiped his mouth, setting the glass on the table. "I think I have good news for you. Rewiring, as you know, can be pricey. But, since you have a basement and an attic, I'm fairly confident I can fish the wires through the walls, eliminating the need to open up them up."

I took a long breath, remembering my conversation with the electrician who thought we'd have to cut through the paneling and ceilings. "That's a relief. How much do you think it will cost?"

He thought about it for a moment. "It's a large house—a lot of square footage and at least two outlets in every room...so materials would be about three thousand."

I nodded. "That's what the guy from Jay's Electric said too. And man hours?" I tried to keep my expression neutral, but I was cringing on the inside, waiting for an answer that would make it impossible for us to move forward on the repairs.

Maybe some of my anxiety bled through the façade, because he asked, "May I ask what Jay's estimate was?"

"Six thousand for the work, so nine total."

"And how much do you have to work with?"

I frowned. "Only seven thousand." And wiring was just the first fix in a long line of repairs this house needed.

"Okay," he said. "I can do it for seven."

I stared at him, taken aback. "That's…that's awfully generous of you."

He toyed with the glass on the table, staring at his hands. "Well… to be frank with you, I could use the work." He looked up at me. "Things tend to slow down for me after summer—with the tourists gone and the rains starting up."

"I imagine you get a lot of roof work."

He nodded. "True. After the big storms. But it's not steady work. Or all that predictable."

"I see." I studied his face, thinking about our list of repairs. Mark would be happy about Jesse's willingness to work within our budget, but would he feel comfortable hiring him? I hoped so. "I need to talk to Mark—my husband—but we do have a lot of work to do on this house. We have limited funds, but maybe once we get through the electrical issues, we could talk about you working on the roof?"

"That sounds fair," Jesse said. "I'd be willing to work on things on your schedule and as you can afford them. Like I said, I could use the income."

"And we definitely need that kind of understanding," I replied.

"Talk it over with Mark, see what he thinks." Jesse reached into his back pocket and handed me a business card. "Call me when you want to get started."

**

It turned out Mark was open to hiring Jesse. It didn't hurt that I approached him with the bad news first, sharing the two more expensive estimates, and then Jesse's offer to honor our budget. I called Jesse the next day, and he agreed to get started once he'd purchased the materials he needed.

Someone else working on the house inspired me to get moving on my own projects. As Jesse installed new wiring and replaced outdated outlets, I focused on sanding and painting the rooms downstairs.

Paint was affordable and went a long way toward erasing years of neglect.

"Looks great," Jesse said as he passed through the living room, headed to the kitchen for a drink. I'd told him to make himself at home, and stocked the fridge with soda and water bottles.

"Thank you very much." I opened a new can of paint. In line with my beach cottage vision, I'd painted the paneling white, giving it a fresh look. The light color made the room less dark and dingy. As I stirred the paint, I said, "I'm hoping, eventually, to restore the fireplace in here. Build it with river rocks, like the other beach houses I've seen in Seaside."

Jesse resurfaced from the kitchen with a bottle of water and studied the fireplace area. There was still a board nailed where the opening had been, and an outline of chipped tile on the floor. "That would look nice." He turned a slow circle, looking at the wood floor. "What's your plan for flooring?"

"I haven't decided. I want to keep the wood, if I can. But I don't want to stain it too light, because of the white walls. If I go too dark, pet hair will show. Our dog sheds like crazy."

"I hadn't noticed." Jesse laughed, looking down at his jeans, which were covered in dog hair. His laugh was infectious, and I found myself chuckling too. Dune had fallen in love with Jesse, following him everywhere but down to the basement. I often had to put her outside while he worked so he wouldn't end up covered in slobber. He didn't seem to mind, sometimes stopping his work to give her an affectionate belly rub. "How about a driftwood color?"

I thought about it. "Gray? Maybe. The hardware store doesn't stock stain like that though—just pine, oak, and cherry. How would I pull that off?"

His eyes twinkled. "A little trick I know. Get gray paint and dilute it with water, then wash it over the boards."

I smiled. "I like it. I might just give that a try."

Chapter Five

S everal days into the project, Jesse informed me he'd need the electricity turned off during most of the day. The girls had the afternoon off from school because of training for their teachers, so I decided to take them someplace where they wouldn't be in Jesse's way. The rain ruled out the beach, so we settled on a visit to the Carousel Mall for a cheap date indoors.

The carousel was in the center of the mall, and the girls were excited to ride it. We'd lived in Seaside for two years, but had never taken them. Sara was immediately drawn to a hippocampus—an aqua-colored horse that was half fish, with fins and a curling, fluked tail. Sophie chose a cream horse with a saddle edged in ochre and violet sea stars. I strapped her in, but she insisted I stand next to her during the ride.

As we circled around, I surveyed the mall. There were several stores that seemed to cater to tourists, selling t-shirts with beach slogans or shells etched with the word "Seaside." One store sold nothing but hats—a birthday cake, a magician's black hat with a white rabbit bursting from the top, and a jester's hat with bells. There was even a hat that looked like a squid. I laughed to myself, thinking about how the girls might enjoy trying on hats. Then I saw a toy store called *Trinkets*.

Sara spotted it too. "Look Mom! Toys! Let's go there next."

I gave her a smile and nodded, suppressing my urge to groan. I knew if I took her in the toy store, she'd see all kinds of things she'd want, and it'd take forever to leave. I wasn't looking forward to hearing her whine when I told her no, we couldn't afford to buy her a new toy right now. Maybe I could pacify her by telling her to put the things she wanted on her Christmas list.

I glanced at Sophie, in wonder at how two kids raised in the same house with the same rules could be so different. When I told Sophie no, she always seemed to take it in stride, nodding wisely, like she understood and wouldn't hold it against me. In some ways, she was more mature than her older sister. I hated to punish her for Sara's behavior. It wouldn't be fair to Sophie to avoid the toy store just because Sara might have an outburst.

The carousel slowed, grinding to a stop. By the time I had Sophie unbuckled, Sara was already standing at the gated exit, hopping excitedly from one foot to the other. "Come on! Let's go!"

"We will," I said, taking her hand as we left the carousel. I stopped next to a park bench and set Sophie down. "One condition, Sara."

"What?" She glanced up at me and then returned her attention to the toy store—tugging my arm, pulling impatiently.

I knelt down so we were face-to-face. "Sara. Look me in the eye." She stopped squirming and raised her eyes to mine. "I'll take you in the toy store, but we're not buying anything today. If you see something you like, you'll have to put it on your Christmas list. And when I say it's time to go, I don't want to hear any complaints. Got it?"

"Got it," Sara parroted back. She looked wounded, like I'd given her a balloon and then stuck a pin in it, but I hoped the message had gotten through.

"Got it," Sophie said, echoing her sister in a more cheerful tone. She reminded me of a sparrow with her tiny frame and bright eyes.

I scooped up Sophie. "Good. Come here, little bird. Let's go see some toys."

As it turned out, Sara mostly behaved herself. She walked around Trinkets with her hands clasped demurely behind her back, like a proper lady from a bygone era. She even said "Excuse me," to a little boy who blocked one of the aisles, stretched out full-length on his stomach as he played with a toy train on the carpeted floor. I worried she'd step on him, but she simply stepped over his legs, said "Thank you," and went about her business.

I was just congratulating myself on a parenting win when she suddenly made a beeline to a glass case stocked with porcelain dolls. Face pressed against the glass, she hollered for me to come look. "Mama! Dolls!"

The tall man at the register shot me a warning look, as though we were in a library and not a store catering to children, and I gave him an apologetic smile. I knelt down next to Sara, Sophie in tow. "I'm right here, honey. There's no need to yell."

"Dolls, Mama," Sara whispered. "Aren't they pretty?"

"Yes," I whispered back. "They're beautiful." The dolls in the display looked lovely arrayed in satin and lace, with delicate features and hair in ringlets. Some of the faces sported fine cracks as though the porcelain were old. I wondered if the hair was real—it must be, if the dolls were antiques.

"Can I put one of these on my Christmas list, Mama?" Sara asked. She almost looked like a doll herself, her wide eyes filled with hope.

I stole a look at the price tag on one of the dolls' wrists. Over a hundred dollars? Ouch. I was about to tell Sara the dolls were too expensive when the man behind the counter walked over. He was an older man, with a potbelly and thinning white hair. Pinned on his red apron was a name tag that said '*Nick.*' I wondered if he went by Saint Nick around the holidays. I bet he did if he ever wore a Santa suit.

"I don't recommend those for children," he said with a scowl, his bushy brows knitted together. "They're collector's items, not toys."

Ironic then, that they're in a *toy* store. Noting the harsh expression on his face, I decided it was best to keep that to myself. I revised my earlier assumption—he didn't seem the type to play Santa after all. With his gaunt face, he seemed much too severe. I stood and gave him a pacifying smile. "They must be very old."

"Indeed, they are," he replied, his large hands splayed on the surface of the counter. He had long fingers and yellowed smoker's nails. He looked down at my daughters, towering over them. "Perhaps when you girls are much, much older, you'll be responsible enough to have something like this." He gave Sara a smile that showed his teeth and held no warmth. "Until then, we've got plenty of other dolls in aisle five."

Sophie looked alarmed at his tone, but Sara looked crushed. Her lip trembled like she was about to burst into tears.

"Thank you anyway," I said, biting back my anger. "We'll keep looking." I took my daughters' hands and walked out of the store. I guided the girls to a bench near the carousel and sat between them. "Are you all right, Sara?"

She nodded, blinking back tears.

I put my arm around her and pulled her onto my lap. "I want you to know I'm proud of you for the way you behaved in that store. You did a good job, and that man shouldn't have talked to you like that."

She sniffed, and pulled at one of her pigtails, winding her hair around her fingers. It was something she did out of nervousness or if she had trouble falling asleep. The ribbon in her hair loosened. "He was a grouch."

I smirked. Leave it to Sara to tell it like it was. "Yes, he was a *big* grouch. Sometimes adults aren't very nice, but that doesn't mean you did anything wrong, sweetie."

"I yelled in the store," she said, looking up at me. "A little."

I nodded. "A little, yes, but then you quieted down when I asked you to." I smoothed her hair and tightened the ribbon holding her pigtail in place. "Why don't we go someplace else? I saw a store with silly hats."

"I saw a store with candy," Sophie piped up. "There were fairies too."

That got Sara's attention. "Candy *and* fairies?" She wiped at her eyes and sat up straight.

Sophie shook her head up and down. "Uh-huh. Boaf of them."

Sara scooted off my lap. She and Sophie were obsessed with fairies. Anything sparkly, really—fairies, ponies with wings, or princess dolls with rhinestone tiaras. I was forever cleaning glitter off the kitchen table after their craft projects. I stood up and held out my hands for my girls. "All right. Lead on, Soph."

Sophie led us across the mall to a store I hadn't noticed as we rode the carousel, but I could see why she had. Tucked between a t-shirt vendor and an old-time photography studio—where women had the choice of dressing either like a high-collared Victorian schoolmarm or a scantily-clad saloon girl, all captured in sepia tone—was a shop with a large window display.

The front of the shop was fashioned as a storybook cottage straight from the Black Forest, the molding on the paned window covered with carved leaves and forest animals. Inside the display window was a faux tree, lit with sparkling white lights. All around the tree were beautiful fairy dolls, perching on the branches, sitting on gnarled tree roots, or captured mid-swing, on a rope swing suspended from the branches.

All six fairies looked like barefoot little girls with gossamer wings. The translucent wings sparkled with glitter, and the dolls had rosy cheeks—each the picture of vitality, frozen in time. Each wore a different color dress that matched the crown of flowers on her head, and each had different colored hair.

Sara and Sophie pressed their faces against the glass, mesmerized by the display. "Can we go in, Mama?" Sophie asked.

I nodded and opened the door to the shop. The girls went around to the other side of the display for a closer look. Behind the counter, a jolly-looking man gave us a wide smile, full of the warmth the toy salesman's lacked.

"Welcome to the Confection Cottage," he said, his voice as rich and welcoming as his smile.

I returned his smile, the anger from the toy store slipping away. "Your display is beautiful."

The man's smile grew even wider. "Thank you! I've invested a great deal of time in it." He came out from behind the counter and crossed his arms over his chest, gazing at the display with pride.

I glanced over at the fairy tree. "You made that?" Every limb on the tree had been carved with intricate detail; every leaf painstakingly formed and painted varying shades of green. The dolls themselves were a wonder—each as different and lifelike as real children.

The man chuckled to himself and looked down at his feet as though self-conscious. "Yes, I did. It's a labor of love, that. Less of a hobby and more of an obsession." He looked up at me shyly. "I suppose it's a bit strange, a grown man making fairy dolls." He tipped his head toward my daughters. "Seeing the joy it brings to their faces makes it worthwhile though. All the children love the Cottage's fairies."

"My girls certainly do." I held out my hand to him. "Tawny Ellis. First visit to the Carousel Mall."

He shook my hand. The man had huge hands. My hand looked tiny enveloped in his. His fingers weren't as long as the toy salesman's, but his nails were in better shape, clean and neatly manicured. "Richard Olheiser. Is this your first visit to the coast?"

"No—we live in Seaside. But we don't get out much."

Mr. Olheiser laughed, a great rolling laugh as big as the rest of him. I found myself grinning—here was a guy who could play Santa Claus. No beard, but thick white hair and a round tummy that suited him. I wondered if he had grandchildren. He looked like a kindly grandpa, or maybe a favorite uncle. The kind of person who puts you at ease, makes you want to open up. Maybe the kind to pull up a chair for you near the fire, and offer you a hot chocolate as you swapped stories.

"We've lived here for a couple of years, but we were renting a place outside of Seaside, so we didn't spend much time in town," I told him. "But we just bought a place, so now we're renovating it."

"Oh, whereabouts?" he asked.

I found myself pausing. Here I was, gabbing to a stranger. Should I really tell him where I lived? I studied his face, his warm smile, and decided he meant no harm. "Holladay and Seventh."

He nodded, seemingly unaware of my hesitation. "Ah—I know the place well. The old Stroud homestead. Saw it was for sale. Glad to hear someone is fixing it up."

I supposed it wasn't all that strange he'd know the house—Seaside was a small town. "Do you know any history about the house, Mr. Olheiser?"

He held up his hands. "Please—call me Richard. Mr. Olheiser is my father, and he's quite elderly. Though I'm no spring chicken, either."

"Richard," I corrected, giving him a smile. "I've been trying to track down the house's history. We're hoping to turn the place into a B&B, and I thought it would be neat to share that with people."

Richard tapped his chin, thinking. "I know Paul Stroud built it, and the Strouds had it in the family until the last son, Nicholas, lost it to the bank," he said. "Nick refinanced to make repairs, but couldn't pay the mortgage when the recession hit. Almost lost his toy store too."

That made my ears prick up. Hadn't the salesman in Trinkets been named Nick? "The toy store in this mall?"

"The very same."

"Oh." I felt like my head was spinning. "That's why he was so rude. He must know we bought his house."

Richard gave me a sympathetic smile. "Oh, I doubt that was it." I shook my head, about to disagree, and he shrugged, conceding. "Well, perhaps he *does* know, but Nick's rude to everyone. Bit of a curmudgeon, that one." He reached over and patted my hand. "If it's any consolation, he's got no love for me either. Not after the Lolly Dollies."

"Lolly Dollies?" I asked. I felt a tug on my pants leg and looked down.

Sara was looking up at me. "Look, Mama." She pointed to a table I hadn't spotted. Sitting on top of it, in a tiered display, were fabric dolls. They wore flowery dresses and had hair made of yarn. Each held a colorful lollipop in her arms. "This store has candy *and* dolls."

I was surprised I hadn't noticed, considering my daughters' love of dolls. Then again, I'd been distracted by my conversation with Richard. Not to mention, the store was chock full of colorful candies and sweet creations—there was a lot to look at. The store's proprietor seemed to pride himself on visual presentation.

"Right you are, young lady," Richard said. "The very things we were talking about." He crouched down to my daughters' level, his hands on his knees. "And what might your names be?"

Sophie, shy as usual, looked away, but she had a sweet smile on her face. Sara, recovered from the upset in the toy store, was the one to speak up.

"I'm Sara, and this is Sophie," she said. "I'm seven, but she's only five."

Sophie looked insulted. "Five and a *half*."

Richard turned to Sophie and chuckled. "Of course you are. Half birthdays are very important."

"Well, it's not her half birthday today—" I began, but he shushed me with a wink.

"Tell me, Miss Sophie, have you been thinking about what you want for Christmas?" he asked.

Sophie blinked and went back to being shy. Sara answered for her. "When we went in the toy store, Mama said if we saw toys we liked we hadta put them on our list. I saw a doll I wanted, but the mean man said I was too little."

"Sara," I warned.

Richard waved me off. "It's all right, Mom. She's just being honest." I bristled a little at that, but softened at his smile. He had such a way with children, I couldn't fault him. "Then what happened?"

"Then we came in here, and I like your dolls much better anyway," Sara finished. She walked over to the display and then looked back at me. "Can I put one of these on my list, Mama?"

I took Sophie's hand and led her over to the Lolly Dollies. Richard rose and followed.

"Mom," Sophie whispered. "The one on top looks like me." And it did. Where Sara's hair was brown and straight, like Mark's, Sophie's hair was like mine. Blond and curly, though my strands were the color of honey and hers were so pale they were nearly white. The doll sitting on the top of the tier had yarn hair almost an identical color to my daughter's.

"And this one looks like me," Sara said, grabbing a doll from the bottom tier.

I dropped Sophie's hand and reached out to steady the other dolls in the display before they could fall over and spill their lollipops to the floor. "Sara, please don't grab things. If you want to see something, ask, and I'll get it down for you." I held out my hand for the doll.

Admonished, Sara passed it to me, and placed her hands behind her back, reverting to my earlier coaching about the etiquette for visiting stores. I could tell she thought she was in big trouble and was now trying to make up for it with good behavior.

"That's all right," Richard said softly. I'd forgotten about him for a moment, I was so wrapped up in the girls and their doll look-alikes. I turned to find him quietly watching us.

I felt faintly embarrassed he'd seen Sara almost upend his display and then me, getting on her case about it. "Um, did you…" I reached for something to say, something to divert his attention from the near miss. "Did you make these dolls too?"

"I did," he said. "The faces are hand-embroidered. Except for the button eyes, of course."

"Ah." I was at a loss for words, so I studied the black button eyes and cheerful smile on the face of the doll Sara had handed me. "That must have been a lot of work."

"It was, but worth it." He smiled. "I cheated on everything else though, using a machine to make the body and the clothes. But the hair is hand-stitched. The lollipops are my own creation as well."

"That's what I want for Christmas," Sara said, her voice soft with reverence. She looked at me with hope in her eyes.

Richard chuckled. "Why wait?"

I stole a look at the price tag. Ten dollars each. Not a lot to spend on a toy, but if I bought one for Sara, I'd have to get one for Sophie, to be fair, and twenty dollars was a lot to spend for people who were trying to save money to fix up their house. "Well," I said with a nervous laugh, as I put the doll back on the table, "that's not something we can afford today, but—" If my hesitation wasn't obvious in my voice, I'm sure it was written on my face.

"Actually," Richard said, "we're having a special sale. All Lolly Dollies are half off."

I glanced at the display. There was nothing to indicate a sale was going on—no signs reading *50% off*, no colorful banners hung overhead directing customers to the sale. I looked back at him.

He held my gaze. "Today only."

I watched Sophie's face as he took the doll from the top of the display. There was longing in her eyes, but I knew she wouldn't say a word. She was like a miniature adult with impeccable manners. It was as if she watched every brash thing Sara did and tried to be better, so she'd never have to be reprimanded. I wanted so badly to reward her for being a good kid and knew the doll would make her happy. A doll would thrill Sara too. And couldn't I afford ten dollars to make my children happy? But... "But there's no sign," I said, eyeing Richard suspiciously. "Are you *really* having a sale, or are you just being nice?"

He brushed off my concern. "Does it matter? That's one of the perks of owning a store. You can have a sale whenever you want."

"But why?" I asked, exasperated. "Why be so nice to us?" It was kind of him to lower his prices just for us, but I felt like I was taking advantage of him. He didn't even know us.

He shrugged. "Why not? I don't spend hours on these dolls to make money. I don't *need* more money." He nodded toward the girls. "I do it to see the smiles on their faces."

Well, that was a good reason. I looked down to find both of my daughters watching me intently. They both seemed to be holding their breath, standing still like they were afraid to move, waiting to see what I'd do.

I turned to Richard. "Okay. You're being too generous, but you talked me into it. Two Lolly Dollies, please."

He grinned at Sara and Sophie and then reached for the doll Sara had grabbed earlier. "Two beautiful dolls for two beautiful girls."

My daughters beamed back at him, both of them jumping up and down excitedly. "Thanks, Mister," Sara said. I laughed, surprised I didn't have to prompt her to say thank you.

"Yeah, thanks, Mister," Sophie echoed.

Richard walked behind the counter and set the dolls down on the surface. "You are quite welcome, my dears." He drew a paper bag out from under the counter and placed the dolls inside. "And, since it's your first time in the store, and you were on your *very* best behavior, here's a little treat." He scooped up a handful of saltwater taffy from a glass bowl near the cash register and dropped them into the bag. Then he handed the bag to Sophie, giving her a conspiratorial wink.

She took the bag and gave him a wide smile. The man was so charming he'd managed to win her over too.

"Can I hold mine?" Sara asked Sophie. Sophie nodded, and Sara pulled her doll out of the bag. She hugged it to her little chest. "I love her. So much."

"Thank you," I said to Richard, handing him a ten-dollar bill. "You're a kind man."

"As my mother used to say, kindness costs nothing. It's good for business, too." He gave my daughters a friendly wave. "Enjoy your dolls, girls. I hope to see you again soon."

We left the shop, and I noticed Nick, the "mean man" as Sara called him, standing near the carousel, chatting with the man who operated it. He gave us a long look, scowling when he saw the doll Sara carried.

I returned his look with narrowed eyes. Serves him right—act like a jerk and people will spend their money elsewhere. If he treated all his customers the way he treated us, it was little wonder he'd almost lost the toy store.

Chapter Six

Whe we got home, the girls were excited to show Jesse their new dolls. He listened patiently, and then I sent them upstairs to play so he and I could talk in the living room.

"The power's back on, and I fixed the light on the front porch. It should work now," he told me.

I gestured for him to have a seat on the couch. "Thanks."

"I worry that you don't have a light on the back porch," he said, brushing off his jeans before sitting on the edge of the couch. "That's a safety hazard."

I raised my eyebrows. "Because I'll probably go out there some night and tumble down the stairs?"

He took off his ball cap and smoothed his hair, brushing it off his forehead. I noticed he wore his hair longer than Mark did. There was a natural wave to it that worked for him. "You might."

It took me a second to register what he said, and then I was embarrassed that I'd been staring at his hair. Great hair, but still—I had no business looking. "Hey, I'm not that much of a klutz."

He laughed. "That's *not* what I was saying. I guess it's more of a security issue than a safety hazard in my mind. Someone comes to the door at night, and you don't have enough light to see who it is. You said Mark works late most evenings."

"He does." It seemed like Mark came home late every night these days. Maybe he was avoiding the construction zone we called our house.

"I suggest purchasing a porch light for back there," he said. I frowned, and he added, "Doesn't have to be expensive, or even pretty, just one to give you a little more light until you know what you want to do with that area."

I thought about what a mess the back porch was, with the toilet and sink exposed to the elements. It looked trashy. "We're hoping to enclose it at some point and get that bathroom working again. I know it looks awful right now."

He gave me a sympathetic smile. "It'll come together. My concern is that you and your girls stay safe."

Here's another kind man. In spite of the incident with our house's former owner, there were good people in this town. Jesse and Richard were proof of that. "Thank you. It's good to have you looking out for us." I thought about the look Nick Stroud had given us as we left the mall, and wondered if he did know we'd bought his old house. What if he was still angry about losing it and came over some night to confront us? I'd hate to be unable to see him if he was standing at my back door, especially if Mark wasn't home. "You're right—we should get a light for back there."

"I can pick up a cheap one for you," Jesse said. "Something inexpensive, but good enough to tide you over until you can get a nicer one."

"How much would it cost?"

"Probably about twenty bucks. Is that okay for me to add to the bill? I know you like to consult with Mark before buying things."

I stared at Jesse. When he put it like that, it sounded like Mark was a tyrant. I wondered if that was how Jesse saw us—me, the mousey wife, trying to meet the overbearing husband's demands. "I'm sure he won't care as long as it's under fifty dollars. It's just with our budget—"

Jesse held up his hands. "No, I get it. When you have limited funds, you want money to stretch as far as it can."

I nodded. Jesse had mentioned his budget was pretty tight too, with his summer clients gone.

"Hey, I got a present for you."

My eyes widened. "What? You didn't have to do that."

He grinned. "Don't get too excited. With that storm coming tonight, I thought I'd loan you my gennie. Don't want you left in the dark when the power goes."

I gave him a teasing smile. "You trying to tell me something about the work you did today? Worried I'll think you screwed up?"

He shook his head, laughing. "Uh, *no*. I stand by my work, ma'am. But this storm's gonna make last week's look like a gentle breeze. Power could be out for a week, and I don't want to come over here and find you all frozen like popsicles because you had no heat."

"That *would* make it tough to find future clients," I said. "And you wouldn't get paid."

"See, purely professional interest," he agreed.

"Aw, and I thought you liked us."

He gave me a smile, and then looked past me. I turned to see Sara standing in the hallway. She ducked out of sight, like she'd been caught listening.

"Sara, honey, what do you need?" I called. Her footsteps retreated back up the stairs. I turned back to Jesse, surprised to see his cheeks flushed. Was he blushing? Surely not. "I…I should go see what she's up to."

He rose to his feet, adjusting his cap as he put it back on. "Yeah. I better pull that gennie off the back of my truck. I'll show you how it works once I get it set up." With that, he was back to work, all business again.

**

The storm did blow in that night. The whole house rattled and shook from the force of the wind, and the lights flickered, but the power stayed on, thanks to the borrowed generator. The noise from the wind scared the girls, so I tucked them together in Sara's bed, along with their new dolls.

At one point, I woke to a loud noise. I opened my eyes, listening intently, trying to figure out what it was. It sounded like something crashing against the side of the house, or maybe a door slamming, but the wind seemed to have died down, blanketing the house in quiet. Lying there in the silence, half-awake, I wondered if maybe I'd dreamed it.

I was nearly asleep again when there was a soft, rustling noise near my feet, and I propped myself up on my elbows to see one of the girls standing at the foot of the bed. The room was dark, so it was hard to tell, but it looked like Sara's silhouette. "Are you okay, honey?" I asked.

Maybe there really had been a noise, and it startled her awake too. I glanced over at the bedside clock. 3:04 am. I turned to tell her to go back to bed, but she already had.

She just needed a little assurance, I told myself. Sara was prone to nightmares, and when she was younger, I'd spent many a night sleep-deprived, comforting her so she'd go back to sleep. Things had gotten better now that she was older. I could just tell her to go back to bed instead of having to get up and tuck her in. With that thought, I slipped into a deep sleep, not waking until well after the sun rose.

Beside me, Mark yawned and stretched. I rolled over, facing him. "Morning. Did you hear that loud bang in the middle of the night?"

"Nope. I slept like a rock." He hopped out of bed and pulled back the curtains.

Bright light streamed into the room, and I squinted, shielding my eyes. "Too early for that much light," I grumbled, pulling the blankets over my face. Mark was the morning person in the family, not me.

"It's after eight," he replied. I peeked out to find him staring out the window. "Good thing it's Saturday. We're going to have a ton of cleanup from this storm." He closed the curtain and started to get dressed, tossing his pajama pants in the hamper by the closet.

"What kind of cleanup?"

"There're branches all over the yard—shingles too." He picked up his phone and studied it. "And the storm's not done yet—there's a high wind advisory until tomorrow night."

I groaned at the thought of the storm wreaking havoc on our roof. Hopefully, the damage was minor. I'd have to ask Jesse to take a look and patch what he could. We couldn't afford a whole new roof just yet, but we'd have to address the damage, so we didn't get a leak. I pushed back the covers and sat up. "I'll call Jesse."

Mark shook his head. "Wait 'til Monday, Tawn. Doesn't make sense to call until the storm's done. Besides, it's the weekend. The guy could use a break."

True—Jesse had spent all week getting our wiring up to code. "Okay, Monday then." I stuffed my feet into my slippers and went to check on the girls.

They were snuggled up together, sleeping peacefully. Sophie was snoring softly, her arms wrapped around her doll. I sat down on Sara's side of the bed and brushed her hair off her face. She was clutching her doll too—tufts of yarn hair peeked out from under the covers. As I stroked her forehead, she opened her eyes. "Hi, sweetie. Did you sleep okay?"

"The wind was scary."

"Yeah. It blew like crazy," I said. "Did it wake you in the middle of the night? You came in my room."

She looked at me, blinking her eyes. "No, I didn't."

I stared at her, puzzled. "Yes, you did. It was three in the morning. You were standing by my bed."

She shook her head. "I wanted to, but Sophie wouldn't let me. She was scared to be by herself."

"Oh." Well, maybe she forgot, or maybe I dreamed that too. "How's your doll? Does she have a name yet?"

Sara smiled and pulled her doll out from under the covers. It was filthy. Its yarn hair looked matted, and it had reddish-brown splotches on its fabric face and dress. One of the button eyes looked like it was about to fall off.

"Sara, what happened?" When she looked at me questioningly, I felt annoyed. "How did your doll get so dirty? We just got her yesterday."

She looked at her doll and then back at me, seemingly as baffled as I was. "I don't know."

I stood up and felt something soft and yielding under my slippers. I looked down and saw a fabric arm sticking out from under Sara's bed. I bent over and pulled out whatever it was. A doll. I held it up, confused. It was the same doll, but brand new. I set the clean doll down on the bed and took the one Sara was holding. If the new doll was the one we bought yesterday, where had this other doll come from?

A flash of realization came to me, and I dropped the filthy doll like it burned my fingers. This was the doll from the basement.

"I thought you said you didn't get out of bed last night," I said. My tone was harsher than I intended.

Sara looked at me, her eyes wide. "I didn't, Mama."

I sighed and sat down on the bed, trying to temper my anger. "Sara, I won't be mad, but I need you to tell me the truth. You got up last night, and you went down to the basement, didn't you? You know I don't want you down there, honey."

"But I didn't go down there, Mama."

"Then where did the doll come from?" I asked, raising my voice. She was lying. She had to be. How many times had I caught her standing at the basement stairs, peering down? I'd told her again and again it was off-limits. It was too dark down there, and she'd get hurt on junk we'd yet to throw away. Not to mention the mold, grime, and whatever else thrived in dark basements. I remembered the flies coming at my face and shuddered. I stared at the filthy old doll with disgust, wondering if my daughter would be scarred for life if I set it on fire.

Sara shook her head, tears welling up in her eyes. "I didn't, Mama. I didn't."

I was frightening her, but I couldn't help it—I was scared too. Because if she hadn't brought the doll from the basement, who had?

Not Sophie. She was terrified of the dark. And not Mark. Why would he go down to the basement, pick up a dirty doll, and stick it in our daughter's bed?

"Okay," I said, forcing myself to take a breath. The kid had enough nightmares already—I didn't need to add to that. "Okay. I'm sorry, Sara. I believe you." I handed her the new doll and gave her a smile. "Tell you what. I'll just take this old doll downstairs and stick it in the washing machine. It's too dirty to play with right now."

That was a lie. I wasn't going to clean up a creepy doll and give it to my daughter to play with. I was going to put it straight in the garbage. But she didn't need to know that.

fter the winds had settled down, I dialed Jesse's number to set up a time for him to patch up the roof. It was unfortunate we couldn't have tackled that project before the storm, but I was just grateful he let us borrow his generator. Without that, we would've been without power. Now, at least, we were on par with the rest of the neighborhood. Jesse's generator steadily roared, chugging along in concert with those of our neighbors. I didn't mind the noise, as long as the lights stayed on.

I needed to talk to him about pest control too. The flies were back, congregating around the back porch. A number of them had gotten inside. They were buzzing around the living room and hallway, clustering near the coat closet and the stairs to the basement. I suspected there were more under the house, but I was still too freaked out about the doll to venture down there. I knew it was ridiculous to be fearful of my own house, but I was.

A woman picked up. "Hello?"

Surprised not to hear Jesse's familiar voice on the other end of the line, I hesitated before answering. "Oh…hello. Is Jesse there?"

"No. He's in the shower." I realized I must be speaking with his wife Keri, the cashier from the grocery store. There was something in her tone I couldn't quite read, but it made me nervous.

"Ah. Well, I was calling about our roof. To see if he could come over and fix it." I remembered the generator, purring on the back porch. "And to thank him, for letting us borrow his generator."

"He lent out the gennie?" Definitely an edge to her voice. I got the impression I'd said more than I should have. I hoped I didn't just land him in hot water with the significant other.

"Uh…yes," I answered slowly. I bit my lip, annoyed that I sounded unsure of myself.

"I see," Keri said. There was a pause. Then, "You know he's married, right?"

What? Where was this coming from? "Um…yes." I groaned inwardly. I sounded caught off guard, submissive. Not just that, I sounded guilty, and I had nothing to feel guilty about. I took a breath and focused on being assertive. "Yes, I'm aware of that."

"What's your name?" I could hear a threat in her voice. It angered me.

"I'm just calling about my roof, ma'am. Tell him Tawny Ellis called." I almost hung up, but then, not wanting to sound intimidated, I added, "You have a good day, now." I ended the call and sat down at the kitchen table, letting out a breath.

What the hell just happened? I replayed the conversation in my mind, thinking about all the things I could've said, like, "I know he's married. I'm married too," or "I have no interest in your husband. So shove off." A nastier retort came to mind, but my big sister was the one with the dirty mouth, and I tried not to emulate her. Keri's accusation had knocked me so off guard, my thoughts derailed, and I couldn't think of anything halfway intelligent to say in reply.

For a moment I considered calling Keri back and chewing her out for harassing a customer. A *paying* customer. And if she didn't want my money…but no. Giving her a piece of my mind was just a passing fantasy. I wasn't going to call her back.

That wasn't who I was, and even if I wanted to hear Keri squirm, I knew that would just stir up trouble for Jesse. He was a nice guy, and I couldn't do that to him, even if his wife was clearly unbalanced. I wondered if she'd ever done this kind of thing before, with other clients of his. That couldn't be good for his business. I felt bad for him. Keri was psycho. How humiliating to have to put up with someone like that.

**

Jesse came by the house that afternoon. When I answered the door, he said, "Saw some of your shingles had blown off. Thought I'd stop by to check on you."

He gave me a smile as he took off his ball cap and stepped inside, smoothing his hair. I thought about my conversation with his wife and felt terrible for him. He'd come to make amends. Avoiding his gaze, I busied myself in the kitchen, grabbing a couple of clean mugs from the dish drainer. "Want some coffee?"

"Sure." He sat down at the kitchen table. "It's chilly out there—nice to come inside and warm up. Glad that wind has finally died down."

"Pretty scary to try to fix a roof with it blowing so hard," I said, my back to him as I filled the mugs with coffee.

He chuckled. "Oh, I wouldn't even try it. My health insurance might cover falling off a roof, but probably not getting blown off one. Either way, I don't want to test it."

I laughed, relieved he seemed to be in good spirits. Maybe I hadn't gotten him in trouble with the wife. I handed him his coffee and retrieved the sugar and creamer from one of the lower kitchen cabinets. "I guess Keri told you I called?"

Jesse poured creamer into his mug and looked at me. "No."

He didn't know. I turned and grabbed a spoon, so he could stir his coffee. "Yeah," I said, handing him the spoon. "I called about the roof this morning. She didn't tell you about our conversation?"

"No. She didn't." He studied my face, a look of concern on his. "What did she say to you?"

Maybe he did know something. I poured sugar into my coffee, thinking carefully about my words. "She answered your phone, and I asked if I could speak with you. She said you were…" I hesitated as I stirred in the sugar—I didn't want to tell him she'd said he was in the shower. "…unavailable. I said I was calling about my roof, and she…well, she kind of warned me off. I guess she was worried I wasn't really calling about the roof." He looked confused, so I added, "She thought I was interested in you."

His cheeks grew flushed—I couldn't blame him. I could feel heat rising to my own. He lifted his mug and took a long drink, like he was hiding behind it. Finally, he set the mug down and said, "I'm sorry about that. She can be—"

I remembered the generator and cut him off. "No, I'm sorry. I think it was because I mentioned you lending us the generator. Which I really appreciate, by the way. But I didn't mean to get you in trouble."

He barked out a laugh. "Trust me, you can't get me into any more trouble than I'm already in."

I took a sip of my coffee. I had no idea what to say. I could see bitterness in his eyes that seemed at odds with his laugh, but I also understood some things could be so ridiculous all you could do was laugh. Hadn't I learned that lesson with my own mother? Mom's ludicrous accusations about Mark—that he manipulated me, isolating me from the rest of the family? Truth was, we moved to get distance from her and my sister, and all the crazy that came from living in close proximity to them.

"Now I get it," he said. "She seemed miffed this morning, but I couldn't figure out why. She was muttering something about not charging customers for services rendered."

"You're saying she wanted you to charge us for using the generator?" I asked. He started to protest, so I added, "Which is fine. I'm happy to pay to use it."

He shook his head. "No, no. I wanted you to have it. You've got kids, and I didn't want you to be without power during that storm." He sighed. "I'm sorry. I've asked Keri not to answer my phone, because I use it for the business. She doesn't get that you don't have to charge for every single thing—that it's actually good business to do a little extra and keep people happy." He looked down at his coffee, his fingers tracing the curved design along the edge of the cup. "That, and she can be a little jealous."

I laughed. "I hadn't noticed."

He looked up to give me an apologetic smile. "It wasn't so bad when we were dating. But once I put that ring on her finger, she turned possessive."

Or maybe she was always like that, but she hid it better before you got married, I thought. I didn't want to interrupt him though, so I just nodded.

"We used to go out dancing at the Tsunami. Do you know it?"

I shook my head.

"It's a bar on the prom. The one with the giant wave on the sign."

I thought about it, remembering the times I'd taken the girls for walks along the promenade bordering the beach. "It's close to the aquarium, isn't it?" I seemed to recall passing a pub when I took my daughters to feed the seals at the quaint tourist attraction. Sophie had fallen in love with a baby seal, and Sara had been fascinated by the giant Pacific octopus.

"That's the one. Anyway, we used to go there until Keri became convinced one of the waitresses liked me. She caused a big scene— almost got in a fistfight," Jesse explained. I stared at him, trying to hide my shock and failing. "I had to carry her out to keep her from brawling. Needless to say, we don't go there anymore." He looked down at his hands, avoiding my eyes. "We don't go anywhere anymore." He laughed to himself. "But hey, I guess I save money, not taking her out to dinner all the time."

I reached over and placed my hand on his. "I'm sorry."

He gave me a weak smile and patted my hand. "It's all right. Just something I need to deal with." He got up from his chair. "I shouldn't have told you all that, but it's the first time she's done this to a customer. Course, most people who call are men. Or old women in need of a handyman. Nobody she'd see as a threat."

It was sort of a compliment. "Is there anything I can do to ease her mind?" I asked.

"No—it's not your issue." He hesitated, as if realizing what he said sounded harsh. "What I mean is, it's not your fault—it's mine. Thank you for telling me."

I nodded. "I thought you should know."

"I'll make sure she doesn't bother you again," he said. He put on his cap and moved toward the door. "I should take a look at that roof."

"Okay," I said, rising from my seat to put my coffee cup in the sink. "Thank you. If you want more coffee—"

"Thanks, but I'm good."

He stepped outside, closing the door behind him. I watched through the kitchen window as he went over to his truck to grab a ladder. As I listened to his footsteps overhead, I thought about what he'd told me and wondered if I'd done the right thing telling him about my conversation with Keri. Maybe I should've let it go, not upset him. I could only imagine how embarrassed he must feel, and

I couldn't fault him for the professional boundary he'd established as he ended our talk. Still, I was glad he'd confided in me. But that feeling of closeness made things awkward when he finished the job and left without saying goodbye.

I was putting dishes away when Jesse's truck started up, and he backed out of the driveway. I thought he was headed out for more supplies and would be back, but he'd taken down the ladder.

I waited until he was gone before venturing outside to inspect the roof. It looked good, and he'd disposed of the shingles that had drifted into our yard after ripping free from the force of the gale. We'd still need a new roof at some point, but it appeared his repairs might carry us through the next round of storms.

I was surprised he hadn't come back in to give me an invoice—maybe he'd call about it later or provide it when he returned to finish the wiring job—if he planned to come back at all. He had to, didn't he? We still had his generator.

I realized I'd forgotten to ask him about the flies when I went back into the house. They weren't buzzing around the back door anymore but had settled along a crack in one of the floorboards on the back porch, zipping in and out of a hole into our basement. The faint smell of rot drifted up from below. I wondered if another rat had died and the flies were feasting on it. I was glad I hadn't gone down there. Maybe I'd make Mark check it out when he got home.

**

I didn't hear from Jesse at all the next day, and frankly, I was afraid to call again. I had no desire to talk to Keri if she answered the phone. That was why I was so annoyed when I went to grab groceries at Joe's and spotted her. I knew she worked there, of course, but I'd hoped to avoid her. In a small town, where there were only so many places to buy food, that was nearly impossible. Still, it wasn't like I'd have to go in her line to check out—there were other cashiers who could help me.

There she was, hanging out by a garbage can near the store's entrance, smoking. Our eyes met, and I could've sworn Keri's narrowed when she saw me, but she was too far away to be sure, and I didn't want to stare. I didn't want to look intimidated either, so I let my eyes slide from hers to focus on the shopping carts lined up inside. I hoped Keri wouldn't recognize me, but I could feel her eyes on my back as I escorted my daughters inside. I reminded myself I hadn't done anything to warrant her reaction to me. I just needed to feed my family, for goodness sakes.

I grabbed a cart and glanced at my grocery list. A few ideas I'd jotted down for this week's dinners, plus the usual staples—milk, eggs, bread, cereal, deli meat for Mark, and macaroni and cheese for the girls—and sticky tape for the flies. Mustn't forget that.

"Okay girls, let's make this quick." I handed Sara the list to keep her and Sophie occupied so they wouldn't get bored. "What do we need first?"

We did all right until we got to the frozen food aisle. There, an older guy rummaged in the freezer for microwave dinners. He shut the door and looked our way. I realized it was Nick Stroud, the man from the toy store—the man who used to own our house. His eyes widened in recognition, and he gave the three of us a scowl.

I returned the look with a scowl of my own and steered my daughters away before he could say anything rude.

Sara didn't seem to notice. As we walked away, she held up the list to me and said, "Mom, we forgot to get pizza!"

"That's okay. We'll come back for it," I told her. "What else do we need to get?"

Sophie looked over the list and said, "Mac 'n cheese. We gotta get that. And the tape for the flies."

I stalled in the pasta aisle and pest control aisle, and then went back to frozen foods. Nick Stroud was gone, but I was wary of bumping into him again. I wouldn't have cared if he confronted me about the house, but I had no intention of letting him be mean to my kids again.

We didn't see him when it was time to check out either, though Keri was at her register. Luckily, the self check-out lane was free. We could do that—the girls liked scanning the barcodes. I congratulated myself on avoiding not just one, but two potential confrontations. How had I managed to make so many enemies in one week? I realized I couldn't avoid conflict indefinitely if Nick Stroud was livid about the house and Keri Hayes was as crazy as I thought she was, but for today I was claiming victory.

Unfortunately, my feeling of triumph was short-lived. The girls and I loaded our groceries in the trunk, and then I went around the side of the car to help Sophie get buckled. Stretching from the grill to the opening of the gas tank was a long, deep scratch in our car's paint, like someone had taken their key and raked it along the side of the car.

I stared unbelievingly at the long gash marring the paint's surface, and then I got angry. I imagined Keri watching us get out, waiting until we went into the store, and then sneaking over and scratching up our car. It seemed like the kind of thing she was capable of. What a wacko. That confrontation I'd been avoiding would be happening a whole lot sooner than expected.

I urged Sophie to get in the car with Sara. "Stay here," I told them and then locked them in. I didn't know what, exactly, I planned to do once I caught up with Keri, but for the moment, I was so angry I wasn't thinking rationally.

I was halfway across the lot when I saw a man standing by his car, watching me. A white compact car, so nondescript I wouldn't have noticed it parked near the store's entrance, if not for the man staring at me. When I turned and locked eyes with him, Nick Stroud jumped as if I'd startled him, and then quickly opened his car door and slid inside.

He started his car and backed out in a hurry, leaving me standing there with just one thought. What if I'd been wrong? What if Keri hadn't been the one to key my car? Maybe Stroud was the wacko I should really be worried about.

**

When Mark came home late that evening, I showed him the damage to the car. "Did you call our insurance?" he asked as we went back in the house.

"No—not yet. I thought maybe I should file a police report first."

"Why? Did you see the person who did it?" He hung up his coat on a peg on the wall, close to the back door.

"That's just it." As I reheated the spaghetti I'd made for the girls earlier, I told him what had happened at the store, and how I wasn't sure who had messed with the car, even though I had two suspects in mind.

Mark grabbed a Fort George beer and sat down at the kitchen table. "So what you're saying is, you don't have any proof either of them were involved."

I opened the microwave and set his plate on the table. "Well… no. I guess I don't, but the way Nick Stroud sped off, he sure looked guilty."

"But it could've just as easily been this Keri person—Jesse's wife, you said?" Mark asked. When I nodded, he continued. "Or it could have been someone else entirely."

I sat down across from him. "I guess, but—"

"Tawny, unfortunate as it is that the car got damaged, I doubt the police would do anything," he said. I started to object, but he held up his fork, cutting me off. "Not without some kind of proof. A witness. They've got bigger fish to fry."

His condescending tone annoyed me. "I realize that, but what if something else happens? Seems like I should at least establish a paper trail in case one of them starts, I don't know, harassing us."

"Maybe, if this Nick guy does something," he agreed. "But I hate to stir things up with Jesse since he's done a good job on our wiring and we could still use his help. You said you already mentioned the phone call, so he's aware of the situation with the wife, right?"

"Right."

"So let it go." He shoveled another forkful of spaghetti into his mouth.

"What about the insurance claim? If I file, our rates might go up," I said.

He chewed and then took a swig from his bottle of beer. "The damage isn't that bad. I bet I can grab some touch up paint from the auto store and take care of it myself."

I frowned, remembering similar promises he'd made, like putting wire screw caps over our exposed wires or installing a door to the basement. He hadn't helped me deal with the insect problem either. The evening before I'd hoped he'd check out the flies in the basement, but when he came home at nine, he said it was too late, he just wanted to go to bed. He promised he'd look tonight, but here he was, late from work again. I ended up getting on a chair and hanging the fly tape myself—a few strips inside the house and several outside, near the back door.

I knew things were getting busy at work—it was close to finals, but I was frustrated. We'd bought the house with the idea we'd take care of it together. Yes, I'd agreed to do most of the work, since he had a job and I didn't. But it felt like his students were taking precedence over his family. I couldn't remember the last time he'd come home before the girls were in bed, and he rarely paid attention to them on weekends either.

I considered broaching the subject while he was captive, finishing dinner, and then decided I'd had enough conflict for one day. If Mark didn't keep his promise to fix the scratch on the car, I'd buy the paint myself. And if I couldn't fix it, maybe Jesse could.

Chapter Eight

My concerns about Nick Stroud deepened when I saw his car parked near our house a few days later. I took Dune out for her morning walk on the beach, and when I returned home, the empty car was parked across the street. Curious, I stayed in our front yard and tossed a ball to the dog, waiting to see if he'd return. I wasn't too worried he was lying in wait for me at the house—Dune would've barked if she sensed a stranger lurking around, and she would've protected me if he threatened harm.

Our dog was generally affable except where her family was concerned. She wasn't fond of our basement though. She wasn't exactly frightened of it, but she avoided the coat closet, hurrying up the stairs after the girls when it was time for bed. She preferred sleeping in Sophie's room over Sara's, but that was because Sophie was gentler with her. Anyway, I didn't mind that the dog stayed out of the basement because she'd get dusty and then I'd have to give her bath before she tracked dirt all through the house. Dune wasn't fond of baths either.

I glanced up at the house, glad to see the roof was holding. We still needed to replace the windows, but we'd covered the cracked one in the upstairs bathroom with a board. Once we dealt with the windows and the rains settled down come spring, I hoped to give the house a fresh coat of paint.

The house was slowly looking better than when we'd bought it, though I wished we had more money so we could pay for more help. Jesse was done with the wiring job and had moved on to installing a heating system, but he was only one guy. I was anxious to finish the restoration project so we could start making money off the house instead of sinking every dollar we had into it.

As I stared at the house, I realized something was wrong. The outside door leading to the basement was ajar. It was set into the foundation of the house and was lower than the level of our lawn, which is why I hadn't noticed it was open until I was closer. When Dune growled, I tensed up. What if the reason Nick Stroud wasn't in his car was because he was in our basement?

I backed away and pulled out my cell phone, debating whether I should call Mark or the police. Mark, I decided. I'd look like an idiot if I called the police and it turned out no one was in the basement. It was possible Mark had made good on his promise to check out the fly situation and had simply forgotten to close the door before he left for work.

I dialed his number, keeping my eyes on the basement door while I listened to his phone ring over and over. Finally, the call went to voicemail. "Hi, it's me," I said, trying not to sound panicked. "I was just curious if you'd left the basement door open." I paused, about to tell him about the car across the street, and then decided against it. Mark would just dismiss my concern, and I hated it when he acted like I was paranoid. "That's all. Love you," I finished.

I hung up, thinking about what to do next, when I heard an engine behind me. I turned to see Jesse's truck pulling into the driveway. The white car across the street was gone.

"Oh, I'm so glad to see you," I called to him as he got out of his truck.

His smile changed to a look of concern as he came around the hood of the truck to where I was standing with the dog. "Everything all right? You're shaking."

I glanced down at my hand, holding Dune's leash, and realized I was trembling. "Just had a little fright. Shook me up more than I thought, I guess."

"What happened?" he asked. Dune pulled on the leash and then jumped up, putting her paws on his chest.

"Down, Dune." I gave the leash a little tug, and she went back down on all fours.

"It's okay," he said, bending over to give her an affectionate rub down her back and sides. She nudged his legs with her head and wagged her tail. He peered up at me. "What happened?" he repeated.

"I went for a walk, and when I came back, the basement door was open. I think someone might have been in the house."

Jesse looked over at the door and then scanned the house before returning his gaze to me. "You're sure it wasn't open before?"

"No," I admitted. "It might have been Mark, but there was this car parked across the street when I came home. I think it belonged to the guy who used to own the house." I told him about my encounters with Nick Stroud, and how he might've been the one to leave that long scratch on my car, with the way he took off in the parking lot. Feeling guilty, I left out the part about me thinking it was Keri. Mark was right—there was no proof either of them did it, but after seeing Stroud's car, I felt more certain he'd been responsible.

"Have you changed your locks since you moved in?" Jesse asked.

I shook my head. "No—just the back door, when Mark installed it."

"You should change them then. Today. Not the back door, since it's new, but the front door and the basement door, for sure." He moved toward the open basement door. "Stay here."

"Where are you going?"

"I'm going to check out the basement and then look over the house. Make sure he's not still around."

I glanced at the street. "But his car's gone. He left."

Jesse frowned. "Maybe. But I want to see where he got in to make sure he won't be able to do it again." With that, he went through the basement doorway and disappeared, leaving me and Dune standing in the yard.

After what seemed an eternity, he came back, appearing around the side of the house. "I went through the house—there's no obvious sign of someone having been there, but I want you to look it over and make sure nothing's missing, okay?"

"It didn't look like someone had been in the basement?"

He hesitated before replying. "I didn't want to alarm you, but there are footprints. I'm hoping they're Mark's. I thought maybe they were mine at first, since I've been stomping all over the place working, but—" He lifted his foot to show me the bottom of his work boots. "The treads don't match."

I nodded slowly, feeling dread pool in my stomach as I walked over to the basement door. It didn't help that my dog started growling again. "Shh, Dune. It's all right." But it wasn't. She and I both knew that.

I didn't have to look long to know the footprints leading from the outside door to the basement stairs inside the house weren't Mark's. I felt numb as I asked, "What size shoe do you wear, Jesse?"

I could feel his eyes on me as I studied the clear imprint of a work boot on the dusty floor of the basement. "Eleven," he answered. He lined up his foot with the print and stepped down, leaving a second impression. "I'd guess whoever was here wears a size thirteen."

Side by side, I could see the differences in the sizes of the footprints and the tread marks. "Mark wears a ten." Jesse was quiet, as though he were letting that sink in. "He was wearing his dress shoes to work this morning. Leather soles, no treads," I added.

Part of me had hoped I was wrong about Nick Stroud. Seeing his car across the street was surreal, like something you'd see in a bad movie. But I couldn't deny someone had been in my basement, and there was a real possibility it'd been Stroud.

"What do you want to do?" Jesse asked quietly.

I laughed. My voice was hoarse, echoing in the basement. "I want to find Nick Stroud and see what kind of shoes he's wearing."

Jesse's mouth quirked up in a small smile. "That's a terrible idea, Tawny." His expression grew serious. "I mean, do you want to call the police?"

I dropped Dune's leash to wrap my arms around myself. "I'm not sure what good it would do. If he didn't steal anything…"

"He was trespassing."

I remembered the conversation Mark, and I had about the car. "If it *was* him. I have no proof."

Jesse nodded toward the footprint. "You have proof someone was in your house." He slid his phone from his back pocket and crouched down to take a photo.

"Good idea."

"Yeah." He stood up and showed me the photo of the two prints side-by-side. "Doesn't hurt to have evidence, even if all you decide to do right now is change your locks." He picked up Dune's leash. "Why don't we go upstairs and you can make sure nothing is missing? Then we'll make a trip to the hardware store."

I gave him a smile. "We?"

He chuckled. "Well, I'm not leaving you here alone after this."

"You're a nice guy, Jesse."

He gave me a grin as he led Dune up the basement stairs into the house. "I try."

**

"All I'm saying is, it was an additional expense that wasn't necessary," Mark said, putting down his sandwich.

"I think it *was* necessary," I replied from across the kitchen table, trying to reign in my anger. When Mark got home, I told him what had happened, and handed him copies of the keys for our new locks. His reaction wasn't what I expected, or wanted. He'd refrained from labeling me as paranoid, but he was thinking it. "And, I tried to call you *before* we bought the locks, but you didn't answer." *You never answer*, I thought, but managed to bite back that retort.

Mark sighed. "Tawny, nobody was in our house. You said it yourself. Nothing was stolen."

"But the door to the basement was open."

He nodded. "Yeah, that was probably me—you know how I am. Sometimes I walk into a room and forget why I went in there. I was probably distracted, thinking about work. Or maybe Jesse forgot to shut it last time he was down there."

I stared at him. Maybe I'd been foolish after all. "So you did go down there this morning?"

"Yes. You asked me to check on the fly situation, and I did." He gave me a look I couldn't quite read and hesitated as though he were mulling something over. Finally, he said, "I didn't see any flies, Tawny."

He thought I was losing my mind—the accusation was in his voice. He thought I was turning into my schizophrenic mother. I clenched my fists, infuriated by the insinuation. "You don't believe me? You think I'm the only one who sees the flies?"

"I didn't say that." But he did. Maybe not out loud, but after you live with someone for eight years, you know what's not being said.

"They're all over the back porch. I'll show you." I leaped up from my seat at the table and marched over to the back door. I threw it open and yanked down a piece of fly tape, intending to prove my point. Then I stopped, staring at the tape. With all the flies that gathered around the back porch, it should've been covered in insect remains. It wasn't. There wasn't a single fly trapped on the tape's sticky surface.

Confused, and with the thunder stolen from my argument, I stood on tiptoe and tacked the tape up on the ceiling of the porch. I went back inside and closed the door behind me. Mark had turned in his chair and was watching me, a look of pity on his face.

"Don't give me that look," I said. "I'm not crazy."

"Never said that," he said quietly. "But it's almost Thanksgiving. You don't get flies in winter."

"Not true. Cluster flies become active after a period of cold temperatures, gravitating toward warmth in winter. Like when you buy an abandoned house that's had no heat and turn the heat back on." I crossed my arms over my chest, feeling smug. "I looked it up." I'd researched the topic as I looked for solutions to our pest problem, and was certain the flies that swarmed me in the basement had been cluster flies. I read that they tended to be bigger than houseflies, but of course, I knew that from first-hand experience.

He glowered at me, showing his distaste for my saucy tone. "Bully for you, Tawny, but the fact remains. I've yet to see a single fly."

"Well, I don't know what to tell you. Your girls have seen them. Even the dog's seen them." The day before, Dune spent ten whole minutes hunting a fly, chasing it around the house, jumping up to try and catch it in her teeth. *See*, I thought, feeling vindicated, *I'm not the one who's crazy. Maybe you're the one who's crazy.*

Mark huffed and went back to eating his sandwich, dismissing me. But I wasn't done with the conversation.

"You're telling me you went into the basement this morning, and you saw zero flies."

He narrowed his eyes. "I'm not sure how this conversation turned into an argument about bugs. I thought we were talking about buying stuff we don't need."

That sounded like a diversionary tactic. I sat down in the chair across from him, folded my hands in my lap, and waited.

He took another bite of his sandwich, chewed, and washed it down with a swig of beer. "Okay, I didn't exactly go *into* the basement this morning."

I raised an eyebrow and waited some more.

"I had a meeting with the instructional council, so I wore my suit jacket," he said, gesturing to the navy-colored wool jacket he'd hung up when he came home. He usually saved that for faculty meetings, preferring to dress down in polo shirts and khakis when he taught. He thought it made him more approachable to students. Tonight, he wore a long-sleeved white button-up. I noted, with annoyance, a dab of mustard on the right cuff. I'd have to address the stain when I did laundry. "I didn't want to tromp around in filth, tracking down bugs," he continued, putting down his sandwich. "So I opened the outside door, poked my head in the basement, saw nothing, and left for work. Sorry if I freaked you out, leaving the door open."

I nodded, thinking. "You didn't actually step inside."

His lips formed a thin, hard line. "No. I just said that. Why does it matter?"

"Because of the footprints. They weren't Jesse's, and they weren't yours. Because it proves someone *was* in our house." The thought was terrifying. At the same time, it proved my point. I smiled to myself. I hadn't overreacted.

"But it doesn't prove the person had bad intentions," Mark insisted. "Maybe it was the meter reader. The gas and electric meters are right there, next to the basement door. Maybe the person saw the door was open and was curious."

"That's still trespassing," I argued.

"Yeah, but the house had been empty for a long time," Mark said. "Odds are the person just wanted to see what we've done with the place, and took off when they saw you come home with the dog. It's an interesting house with a lot of character. I'd want to look. Wouldn't you?"

I threw up my hands, frustrated. It didn't matter what I said, I'd never convince Mark a stranger coming into our home and wandering around was an issue. Clearly, he thought of it as a benign, one-time event. I saw it as a warning. "Look, I can see we're never going to agree on the seriousness of this. But I'm here by myself. A lot. And I want to feel safe in my own home. *That's* why I got the locks changed."

I was so mad I wanted to throttle him. He didn't know what it was like having to be afraid. We lived in a small town with almost no chance of ever getting mugged or assaulted—if you were a man, and you stayed away from the sketchier parts of town. As a woman, I didn't have the luxury of being nonchalant about safety. Women get raped and murdered all the time. Maybe not every day in a town like Seaside, but still. It can happen, and not because you walked down a dark alley at two in the morning. You could be assaulted in your own home, by a neighbor or a door-to-door evangelist. By someone you thought you could trust. I felt angry tears pricking my eyes.

Mark reached across the table and took my hand. "I'm sorry, Tawny. You're right. Your safety—and the girls' safety—is important. If changing the locks makes you feel better, I'm all for it."

I looked at his hand holding mine, and then into his eyes. The look on his face was tender, full of concern. I wiped at my cheeks, brushing away my tears.

"I didn't mean to discount the safety issue. It's just that I assumed Peterson had changed the locks when he came into possession of the house," he said.

"You assumed. But you don't know."

"I don't." He let go of my hand and rubbed his temples like he had a headache. "It's fine that you changed the locks. I just wish we'd had a chance to talk about it first." I opened my mouth to object, and he held up his hand, silencing me. "I know—you said you tried to get a hold of me, and I didn't answer. I appreciate that you tried. But I'm worried about our finances." He held his head in his hands. "I'm really worried. You have no idea the pressures I'm under at work."

He was quiet for a moment, so I put my hands back in my lap, waiting for him to continue.

He looked up at me. "There are more rumors about budget cuts. They might let some faculty go. And here we are, sinking everything we've got into this house. What if I lose my job? Will we be able to sell this place?" He gestured to our as yet untouched kitchen. "Not the way it looks right now."

"But we're working on that," I said. "The heating job is almost done, and then we'll start on the windows."

"And in the meantime, we're getting nickeled and dimed with other expenses. The porch light, the locks...each thing on its own isn't that much money, but it adds up, Tawny. It adds up."

I stared at him. "You're saying it was a mistake to buy this house."

He shook his head. "I'm not saying that. Not yet. But we've got to invest thousands of dollars into new windows, and I don't know how we're going to afford to get them installed."

"Jesse's open to working with us on that."

He gave me a weak smile. "I know. I appreciate his willingness to help out, and he's done a good job with the electrical and heating. But labor costs money. We're going to have to pay him or someone else to install the windows because you don't have the expertise, and frankly, I don't have the time I thought I would. I need to spend the next few weekends working, so I'm ready for the end of the term."

I felt my mouth drop open. "Even over Thanksgiving break?"

"Yes. Not on the holiday, but over the long weekend, for sure. I need to do everything I can to be prepared for class and get glowing reviews from my students. I'm one of the newer faculty, and as you well know from the last round of cuts, in this college, it's always the newbies who are first to go. Unless people really like you."

"Okay," I said quietly. "I understand. Do what you have to do."

He reached over again and gave my hand a squeeze. "I always do."

"Do you want me to resume the job search?"

He shook his head. "At some point, you might need to, but this time of year, I doubt anyone's hiring."

"I could do retail. There've got to be openings with the holidays coming."

His smile was bittersweet as he let go of my hand to get up and set his dinner plate in the sink. "You are much too educated for a retail job. No, hold off until the new year, and maybe there'll be an opening at the middle school or high school. Then, at least, you'd be on the same schedule as the girls, and we wouldn't need to pay for a sitter over the winter break."

I thought about it. "True. But can we afford to wait that long?"

"If things go well with my job, yes. Cuts won't be announced until the middle of spring term. I've just got to keep it together. By then, maybe the house will be ready for paying guests."

I looked up at him, confused. Didn't he just say he was worried about having money to fix up the house? "So we ask Jesse to keep working with us on the house?"

"Maybe." He put the plug in the sink and ran the water, adding a few drops of dish soap so he could wash his plate and several other dishes. "We pay him the money for the work he's done, and make sure we're squared away with those other, smaller invoices he gave you. Then we ask if he's willing to set up a payment plan with us, to fix the windows and install the new roof."

I rose and began putting away the sandwich fixings, securing the clip on the plastic bread bag and setting it on the kitchen counter. "I think he'll go for that."

"Ask him for a quote on both jobs," Mark said. "I like the guy, but if we can get the labor done cheaper, we're going to have to do that. We can't make him any promises."

I covered the deli meat and cheese and stuffed the containers in a refrigerator drawer. "You want me to get estimates from other contractors? I doubt anyone will cut us a deal like Jesse will. He was two thousand less than that other electrician. And he got a good price on the materials for the heating system."

Mark rinsed the dishes and set them in the drainer to dry. "Just ask him for an estimate, and then we'll google labor costs for the area. You're probably right—he's got the cheapest rates, but I'd feel better researching it. We're already giving him most of our savings."

I screwed the lid on the mayonnaise and put it and the mustard back in the door of the fridge. "At least the mortgage is less than we used to pay in rent. We've got some savings there."

Mark pulled the plug on the sink and let it drain, rinsing it out. "Yes. There's that, thankfully. But most of that is going to get eaten when we purchase windows." He dried off his hands and set the dish towel on the counter.

I crossed the room and slipped into his arms. "It'll work out. I don't know how, but it will."

He kissed my forehead. "It has to."

Chapter Nine

The next morning, I called Jesse and asked him to stop by for his check. I planned on taking Dune for her morning walk before he arrived, but it was raining so hard, I decided to wait until the skies cleared. As I glanced out the living room window, checking on the weather, I noticed the white car parked near our house again. Nick Stroud opened the driver's side door, looked up and down the street, and then crossed over to our side. He stared at our house for a moment and then walked toward the corner of Holladay and Seventh.

What was he up to?

I lost sight of him as he rounded our tall hedges. I went over to our guest room and peered out the window. I saw him briefly as he moved past the house and then lost him again as he walked further down the street. Maybe he was visiting someone down the block and wasn't stalking us after all. But then, why would he park in front of our house? There was plenty of parking along Seventh.

There was a knock on the front door. I jumped, startled out of my thoughts. The knock came again, more insistent this time. I padded into the hallway toward the front door. We hardly ever used that door, since the back door was close to where we parked our cars. Our few visitors used the back door too, so I knew it wasn't a friend knocking. Toenails clicked down the stairs as Dune joined me in the hall. She didn't bark, but her ears were pricked, her eyes locked on the door.

The knocking stopped, and I held my breath, waiting for it to start again, wondering if the person gave up and went away. A metallic rattle startled me as someone tried a key in the lock. I sucked in a breath. It had to be Stroud. He hadn't passed the house. He was standing outside my door, trying to get in.

Dune's ears flattened, and she growled. Heart pounding in my ears, I silently slipped over to the door. The deadbolt was still in place, but I put the chain on the door anyway. The sounds of the key in the lock ceased, and everything was quiet.

Then it occurred to me he might try another door. I knew the back door was locked—I'd made sure when I came back in from walking the girls up the driveway to the school bus.

But what about the basement door?

After our argument the night before, Mark and I had gone into the basement so I could show him the footprints. He'd shown a little more concern after seeing them, and went over to the door to look at the new lock. He'd opened the door and shut it to test the mechanism, but had he actually locked the door?

Panicked, I ran to the back door, where I'd left my shoes. I slipped them on, grabbed a flashlight from a drawer in the kitchen, and ran two steps at a time down the basement stairs, Dune on my heels.

I slid to a stop in front of the basement door that led outside, and then breathed a sigh of relief when I saw it too was locked. Okay. Stroud could try to get in, but he wouldn't have an easy time of it.

Even so, I let out a small scream when there was a loud bang against the door. I clamped my hand over my mouth, holding in my terror, as Dune started barking wildly. The bangs continued. What was he doing? Trying to bust his way in? With the way Dune barked, he had to know someone was home. This man was nuts—certifiable.

Maybe he wasn't going to stop until he broke the door down. In that case, it made no sense to stay here in the basement. I needed to call the police. I ran back up the stairs and grabbed my phone off the kitchen counter. As I did, I realized I might be able to catch Stroud in the act. The basement door was positioned just under one of the kitchen windows, the one facing the street. I pressed up against the window, trying to get a view of the man in my front yard, but I couldn't quite see him. The banging continued though, the glass against my cheek vibrating from it.

Maybe if I had a wider shot. I looked toward the back door. If I moved quickly, I could slip around the house, snap his photo, and then come back inside, lock the door, and call the police. He was making so much noise, he wouldn't hear me, and if he was focused on the door, chances were he wouldn't be looking my way. It was a reckless idea, but I wanted proof he was harassing me, so it wouldn't be my word against his.

I went to the back door, opened it cautiously, and whispered for Dune to stay. I closed the door and stalked down the back steps and around the side of the house.

Just before I turned the corner, the banging stopped. I peeked around the side. No one was there.

I looked around, frantic. Where'd he go? The hair on the back of my neck rose, and I was certain he'd somehow seen me coming and was about to ambush me. I turned to run back into the house, and a car engine roared to life behind me. I whirled around as the white car sped off.

I sprinted toward the street. By the time I got there, all I could see were the glow of red taillights in a gray haze of rain. Defeated, I wracked my brain, trying to understand what just happened.

There was no way Nick Stroud could've been banging on my basement door and then run all the way across the street to his car without me seeing him. Scratch that—without me catching him. He was an old man. I was no runner, but I was certain I could move faster than he could.

I started back toward the house, looking at the basement door, and then up at the kitchen window, where I'd first tried to catch a glimpse of Stroud. I stopped dead cold. Sitting on the sill inside the kitchen window, where I'd *just* been, was a fabric doll.

The one I was sure I'd thrown away.

**

I admit it—I was spooked. I'm not sure how much time passed before I worked up the courage to go back in the house, but when I did, I was soaked from the rain. I opened the back door, sure the doll would be gone, that I was just seeing things. Maybe the adrenaline rush from trying to catch Stroud temporarily pickled my brain.

But the doll was still there, gazing serenely out the window. I, on the other hand, felt anything but serene. I grabbed a dish towel to pat myself dry, keeping my eyes on the doll. Dune got up from under the kitchen table and bumped my leg. Absently, I rubbed her head, not yet daring to take my eyes off the doll. It helped, a little, that the dog wasn't freaking out too.

Someone knocked on the door behind me, and I yelped. I looked down at Dune—no reaction from her. Was I hearing things now too? I thought about my greatest fear—turning into my mother. Seeing and hearing things that didn't exist, unable to trust my own senses, watching as my family pulled away from me, weary from dealing with my illness. Reluctantly, I turned my gaze from the doll to the back door. A ball cap was visible through the window at the top of the door. *Jesse.* I'd completely forgotten he was coming.

I opened the door for him. "Jesse. Hi."

His gaze went from my soaking hair to the sopping dish towel in my hand, and he raised his eyebrows. "Uh, hi. How's it going?"

"Kinda crazy," I answered. He stared at me, and then quickly averted his eyes. I realized my wet clothes were clinging to me. Feeling self-conscious, I said, "Um, come in, grab some coffee. I got caught in the rain. Be right back." With that, I ran off to change.

**

When I came downstairs ten minutes later, Jesse sat at the kitchen table, talking softly to Dune as he stroked her ears. She leaned her head in his lap and gazed at him adoringly. He looked up at me when he heard my footsteps.

"Hey," I said. "Sorry about that." I worried I'd made him uncomfortable, but he didn't seem as embarrassed as I felt. Instead, his eyes were watchful and concerned as I scooted past the dog to grab a mug. Wary of the doll still sitting in the window, I gave it a wide berth as I poured my own cup of coffee. I joined Jesse at the kitchen table, taking the seat next to him rather than my usual place across from him. I had no desire to sit with my back to that doll.

"It's fine," he said. He waited until I took a drink before adding, "You don't seem yourself today. Everything okay?"

"It's been an exciting morning." I gave him a weak smile.

"What happened?"

I swiveled in my chair toward the doll. "You can see the doll, can't you?"

He nodded, taking a sip of coffee.

I let out a shaky laugh. "Oh, thank goodness. Thought I was losing my mind." He quirked an eyebrow. "You didn't retrieve that from our trash, did you?" I asked. When he shook his head, I sighed. "Yeah. I didn't think so." Maybe Mark saved the doll from its fate in the landfill. That made more sense than it somehow crawling out of the garbage can on its own. I made a vow—if that thing was possessed, I was setting it on fire.

I told Jesse what happened—the knocking on the front door, the key rattling in the lock, the banging against the basement door, the white car speeding off, and finally, the reappearance of the mystery doll. When I was done, I figured he'd leap up from the table, tell me to mail him the check, and say I should never call him again.

He didn't, and I liked him all the more for that. He looked from me to the doll and scratched his chin. "Wow. No wonder you seemed frazzled. I probably would've wet myself."

I burst out laughing. "Just for the record, it was the rain that got me all wet."

He grinned. "Glad you cleared that up." He thought for a moment and said, "Lemme get this straight. This doll—you said it was in Sara's bed first. You threw it in the trash, but all of a sudden, it mysteriously reappears in the kitchen."

"Yes. I *swear*, Jesse, it wasn't there when I looked out that kitchen window, not five minutes before."

"You think maybe somebody's gaslighting you?" he asked.

I stared at him. "Gaslight—what?"

"You know, when someone wants you to think you're going crazy, so they hide your keys or your wallet or whatever. You go looking all over the house, and while you're busy doing that, they put your keys right back where they're 'sposed to be."

I considered the idea. "I guess that makes more sense than the doll being haunted. But why would somebody do that?"

He shrugged. "Maybe they think it's funny. I had a roommate like that." He frowned. "Stood up as my best man at my wedding."

"How'd that work out?"

He laughed, but I couldn't hear any humor in his voice. "Not so well."

I thought about all the things that could go wrong during a wedding ceremony. "I hope he didn't hide the rings."

"Nah. He set off a bunch of Black Cats when we were cutting the cake. Firecrackers scared Keri's mom half to death. Keri wasn't happy about it."

I'll bet she wasn't.

I don't think any woman would be thrilled by a prank at her wedding, but remembering Keri's icy tone on the phone with me, I imagined she wanted to gut the guy. "What happened?"

Jesse looked at his hands, avoiding my gaze. "She laughed it off at the time, but she was ticked. As we were leaving for our honeymoon, she told me her parents hadn't spent a fortune giving her the perfect wedding to have it ruined by my idiot friend. She said she didn't want me hanging around him anymore."

"I'm guessing you gave her what she wanted."

He looked up at me. "You know how marriage is. You do what you have to, to keep the spouse happy. Otherwise…."

I nodded. "Otherwise there's trouble in paradise."

He gave me a small smile. "Yep." He took another drink of coffee and asked, "So who do you think it is?"

"Pardon?"

He gestured to the doll. "The person who's gaslighting you. Who's doing it?"

"I don't know." I thought about it. "They'd have to know about the doll, for one. And they'd have to have seen me leave the house to check out the banging noise, and had the opportunity to slip into the house and put the doll in the window."

"Did you leave the back door open?"

I shook my head. "I closed it, so Dune wouldn't get out. But it wasn't locked."

He nodded. "It would have to be someone the dog knew. So she wouldn't freak."

"Makes sense."

He looked at me. "That rules out Stroud, you know."

"Does it? I'm pretty sure he was the one banging on the basement door."

He rubbed the back of his neck, thinking. "It does, because he couldn't bang on the door and put the doll in your house at the same time. And I don't think Dune would take to him. Any friends who'd want to prank you?"

"None that I can think of. And anyway, they'd have to have access to the house so they could put the doll in Sara's bed. In the middle of the night." I stopped. "The only people who know about the doll are you and Mark."

Jesse sat back in his chair, hands raised. "Don't look at me. I only found out about the doll today."

I felt defensive about the insinuation. "Are you suggesting it's Mark? That my own husband is trying to make me think I'm insane?"

Jesse held my gaze, a sad look in his eyes. "I'm saying married people can do some pretty awful things to one another," he said quietly.

Looking at him, thinking about Keri's ultimatum about his friend and wondering what other terrible things she'd said to him throughout their relationship, I felt my anger deflate. I thought about the horrible things Mark and I had said to each other during our last fight, only the most recent in a long string of arguments. My marriage was in trouble—it had been for a while. Maybe Jesse understood more about me than I realized. Maybe we were going through the same thing.

But the idea of Mark intentionally making me think I was crazy, given the mental illness that ran in my family? He wouldn't go that far, no matter what kind of problems we had. He acted like I was off sometimes, like when he said he hadn't seen any flies, but he'd never actually say I was insane. "Sorry. I'm not mad at you. It's just hard to imagine Mark doing something like that. I mean, we've got issues, sure. But doesn't everybody?"

"Yeah. I'm afraid so."

Thankfully, Jesse seemed unwilling to press me on the matter, and I changed the subject. "You know, I didn't ask you over to talk about crazy stuff." I got up and went over to my desk in the living room. "I have a check for you."

"Appreciate it." He rose from his chair and placed his empty mug on the kitchen counter, like he was ready to leave. I didn't want him to go just yet.

I held out the check to him. "Do you have time to talk about other projects? If you have another job waiting, I understand."

He took the check, folded it, and stuffed it in his shirt pocket without looking at it. He trusted us, I guess. He glanced at the clock on the microwave. "I've got something set up for this afternoon, but I've got a little more time."

We started talking about the roof and replacing our windows. I was careful not to make any promises, emphasizing that I just wanted an estimate for now. Given our topic of conversation a few minutes prior, I wasn't about to admit that the hesitation to have him do the job was all Mark's, not mine. A united front, I told myself. That's what's most appropriate in a situation like this—presenting a united front. I felt guilty for opening up to Jesse as much as I had—like I'd betrayed Mark.

"Ideally, I'd like to go with a metal roof," I told him. "I think it would stand up against these winter storms better than the shingle roof we have right now. Plus, it would give the house that classic beach cottage look we're going for."

He nodded, considering. "That would look nice. How much do you want to spend on it?"

"Well, that's the thing. I don't know how much something like that would cost." I got up from the table to grab a notepad and pen from my desk so I could take notes. Mark would want to discuss it later, so I wanted to make sure I jotted down details from the conversation.

Jesse scratched his chin. "Metal's a lot more expensive than asphalt shingle. I'd say upwards of twelve thousand."

Ouch. That was a lot pricier than I'd thought. "Oh." I sat back down at the kitchen table. "That's more than we'd want to spend. What about an alternative? I saw a house near the beach that used slate."

He shook his head. "Slate's going to cost about the same as metal."

"I see." I scribbled his estimate on the page in front of me, trying to hide my disappointment.

"I know you're not fond of shingles, but the way they make them now, they can look really nice," Jesse said, trying to console me. "It's just that the ones you have up there now are about twenty years past their shelf life."

"Won't the wind just rip the new ones off?"

"No, not if they're installed correctly. I'd take off all the old ones, check to make sure there's no water damage on the boards, and lay down a moisture barrier before putting on the new shingles," he said. "The new roof should last you a good twenty years. Granted, a metal or slate roof might last you fifty, but you pay a lot more upfront."

Yeah, and our budget was tight anyway. "So, if we went with the shingle roof, how much would that cost?"

"I'd guess that roof is about twelve hundred square feet," he said, more to himself than me, "which isn't too bad. If you had a single story this size, you'd have more roof, but since it's a two-story house...I'd say it would cost between four to six thousand, labor included. Closer to four if there's no water damage up there, and I hope that's the case. I didn't find any places where the boards felt soft when I was making repairs, but I wouldn't know for sure until I stripped off the old materials."

"Okay—I'll have to talk it over with Mark," I said.

He gave me a knowing look, and I bowed my head over the paper to make another note, regretting that I'd shared so much before.

"That's fine," he said. "Probably best to wait out some of these winter storms anyway, since we'd need to tear off what's up there now. You mentioned replacing the windows—what do you want to do about that?"

I swallowed, avoiding his eyes. "Uh, yeah. The ones we have now leak, and Mark says we're losing heat because they're single pane. He wants to replace them with energy efficient vinyl windows."

Jesse rubbed the back of his neck. "I don't want to tell Mark what to do, but I have to say, I disagree with his thinking there."

I looked up from my notebook. "You do?"

"The windows you have aren't bad, actually. They're old, but they're solid—probably built better than what gets produced these days," he said. "I could caulk them, replace the glass in that window upstairs, and I think you'd be all right. You'd save money and be able to preserve some of the house's history."

I liked that idea. "That's good to hear—but what about losing heat?"

He shrugged. "You'd do better adding insulation to your attic. More heat gets lost through your roof and walls than through windows. We could always add storm windows though."

"And you really think we'd save money?" I asked.

"I do. But again, it's up to you and Mark."

I nodded, mulling it over. "If we saved money there, we'd have more for the kitchen and bathrooms." I hesitated, afraid to ask my next question. It seemed like he was being straight with me though, so I had to be honest with him. "I'd really love to work with you on this—I feel like you're looking out for our interests."

He held my gaze. "Thanks. I am."

I believed him, and that made me smile. He returned my smile and warmth washed over me. "You know our budget is limited, but I'm not sure if you know *how* limited." He stayed quiet, waiting for me to continue. "If we decided to continue working with you—that is, if you wanted to keep working with us too—we wouldn't be able to pay in a lump sum like we did with the wiring and heating. I could do monthly payments, but...."

He nodded, like he wasn't surprised. "I'm okay with that. I like working with you, Tawny, and I know you're good for the money."

I hoped we were good for the money. What Mark said about possible cutbacks at the college scared me. I hated the idea of starting these new projects with Jesse and then having to stop because we didn't have the money. I trusted him—he was honest, and I wouldn't want him to think I wasn't. But I couldn't tell him all that, not when he was open to helping us. Instead, I said, "All right, then. I'll talk to Mark and get back to you. Deal?"

He grinned and held out his hand for me to shake. "Deal."

**

Mark didn't agree with Jesse's assessment of our windows—not at first. He insisted on researching it himself over the course of the next few days, which made me nervous for two reasons. One, I felt bad for leaving Jesse hanging about our decision, and two, I worried Mark would call the whole thing off and go with a different contractor. I held my peace, though, knowing if I pushed Mark, he probably wouldn't go in the direction I wanted. Not out of spite, exactly, but just because he hated getting backed into a corner.

In the meantime, I spotted Stroud's white car across the street several more times. He never approached the house, but I stopped taking Dune for walks. I hated to admit it, but the thought of getting caught alone with Stroud frightened me. I guess Mark wasn't the only one who didn't want to get cornered.

I asked Mark about the doll, and he denied retrieving it from the garbage can. I didn't tell him about its sudden appearance in the kitchen. Instead, I secured it in the antique trunk in the basement. Closing the lid, I thought, *See if you can get out of that, demon doll.*

Standing there in the dark basement, I wondered if maybe it could.

Chapter Ten

I felt bad for making Jesse wait so long for our decision, so I decided to make it up to him. I went down to Confection Cottage to buy him candy as a thank you for working with us. I also had an ulterior motive—to ask Richard Olheiser what else he knew about Nick Stroud.

I was uneasy as I passed Trinkets on my way into the Carousel Mall, but didn't see Stroud. Richard had several customers when I entered the candy store, so I busied myself looking at his wonderful displays.

Besides Lolly Dollies and saltwater taffy, he sold homemade fudge, bonbons, and peppermint bark, among other confections. I wasn't sure what Jesse liked, but I could easily put an assortment together. The store sold gift bags for just that purpose.

I was looking at a creation labeled as 'sea foam' when Richard finished at the register and came over to where I stood. "Would you like to try a sample?"

I smiled. "Sure. The sea foam, please."

"Okay, coming right up." He was friendly, but not overly so. I wasn't sure if he recognized me from our last visit. He grabbed a pair of tongs, placed a piece of sea foam on a sheet of wax paper, and set it on top of the glass display case. "Enjoy."

The candy was dipped in rich dark chocolate, but the insides were light and airy. "Wow," I said, between bites. "This is really good."

"Thank you very much," he said, smiling. "My mother's recipe." He studied my face and then asked, "No girls this time, Tawny?"

He did remember me. I shook my head. "They're in school today."

For a fraction of a second he looked disappointed, but then he asked, "How's the house coming along?"

"It's coming. That's actually why I'm here." I selected one of the gift bags hanging near the counter. "I wanted to put together a thank you gift for our handyman. He's been doing a great job."

"What a nice sentiment. As you can see, we've got a wide selection of handmade candies." Richard opened his arms, gesturing to the many candies on display. He was such a large person, his arms spanned the length of the case. Funny to think of such a huge man delicately drizzling white chocolate over a tiny bon-bon. "Any idea what he'd like?"

I shook my head and handed him the bag. "None. But maybe you could recommend some? An assortment might be good."

"Of course. Our peanut butter fudge is a favorite unless he has allergies."

Did he? I tried to recall what Jesse usually ate for lunch. I was sure he'd had PB&J before. "That sounds fine, and some of that sea foam as well."

Richard placed my selections in wax paper bags and then arranged them in the gift bag. "Anything else?"

"Perhaps two or three other kinds—you choose," I said.

He nodded and got to work selecting another type of fudge. "Are the girls still enjoying their Lolly Dollies?"

I grinned, thinking about how Sophie clutched her doll tight each night and Sara dragged hers everywhere. "They are. The girls play with them constantly. I couldn't part them if I tried."

Richard chuckled. "And why would you want to?"

I could think of one reason, but it was locked in the basement. "Oh, I wouldn't dare. Thank you, again, for your kindness. You made Sara's day."

He waved me off and wrapped up several pieces of peppermint bark. "It was nothing."

"It's funny. I think whoever lived in the house before us had one of your dolls. We found it in the basement when we moved in."

He froze, tongs held up in the air. He'd been about to select some chocolate-covered cherries, but he set the tongs down and looked at me. "Stroud had one of my dolls?" There was something behind the question, something I couldn't read.

I shook my head. "No, I think it belonged to a young girl who'd lived there. There were squatters in the house, and they left a bunch of their things behind when they moved. Not to worry though—the girls were thrilled to have a third doll. They're taking good care of her." That was a lie, but I didn't want to insult him by telling him I'd put the doll in the trash. Besides, she wasn't in the trash anymore.

He held my gaze for a second and then chuckled, picking up his tongs. "Well, that's good to hear. I'm glad she's been adopted by nice children." He plopped four more candies in a wax paper sack and placed it in the colorful gift bag.

"You never finished your story, you know," I said as he moved over to the cash register.

"Which story was that?" he asked, ringing up my purchase.

I put my purse on the counter and retrieved my wallet. "About the Lolly Dollies. How Nick Stroud was mad at you because of them."

"Oh, *that* story." He gave me a broad smile, looking more like the jolly man I'd met the first time I visited. "It'll be $14.95, dear." I handed him my credit card. He swiped it in the card reader and handed it back to me. "Stroud and I were friends when we were kids—hung out in the same neighborhood. But people change. About ten years back, when I introduced the Lolly Dollies to my inventory, Stroud threw a fit."

"Why?"

Richard's smile turned conspiratorial. "Because he felt I was infringing on his territory. He argued that I shouldn't be allowed to sell toys *and* candy. Though he sells those glitzy plastic rings with gemstone suckers on them. Keeps them right next to his till."

"That's hypocritical of him," I said.

Richard nodded. There was anger in his eyes, but he seemed pleased with my assessment of Stroud's character. "Yes, and that tourist trap between us sells all kinds of things. T-shirts, souvenirs, toys, and taffy. Stroud took up his cause with the landlords, trying to ban my dolls, but he didn't have a leg to stand on. He's still bitter about it."

"I could tell. He gave us quite the look when he saw us walking out of here with our Lolly Dollies."

Richard gave me a grim smile. "Best to stay away from that one. Grumpy old goat."

"I've tried to, but I think he's angry about us buying his house. I've seen his car parked out front a few times." I didn't mention the banging on our doors or the footprints in the basement. It sounded crazy, saying all that out loud.

Richard huffed. "Doesn't surprise me."

I wondered what else Stroud was capable of. "You don't think he'd try to hurt my family, do you?"

Richard stared at me a moment before answering. "Let's put it this way. I wouldn't trust him. Not a single thing he says or does."

That didn't make me feel better at all. I thought about standing in the basement with Dune, listening to the violent banging against the side of our house. Even though I hadn't seen Stroud's face on the other side of that door, I'd known it was him, felt his rage like it was something tangible. He scared me more than I cared to admit.

My fear of him was even greater than what I'd felt in the basement with the flies or over the doll mysteriously reappearing. I'd been startled by those things, to be sure, but aside from that, had experienced a general sense of unease, something abstract I couldn't quite define. This thing with Nick Stroud was concrete and dangerous. There was sharpness to the fear like it could cut, and if it did, the wound would be deep. I had another question for Richard Olheiser.

"Richard, did something bad happen in my house?"

He blinked at me, eyes wide. "Why do you ask?"

I held his gaze, studying his face. "Odd things have been happening in the house—things I can't explain. I wonder if they have something to do with Nick Stroud." Richard didn't answer at first, so I asked, "Did someone die there?"

He looked away, busying himself by grabbing a tea towel and wiping down the counter behind his display case. Finally, he said, "His mother."

I swallowed, processing this information. "How did she die?"

"Papers said it was an accident." He looked up at me. "But I always thought he pushed her down those stairs."

I froze. "Which stairs?"

"The ones to the basement."

Everything clicked into place. I hadn't wanted to believe it, but there was a reason I felt uneasy about that basement, a reason I'd sometimes sensed someone was standing just outside my field of vision when I was alone in the house. I thought about the phantom footsteps I'd heard on the stairs on more than one occasion. His mother. We were being haunted by Nick Stroud's mother.

"Tawny, dear, are you all right?"

I looked up to see Richard watching me with concern. "I just... thank you." I grabbed the gift bag and hurried out of his shop.

I didn't know if Nick Stroud's mother had been the one to rescue the doll from the garbage, but if Richard's suspicions about Stroud were on target, and if there really was a ghost in my house, my guess was she was the one who'd been gaslighting me. The question was, was she doing it to warn me about her son? Or was she doing it because she wanted to harm my family?

**

"You didn't have to do this," Jesse said, opening the gift bag I gave him when I answered our back door.

I shrugged. "I want you to know you're appreciated." That was true. I was grateful he was still open to helping us, despite the delay. I was also thankful his wife hadn't picked up when I called him.

"Well, thanks." He gave me a smile. "How do you feel about working on windows today?"

"You don't want to work on the roof first?" That seemed like a priority to me, but what did I know?

He shook his head. "It's been so wet this week, and there's more rain coming in the next two days. I say we wait until we have some sunshine."

I cocked my head at him, skeptical of the plan. "When will that be? April?"

He laughed. "Forecast says next week. Once I start taking those shingles off, we're going to have to tarp the roof to protect those boards."

That made sense. "Windows it is, then."

"Cool. I was thinking we'd start with that upstairs bathroom. Get new glass on the window. I could use some help, if you're willing."

I was willing—that window looked awful with a board nailed over it. It was dark too with just the light over the sink. It sure would be nice to let in natural light. I nodded. "I don't mind learning something new."

We went out to Jesse's truck for supplies and then got to work. He removed the plywood board and handed it off to me. I leaned it outside the bathroom door and then watched as he used a putty knife to scrape off the old putty on the window.

As I perched on the side of the claw foot tub, watching him work, I became aware of a buzzing sound. I turned, tracking the sound, and saw a fly crawling out of the drain. It flew up, circled around me, and then landed on the mirror over the sink. "You see that, don't you?" I asked Jesse.

"That's the second time you've asked me that." He was trying to free a broken shard of glass from the window, but he looked up. "The fly? Yeah, I see it. Why?"

I laughed bitterly, recalling the argument Mark and I had about the flies. I sat back on the edge of the tub and kicked my feet. "Just something Mark said to me."

Jesse gave me a questioning look and returned his attention to the window. He wiggled the shard back and forth, but it was stuck. He grabbed his chisel and gently worked to remove the remaining putty gripping the glass.

I told Jesse about the flies swarming me when we first looked at the house, and how Mark hadn't believed me when I told him we still had an infestation. How the fly tape I'd hung up hadn't worked and how Mark accused me of seeing things that weren't there.

Jesse stopped and looked at me. "He said you were crazy?"

"Not in so many words. But he said he didn't see the flies."

Jesse scoffed. "All due respect, but maybe he's the one who's crazy. I saw flies crawling all over the place when I was rewiring the basement."

I grinned. "That's why I like you." I felt guilty the second I said it, but still, it felt good to not have someone question my sanity, to actually be on my side for once.

Jesse smiled, gave the shard a yank, and pulled it free. "Victory at last." He held it out to me, and I dropped it in the garbage can we'd brought up from the kitchen to dispose of glass and gunk from the window. "Probably shouldn't have said that about Mark, but that was wrong of him to dismiss you like that."

I shrugged. "I won't tell if you won't."

"You have yourself a deal," he said. "Can you hand me the sandpaper?" I grabbed some from his tool box. "You want to make sure there's no leftover putty, because otherwise, the new glass won't fit right."

"Got it."

He took a moment to secure his protective face mask and gestured for me to do the same with mine. I watched him sand the wood smooth, and then clean off the resulting dust. We were both quiet for a while, me alternating between watching the fly and watching Jesse work, and him focusing on the job. I wondered what he was thinking about, but didn't want to interrupt him. He installed a new pane of glass and caulked the window.

When the fly landed on his arm, he shooed it away. "You may need a professional for your bug problem." His voice sounded muffled with the mask.

"We might."

"I could recommend someone." He removed his mask, stepped back, and inspected his work. "Okay, I think we're ready for primer." I handed him a small can and a paintbrush. Our hands touched briefly, and his eyes met mine. Then he broke eye contact and gestured to the primer. "Want to give it a try?"

I nodded, and we switched places. I could feel his eyes on me as I opened the can and stirred the primer. "Remember when we talked about gaslighting?"

Jesse crossed his arms, leaning against the edge of the tub. "Yeah."

I dipped in my brush and got to work on the window. "I don't think it's Mark, but I think I know who it is."

Jesse sat up, staring at me. "Who?"

I laughed, shaking my head as I brushed primer over the wood. "Mark would say it was ridiculous to even consider the idea."

"I'm not Mark."

I paused, my brush still as I studied his face. "No, you're not." Mark had a lot of great qualities, but he was never one to entertain my off-the-wall theories. He and Jesse were complete opposites in that regard. A drop of primer fell on the tile floor, and I hurried to clean it up with a paper towel.

As I stood back up, Jesse eyed the dripping brush in my hand and smiled, gesturing for me to give it to him. "Here—you talk, I'll paint. I listen better when my hands are busy anyway."

I relinquished control over the paintbrush and took up my post on the edge of the tub, tossing the used towel in the garbage. "Crazy question, but…do you believe in ghosts?"

Jesse stopped a second, considering. "Maybe." He dipped the brush in the primer and turned back to the window. "I've never seen anything like that myself, but that doesn't mean they don't exist. You?"

"I'm starting to believe more than I used to." I told him about the strange things I'd experienced in the house, besides what I'd already shared about the doll. Then I told him what Richard shared with me, about Nick Stroud's mother dying in the house. "What do you think? Could she be behind all this?"

Jesse stood back from the window, eyeing his work. "I think we're done for now—this needs to dry." He turned to me. "I don't know, Tawny. Anything's possible, I guess."

"You've been here by yourself a few times. Anything strange happen to you?"

He put the lid on the paint can and placed the brush in a plastic bag to keep it moist, in case we needed it again. "One thing. That day you went to the mall, when I had the electricity off. I was working on the light in the stairwell up here, and I thought I heard someone downstairs. Walking around." He shook his head, laughing to himself. "I thought it was you and the girls, but you didn't come home until later."

"Weird."

"Yeah. Didn't freak me out, but it was weird." He looked around the room and then back at me. "Old houses like this though, they make *lots* of weird noises. Maybe that's why it didn't scare me."

He moved past me to put his tools away. "At the same time, I've sometimes wondered about places I've worked. Just that feeling you get sometimes, like you're not alone even though you know full well you are. Guess that's why it's not hard to believe your story."

Gratitude washed over me. "So you do believe me."

"I do." He gave me a reassuring smile. "Maybe you have a good imagination that sometimes runs away with you, but I don't think you're a liar. I saw that doll and how much it scared you, and I don't think you're the one who put it there. But *someone* did. Maybe it was someone who's alive, maybe it wasn't. But the thing I wonder about is why. Why are they trying to scare you?"

"Because they don't want us in the house?" I asked.

He looked doubtful. "Maybe. Have to say though, if it were my house and I was dead, I'd be happy someone cared enough to fix up the place. Have you looked it up?"

"Looked what up?"

"Her obituary. Maybe you should do a little digging, see what you can find out about Stroud's mom."

Not a bad idea. "Maybe I should."

**

Jesse was right. Arlene Stroud's obituary was a good place to start. Browsing our local newspaper archives online, I discovered she'd died in 1995 at the age of 72. If I had to guess, I'd say Nick Stroud was about that age now, so he was in his early fifties at the time of the accident—if it had indeed been an accident. The obituary didn't talk about that. It merely said Stroud was her only surviving child. She'd been preceded in death by her husband and a daughter. That piqued my interest. I wondered how old the daughter had been when she died.

I searched for other articles about the Stroud family, jotting down notes. One did cover Arlene's fall, though the details were sparse. There was no mention of the basement stairs, nor any suspicion it was anything other than a tragic accident. Elderly people do sometimes fall, so maybe no one had a reason to think otherwise. In any case, no one but Richard Olheiser seemed to suspect Nick Stroud was responsible for his mother's death.

The sister's demise, on the other hand, had been covered in depth. MaryAnn Stroud had drowned in the Necanicum River, which was a block west of the house. She was only ten years old and vanished from the house in the middle of the night. There was nothing to indicate she'd been abducted—no signs of forced entry, at least—but no one seemed to understand why she'd left her bed either. I did some math. If I guessed right, Stroud would've been in his teens. Was it possible he'd had something to do with her death? If he had, that would explain why no one had broken into the house and taken the girl. He wouldn't have had to.

I studied the article. It seemed like big news at the time, especially for a small town like Seaside. Why hadn't Richard mentioned her? Maybe because it happened a long time ago, and maybe because I'd only asked him about deaths inside the house. Still, there was no doubt the house was linked to tragedy. I could only imagine the sense of loss the Strouds must've felt. I couldn't bear it if something like that happened to one of my children.

I kept looking, but only found a few other articles mentioning the family. Nick Stroud's grandfather opened a clothing store in the 1940s, and later, just before his mother's death, Stroud opened his toy store. I knew Mr. Peterson bought the house in 2010, so Stroud must've lost it sometime between opening his store and then. Again, I wondered if Arlene's deadly fall could somehow be linked. Perhaps Stroud thought he could get insurance money from her death. Richard did mention he'd had money trouble with the house and his store.

I thought about Richard. How much did I know about him? Not much, but he'd given me no reason to distrust what he'd said. I looked for articles about the Olheiser family. There was a photograph of his parents, opening their candy store in 1957. His mother was plump, but pleasantly so. The weight softened her features. She had Richard's jolly smile and kind eyes. I could see why he spoke fondly of her.

The father was tall and thin, towering over his wife and a young Richard. Clearly, Richard favored his mother's looks, though he got his height from his father. Where his mother looked warm, Richard's dad looked stern, his mouth set in a hard line. How strange to see a sour expression on his face on a day that seemed like one of celebration. I seemed to recall Richard talking about his father being alive, but I wasn't sure about his mother.

Then I found her obituary. She died a year before Nick Stroud's sister in 1962. How sad. Richard couldn't have been more than thirteen. Seemed like he'd been trying to carry her legacy ever since.

**

While I did research, Jesse continued working on our windows. Re-sealing them was a long process, and I helped when I could. I felt safer with him around every day, so I started taking Dune for walks again. I kept an eye out for Stroud's car, but he seemed to be staying away. Maybe seeing Jesse's truck parked in front of the house was a deterrent.

One morning I woke early again to a banging noise. I sat up in bed, listening in the dark. Mark breathed steadily, undisturbed by whatever woke me. The digital clock on my nightstand read 5:30. I slipped out of bed and went to check on the girls. Sophie was fast asleep, Dune lounging at the foot of her bed. I smiled. Nothing would disturb her while her guardian was around.

I checked on Sara. She too was sleeping, though she moaned and rolled over, as though she were having a bad dream. I brushed her hair off her face, and she quieted. Her breathing grew measured, and she clutched her doll to her chest. Without thinking, I lifted the covers, checking to make sure the doll was hers, and not the one from downstairs. It was. I let out a long breath, relieved the evil doll had made no further appearances.

I considered going back to bed, but I felt wide awake. I grabbed my robe and slipped it on. Might as well go downstairs and make coffee. Maybe I'd read for half an hour before Mark and the girls got up.

I drew open the curtains and looked outside. It was still dark out, and the streetlights were on. There was a truck parked across the street. It was hard to tell the color in the orange glow of the lights, but I knew who it belonged to anyway—Jesse.

That was odd. Why would he park in front of our house, when he wasn't supposed to come over until seven-thirty? I usually saw him around the time I walked the girls to the bus.

Toenails clicked on the floor behind me, and I turned. Dune had followed me downstairs and was standing by the back door, needing to go outside. I slipped on my shoes and let her out, following her into the yard where she did her business.

I found my gaze returning to Jesse's truck. Maybe it had broken down, and Keri picked him up last evening. I was surprised he hadn't said anything. I would've driven him home. His surfboard was still in the back of the truck, and I wouldn't think he'd want to leave that out overnight. It would be easy for someone to steal.

My curiosity got the best of me, and I crossed the street for a better look. I peered in the window and then jumped back, startled when I realized the cab of the truck was occupied. Someone was sleeping inside, and I was pretty sure I knew who it was, even though a sleeping bag covered his face.

Quietly I returned to the house, bringing Dune back inside. The clock on the microwave told me it was a little after six. That was close to the time I usually got up anyway, so I headed back upstairs to get dressed.

I glanced out the window again as I made breakfast for Mark and the girls. Jesse was up and moving, his back to the house as he grabbed something from the bed of his truck. I hoped I hadn't woken him. That thought brought heat to my cheeks. I hadn't meant to trespass, but now I was worried about him. Why was he sleeping in his truck?

**

Jesse showed up at seven-thirty as usual, saying hello to the girls before they boarded the bus for school. I felt like I was walking on eggshells around him, but he didn't seem to notice. Maybe I hadn't disturbed his rest. I managed to hold my tongue until after Mark left for work, and then I couldn't take it anymore.

Jesse was working on the windows in Sara's room, so I brought him a cup of coffee. He set his putty knife on the window sill and gave me a smile as he accepted the mug and took a sip. "Thanks."

I wondered if he'd eaten anything today. I didn't see how he could've unless it was something he didn't have to cook. "Did you eat breakfast?" I asked. "I could make something if you're hungry."

He placed his mug on Sara's dresser and got back to work. "I'm fine, but thanks for the offer." He didn't answer my question.

I sat down on Sara's bed and ran my fingers along the satin edge of her blanket, trying to decide what to say, or if I should even broach the subject. I didn't want to embarrass him, but it was awfully cold outside to be sleeping in a truck. "Jesse?"

He looked up from spreading putty between the glass pane and wood frame of the window. "Hmm?"

"I don't mean to meddle, but I, uh…" *Oh, stop dancing around and just say it,* I told myself. "I couldn't help but notice you slept in your truck last night." He stiffened, and then focused his attention on pushing the putty into place with the tip of his knife. My grip tightened on the blanket. This was a bad idea—why did I have to barge into his business and ask? Because it was December and I didn't want him freezing to death, that's why. "You don't have to tell me anything, but I need to ask. Is everything okay?"

He put down the putty knife and stared out the window. Outside, rivulets of water slid down the glass from the rain. "Not exactly, no." I stayed quiet, watching his reflection in the glass since he wouldn't look at me. He grabbed his coffee and took a long drink. When he set it back down, he said, "Keri kicked me out of the house."

I nodded. I'd suspected that much—why else would he be staying in his truck? "When?"

"A couple days ago," he said.

I took in a breath—he'd been spending nights in his truck for days? How could I not have noticed? *Would* I have noticed, if I hadn't woken up early? Probably not. I felt terrible for him. Guilty too, for being so oblivious.

He turned to me. "It's temporary—just until I find an apartment."

"Do you need any money?" We'd planned on paying him month to month, but surely we could find a way to pay him more up front so he could get back on his feet.

He shook his head, waving me off. "She cut off our credit cards, but I had a little money tucked away she didn't know about." His smile was grim.

"What happened?" I asked. Wow, could I be nosier? I resisted the urge to clamp my hand over my big mouth. "If you don't mind me asking," I added.

He turned away and resumed his work on the window. I started to get up, thinking I should leave, give him some space. "It's fine," he said, and I sat back down on the edge of the bed. "She kicked me out 'cause she's got a boyfriend." He laughed, his tone angry. "Three's a crowd, you know, when you're sharing a bed. Someone had to go."

I didn't know what to say, so I just said, "I'm sorry."

He shrugged. "It's fine," he repeated. "She did me a favor actually, ending it. We hadn't been happy for a long time. I see that now. I'd never be able to make enough money to keep her happy. Maybe he can." He gave me a sideways glance. "You know the worst part?"

I shook my head, afraid to speak, to say anything that might make him stop talking. I was scared he'd clam up, shutting me out.

"She's keeping my dog." His voice sounded hoarse, like he was choking back sadness. "Stupid mutt was the best part of that relationship."

I rose and put my hand on his arm. He scrubbed at his face and stared out the window, refusing to look at me. "You could fight her on that," I said. He was clearly in pain, and I hated seeing him like that. I hated Keri for hurting him.

He seemed defeated, his shoulders rounded, his eyes bruised with dark circles. He probably hadn't slept much—I couldn't imagine the cab of his truck was comfortable. "He's better off with her," he said. "None of the apartments I can find allow pets."

I withdrew my hand from his arm, and glanced at Dune, watching us from the common area between the bedrooms upstairs. Her head lay on her paws, but I could tell she was listening—her pupils were big and she had a look of concern on her sweet doggy face. I considered telling Jesse his dog could stay with us, but I had no idea how Dune would react. What if Jesse's dog was aggressive toward her or the girls? Plus, I didn't want to invite conflict from Keri—she was crazy enough as it was. What a witch—cheating on him, and then demanding the dog stay with her. "What about your stuff?"

"I have a few changes of clothes. She said I could come back for the rest once I've got a place."

"What about furniture?" I asked.

He looked at me, finally. "Got my tools and my board. Don't need much else."

"Well, you can't keep staying in your truck. You'll freeze."

He shook his head. "Nah. My sleeping bag's thermal. I'm nice and toasty." I opened my mouth to object, but he held up his hand, cutting me off. "And don't say my truck's not comfy. I've been sleeping a whole lot better than I did sharing space with her." He barked out a bitter laugh. "Especially these last few weeks. I knew she was hiding something."

I studied his face. It looked gaunt and tired. He was lying about sleeping well, of course, putting on a brave face. I wondered if he was punishing himself, feeling like it was his fault things ended. From my perspective, that wasn't the case—not at all. In fact, I thought he should be granted sainthood for putting up with that woman in the first place. I put my hands on my hips. "If you say so, but I doubt you've been eating much." I marched out of the room.

"Where're you going?" he called after me.

I stopped at the top of the stairs, my hand on the banister. "To make you a decent meal."

He came out of Sara's room, wiping his hands clean on a rag. "You're a good person, Tawny."

I crossed the room to stand in front of him. He towered over me by a good six inches, but at that moment I felt taller, stronger— protective of him. "I'm your friend. I hope you know that."

He looked down at me, nodding. "I do. Thank you."

We didn't talk about it after that, but he ate the bacon and eggs I fried, and thanked me again before going back to work. While he was busy, I fired up my computer and browsed the classifieds, looking for an apartment for him. I was surprised by how expensive they were in Seaside, and, as Jesse noted, how few allowed pets. The ones that did were even pricier, tacking on additional fees. I'd hoped I could help him by looking, but my research wasn't going to pay off. I decided not to mention it to him. Instead, I'd talk to Mark when he came home—see if we couldn't at least offer the guy our guest room or the couch. It wasn't much, but it had to be better than sleeping in a truck.

Chapter Eleven

It surprised me that Mark was open to inviting Jesse to stay with us—he wasn't big on houseguests, though he was going to have to get comfortable with the idea if we were ever to open our B & B. What interested Mark was the opportunity to negotiate. He called Jesse and offered him room and board for a month in exchange for a discount on the labor costs for our renovation projects. Jesse was open to the idea as well, so that night he had a roof over his head and a warm shower, instead of having to use the facilities near the beach.

Jesse got settled in our guest room, bringing in his sleeping bag, surfboard, tool box, and a duffle bag stuffed with clothes.

"That's it?" Mark asked him.

Jesse looked embarrassed. "For now. I haven't gone back to the house yet."

"Not looking forward to seeing the missus, I take it?" Mark asked.

Jesse grimaced. "Soon-to-be ex-missus." He set down his duffle bag and surveyed the guest room. "I'll go get the rest of my clothes and albums this weekend. But don't worry, I won't junk up your place with furniture or anything. She can keep all that."

"Not worried a bit," Mark said, giving Jesse a sympathetic pat on the shoulder. "We've got plenty of storage in the basement if you need it. I'm just sorry we don't have more to offer in the way of a bed." Mark had ransacked our camping gear to pile foam cushions into a makeshift bed. It looked shabby, but it was better than sleeping on a hardwood floor.

"We were planning on getting a bed for this room before we opened the bed and breakfast," I said, handing him a pillow and a spare quilt, "but we haven't yet. Not with our other expenses."

Jesse unrolled his sleeping bag. "This is just fine. Thank you both." He laid the quilt and pillow on top of the sleeping bag. "I'm sure I'll be able to find an apartment by the end of the month. I hate to put you out more than that."

"You're not putting us out," Mark assured him.

Jesse gave him a doubtful look, but nodded. "Well, thanks anyway."

Jesse's transition into our household was surprisingly easy—it felt nice having him around. He and Mark seemed to be getting along, though they didn't see each other much—not with Mark working late almost every evening. When Mark did come home, Jesse made it a point to make himself scarce and give us time as a family. He'd excuse himself and go read in his room. We usually had breakfast all together though—Mark scurrying off to teach and Jesse getting to work on house projects. The girls seemed to like having him around, regaling him with stories when they got off the bus each day.

The next Saturday, I woke to the sound of voices downstairs. Light streamed in the window, the branches of the tree outside making shapes on the wall. I yawned and rolled over, intending to snooze a little longer—no reason to get up just yet.

Instead, I found myself face-to-face with a doll. The one I'd locked in the trunk in the basement. I sucked in a breath, startled. Then I got mad. The guys were playing a joke on me—I was sure of it. I grabbed the thing by the leg and hurled it across the room, grumbling under my breath.

For a moment, I considered simply pulling the covers over my head, but I was too annoyed to sleep. I tugged on my robe, smoothed my hair, and marched downstairs, holding the doll by the foot.

Mark and Jesse were sitting at the kitchen table, talking over coffee. The girls were sitting in front of the TV in the living room, watching cartoons. Mark had fried up eggs and bacon, and on the table was a plate loaded with food, presumably for me.

That was nice, except the stove was a wreck, grease splattered everywhere. Dishes covered the table and pans were stacked in the sink. Mark was a wonderful cook, but not great about cleaning up after himself, leaving messes without a thought about who would have to clean them up. That only served to annoy me further, after being so rudely awakened. I cleared my throat.

Mark and Jesse turned to me. "Morning," Mark said, giving me a smile.

I ignored him and held up the doll. "Very funny, guys. *Very* funny." They both looked at me with wide-eyed innocence, infuriating me.

"What?" Mark asked. Jesse, apparently sensing trouble brewing, held his tongue.

I shook the doll at Mark. "This, that's what. You know I hate this thing."

Mark maintained that expression of being dumbfounded a second longer, and then burst out laughing, shaking his head. I glowered at him as he held up his hand, bowed over with laughter. "I'm sorry," he said between gasping breaths, "I couldn't resist."

Jesse's gaze went from him to me, and then over to the French doors leading to his room. He looked like a rabbit about to bolt for cover. To his credit, he put his hands in his lap and stayed put.

"Seriously, Mark?" I tossed the doll at his feet and struggled to keep from raising my voice. It wasn't easy. I felt embarrassed about having Jesse there to witness all this, but I was too angry to reign myself in and not confront my husband. "Why would you put that in our bed? You know it freaks me out—and it's gross!" The thought of that filthy doll on my freshly laundered bed sheets annoyed me even more. It'd been dirty when we found it, and its recent trips between the garbage can and the basement trunk hadn't done it any favors.

Jesse looked like he was trying hard to become invisible. I caught his eye, and he gave me a commiserating look. He held up his hands and shook his head, silently pleading innocence. I nodded—based on Mark's reaction, I'd already guessed Jesse had nothing to do with the prank.

In the meantime, Mark had gotten quiet, finally recovering from his fit of giggles. I turned to find him watching with keen interest the unspoken conversation between Jesse and me. He scowled at me. "It's just a doll, Tawny. I don't see what the big deal is."

"You *know* it bothers me," I said quietly. "I don't understand why you'd do something like that when you know how much it bothers me." Of course, that was the question, wasn't it? Did he know how much the doll freaked me out? He'd been there for my meltdown when I found the doll in Sara's room, but I hadn't told him about the kitchen window incident—just the parts about Nick Stroud banging on our doors and the footprints in the basement. I hadn't said anything because I was afraid he'd say I was being silly and dismiss my suspicion that something strange was going on, something I couldn't quite explain.

Mark didn't answer. Instead, he got up from the table and started clearing plates, angrily stacking them on top of each other. I cringed at the ringing sound they made banging together. He was going to chip them, if not break them if he wasn't careful.

I sighed. "Look—just tell me this. I put the doll in the trunk in the basement. Why'd you take it out?"

Mark set the dishes in the sink, more gently this time, and gazed out the window. "I didn't."

I stared at him. "What?"

He turned. "I didn't take the doll out of the freaking basement. It was in Sara's room, okay?"

That took me a second to process. "Well, how'd it get there?"

Mark glared at me. "How should I know?" He nodded toward Jesse. "Why don't you ask him?"

I turned to Jesse, and he shook his head. "I didn't take the doll out. I swear, Tawny, I didn't even know you'd put it down there."

I froze, trying to find a reasonable explanation for what had just happened. If Mark was telling the truth and hadn't taken the doll from the trunk, and Jesse hadn't even known where I'd stashed it, the only other person who could have taken it out was me—and there's no way I would've sprung that creepy little doll from her makeshift prison. I turned to look at the girls, watching their show, oblivious to the tension in the kitchen. It just wasn't possible for the doll to have ended up in Sara's room unless one of them had snuck downstairs and gotten into the trunk. I couldn't see that happening. Sophie was terrified of the dark, and I'd forbidden Sara from going into the basement. I was fairly certain she'd complied with my wishes. Even if she'd gone down there, there was no way she could've known where I'd put the doll. I doubted she'd have been able to open the trunk, with its antique latches. That led me to an even more frightening thought. If the doll had somehow gotten out on its own, it had found its way into Sara's room. So what did that demon doll want with my little girl?

I looked up to see Mark watching me. He directed a disgusted huff in my direction and rolled his eyes, shaking his head. Then he left the room, no doubt intending to hole up in the office space we'd carved out of the common area upstairs. I turned my attention back to the kitchen. He'd left everything for me to clean up. Again. I sighed and grabbed a paper towel to mop up the grease on the stove.

Jesse stopped me, gently taking the towel from my hand. "Hey, you need to eat. I'll take care of that."

I glanced at the untouched plate on the table. I wasn't all that hungry after fighting with Mark, but I sat down anyway. "Thanks."

He nodded. "Coffee?"

"Orange juice, if there's any left."

"There is." He took a glass from the cabinet and filled it for me.

"Thank you," I said as he handed it to me. I took a swig and set it down, staring at my breakfast. "I'm sorry about all that."

He waved me off and turned to attack the grease-spattered stove. "Keri and I were worse, believe me."

As I chewed a piece of bacon, I watched Jesse methodically wipe down the stove and address spots of grease that found their way onto the handle of the fridge. Then he turned his attention to the dishes. I couldn't believe Keri kicked him out for someone else. He was such a sweet guy—how could she take him for granted? If Mark were half as considerate, we wouldn't fight nearly so much. Then again, I didn't know Jesse that well. I imagined it was easy to get along with people when you weren't emotionally invested in a relationship. He was polite to me, but it wasn't the same as when you're married to someone. We'd only been living under the same roof for a week. Who knew—we could be at each other's throats by the end of the month.

"Going to get your stuff today?" I asked.

He nodded, rinsing off a plate. "Yep. Going to try, at least. With any luck, she won't be home, and I can just go in and get out."

"I'm so sorry."

He gave me a small smile. "It's for the best. I'm already better off, getting away from all her drama." He laughed. "It's funny—you don't realize how tense things are until you get away from it."

I nodded, thinking about the drama my family brought into our lives. How many times had my mother's illness introduced conflict? When we lived in the same town, I played referee between her and my sister, who meant well, but tended to argue with doctors over our mother's care. There was no cure for schizophrenia, so all we could do was manage her symptoms.

Between Mom's delusions of being watched, her refusal to take meds, and her suicide attempts, it was no wonder tension leeched into my relationship with Mark. The situation was tough on my daughters too, as Mark often reminded me. Being away from my family was definitely an improvement, but it didn't solve everything.

"Marriage is hard." I laughed to myself, trying to lighten the mood. "As you witnessed today, unfortunately."

Jesse smiled, brushing it off. "It happens. Don't worry about it." He busied himself drying dishes and putting them away.

I stood up, surprised I'd eaten most of what had been on my plate, and dumped the rest in the garbage. I went over to the sink to wash off my dishes.

Mark came through the kitchen, grabbing his car keys off the hook by the door. He had changed from pajama pants and a t-shirt to jeans and a henley, and had his briefcase in hand. He set it down and slipped on his coat. "Headed to the office," he said gruffly.

"But it's Saturday," I objected. "I thought you wanted to do something with the girls today."

"Can't. Papers to grade." He brushed my cheek with a quick kiss and headed for the door.

"Can't you do that here?" I called after him, but he didn't answer. He closed the door behind him. Soon after, an engine turned over, and I watched out the window as he drove away. I grabbed a paper towel to wipe down the table, hiding my disappointment from Jesse.

"You okay?"

I nodded. "He just needs time to cool off."

"Yeah." Jesse spread the dish towel he'd used on the counter to dry. "I better get going too." He looked at me, holding my gaze. "Maybe if it's not raining when I get back, we could take the girls to the beach."

I knew he was just trying to make me feel better, but I appreciated it. If the sun was shining and it wasn't too cold, a walk would be good for all of us. "Yeah, okay. That sounds nice."

He nudged the ragdoll on the floor with his foot. "What are you going to do with that now?"

I eyed the demon doll from a safe distance. "Burn it."

He smiled. "Ha-ha. Hilarious."

I shook my head. "I'm not kidding."

He picked it up. "Tell you what. Instead of setting it on fire, I'll throw it in the dumpster in the park on my way home. It won't find its way back. Promise."

The doll didn't come back, but that hardly mattered because of the other weird things that happened. Some I could explain, chalking them up to stress and a tired mind—others I couldn't.

**

The cold shoulder from Mark continued into the week. I knew he was busy with finals—students were turning in term papers and taking exams—but it irked me anyway. Christmas was two weeks away, and we hadn't even bought a tree, hadn't talked about gifts for our kids. I used the time the girls were in school to shop for gifts.

On my way home from Beach Books, where I'd picked up my gift for Mark, a tome on the history of Fort Clatsop and the Corps of Discovery, I stopped by Joe's for a gallon of milk and stocking stuffers for Sara and Sophie. I hadn't yet picked up a gift for Jesse. Maybe a book for him too, after I had a chance to ask him what he liked to read. I hadn't asked him about his plans for Christmas either.

I was steering my cart toward the checkouts when a Santa carrying red velvet bag over his shoulder stopped me. "Hi Tawny," he said cheerfully.

"Um. Hi." How did this guy know my name? I mean, I know about the nice and naughty lists, but I had a feeling this wasn't the real Santa.

The man pulled down his fake beard, revealing his face. "Sorry—it's me." Underneath all that white hair was a grinning Richard Olheiser.

I burst out laughing. "Oh! I didn't recognize you." I put my hands on my hips. "Though I always suspected you could play Santa."

He chuckled and patted his belly. "I'd like to say I'm using padding, but I'm afraid this is all natural. How're the girls?"

"Good. They're in school, so I'm running errands. What are you doing here? Not grocery shopping, I see."

"Volunteering. I do this every year."

I cocked my head at him, studying his suit. "That's awfully nice of you. Though I'm surprised you're able to close up shop this time of year. I imagine there's a big demand for holiday goodies."

He smiled. "You imagine right, but I love doing this. It's worth a day of sales. Plus, it's good advertising for the Cottage, you know." He patted his velvet bag. "I give each child a treat from my shop, and I get listed as a sponsor."

"That's smart."

He nodded, tapping the side of his head. "Good business sense in here." His smile broadened. "You should bring the girls by. I'll be here 'til nine."

I returned his smile. "They would love that. Though I have to warn you, Sophie's a little scared of Santa. She's wary of sitting on a stranger's lap."

"Understandable. I'm not a stranger though."

"No," I agreed. "If I tell her it's you, she'll probably be all right."

He gave me a serious look. "Do they know about Santa? That wouldn't spoil it, would it?"

I laughed. "Yeah, they made us fess up last year. But they still like the idea of him coming, bringing gifts, so they haven't quite outgrown Santa."

He nodded, smiling. "Good. Smart girls."

"Okay, I'll bring them by if I can," I told him. "I'd better check out, but I hope you have fun, Santa."

His eyes twinkled as he pulled his beard back in place. "I always do." With that, he made his way across the store, whistling *Jingle Bells*, the large bag jouncing on his back with each long stride. He did make a jolly Santa with his substantial frame and white-gloved hands. *A gentle giant*, I thought, smiling to myself.

After I checked out, I stopped in the lobby to put my cart away. With only two bags in hand and rain pouring down outside, I didn't want to roll the cart all the way across the parking lot and then haul it over to the cart corral. As I parked the cart, I noticed a table near the store's entrance.

The red and green banner along the edge of the table read:

CARNIVOROUS PLANTS!
<u>*Great*</u> *gifts for Christmas!*
Support your local branch of Young Gardeners!

Lined up on the table were various kinds of plants. Some I recognized, like the Venus fly trap, most I didn't. A woman with a long braid sat next to a couple of skinny tweens wearing t-shirts identifying them as Young Gardeners. I wasn't sure if a carnivorous plant would make a great gift, but I still had a fly issue at the house, and fly tape and bug spray had done nothing to alleviate the problem.

I walked over to the table and read the placards in front of each type of plant. There was one with sparkling drops of moisture called a sundew, and another that had odd, bulging growths that resembled a bladder. Above each bladder was a leafy flap that looked like a trap door. The sign for that one read, *Pitcher Plant*. The boy sitting behind it gave me a hopeful smile.

I returned his smile and asked, "Which one of these plants would be best for catching flies, do you think? The fly trap?"

"Maybe," he said, considering my question. "But the traps only close a few times and then they die."

"Oh." Probably not an effective solution for my problem.

"They grow new ones," he assured me. He was probably only eleven or twelve, but the serious look on his face made him appear older, like a miniature adult. "But I think a sundew might be better. They have sticky stuff that traps bugs."

I picked up one of the sundews and studied it. The plant had already caught a gnat, and one of its leafy limbs was curling over the insect's body. I wondered how many flies the plant could capture. "What if there are a *bunch* of bugs?"

The girl sitting next to the boy piped up. "You could get a pitcher plant." She was all business, just like the boy. I was impressed by her professional demeanor in talking with an adult. I had a feeling that ability would serve her well.

I put down the sundew and studied the pitcher plant. "How does it work?"

"Bugs are attracted to the way it smells." She pointed to the bladder. "They crawl into the pitcher, and the insides are slick, so they slide down into the liquid and drown."

The boy grinned. "Then the plant eats them!"

I laughed. He was really into this stuff, and his enthusiasm made him look his age.

"And this plant can eat a *lot* of bugs? Because I have a big fly problem."

"It can," he said, giving me two thumbs up.

"Okay," I said, thinking, "how much is your pitcher plant?"

"Ten dollars," the woman with the braid said. Noticing my hesitation, she added, "It's for a *very* good cause, educating youth."

I was desperate to be rid of the flies, and how could I say no to a cause like that? I handed a ten-dollar bill to the boy and selected a large plant with seven pitchers.

He gave me a broad smile. "Thanks, lady! You won't regret it."

I nodded, chuckling. "I hope you're right. Merry Christmas."

"Thank you. Merry Christmas," the kids sang in unison, as they'd no doubt been coached to do.

Slipping my grocery bags over one arm, I balanced the plant and my car keys with the other and headed to the parking lot. By the time I got to the third row, I was soaked, and it was hard to see with the wind whipping my hair in my eyes. I quickly unlocked my car door and placed my grocery bags on the floor of the passenger side. Then I got in, closed the door, and inspected the plant I'd purchased. I worried the wind had damaged it, but it seemed like it had survived. I bent forward and nestled it between the grocery bags so it wouldn't tip during the drive. *You've got a big job ahead of you little plant,* I thought. *Hope you're hungry.* I straightened up and buckled my seat belt.

In the rearview mirror, I saw a white car parked, its blinker flashing. Somebody waiting for a parking spot—they were lucky I was leaving since the lot was so full of holiday shoppers. I started my car and put it into reverse, intending to back out and relinquish my spot.

Before I could, the car pulled in directly behind me, blocking my path. I turned and waved. "Okay, I know you want my spot, but you gotta give me room, buddy," I muttered. Holiday shoppers—zero patience.

I turned on my blinker, hoping the person would understand what I was trying to do, but the car didn't move. I put my car in park, and turned and waved again. I considered honking my horn when the driver's door opened, and someone in a dark, hooded raincoat got out. With the rain, it was hard to see—water streamed down my rear window. I stared at the vehicle behind me and realized it looked a whole lot like Stroud's car. "Oh no…" Feeling panicked, I locked my doors.

The person walked up to my car door and rapped on the window. It wasn't Stroud after all. It was Keri Hayes.

"Oh no," I whispered again. She was the second to last person I wanted to see. I took a breath and turned in my seat to face her. I forced a smile as I rolled down my window an inch. "Yes?"

"You think I don't know?" she asked, glaring at me through the glass.

Know what? "Uh—you want my parking space?"

"I know all about the two of you, shacking up," she spat, her face twisted with rage.

What? "I'm sorry," I told her. "I have no idea what you're talking about."

"Don't patronize me!" she screamed. "Don't you dare, you stupid whore. I *know* he's living with you."

I stared at her, realization dawning on me. She thought Jesse and I were having an affair. Which was pretty funny, actually, since she was the one who kicked him out after cheating on him. Except it wasn't funny at all, because she looked like she planned to claw my eyes out.

I know you can't reason with crazy, but I tried anyway. "Look, you've got it all wrong. I'm married. Jesse's staying at our house, but there's *nothing* going on between us. Now please, move your car."

"Liar," she said, her fist pounding my windshield. "*Liar.* You can just sit there, liar, and think about what you've done."

What was that supposed to mean? She was blocking me in, putting me in time out, like I was some naughty child? As I sat there, dumbfounded, she gave me a wicked grin and held up her car keys. Then she raked them up and down over my car door. Well, that was one mystery solved. Now I knew for sure who had keyed my car.

I couldn't just sit there, watching her destroy my paint job, and I wasn't about to get out and tussle with her. I was pretty sure I could take her, but I didn't want to end up in jail for assault. Anyway, I thought my eyes were my best feature and didn't want them scratched out. I grabbed my phone, intending to call the police, when I realized—I could drive away. Yes, she had blocked me in, but she hadn't thought about the island I'd parked beside. It was full of rocks and small shrubs, but there was enough room to drive over it without nailing the car in front of me. I thought I could clear the parking island, if I were careful. The idea of outsmarting her had more appeal than calling the police. In retrospect, it was a terrible idea, but I was mad.

Smiling to myself, I rolled up the window, put the car in drive, and turned my wheel as far to the right as it would go. Then I backed up, just enough so I wouldn't hit her car, and did it again, getting the car to slowly turn. Keri stared at me, a smug expression on her face. *Awfully sure of yourself, sweetheart,* I thought, all the while praying I wouldn't high center my car on the parking island.

I put the car in reverse one more time and turned. This time, I had enough space to get the car over the island without hitting the car parked in front of me. I turned the wheel hard and gave the car some gas, hoping for enough momentum to clear the island.

For one awful moment, I thought I was going to get stuck, but then I made it, free and clear. Elated, I started laughing. It was a manic laugh, probably the result of too much stress and adrenaline, but I couldn't stop. In my rearview mirror, I watched Keri's smug grin turn to infuriation, and that made me laugh even more. I gave her a cheerful wave and drove off, giggling all the way home.

**

I was still smiling when I got home. Jesse was working on the window over the sink, and I slid past him to put the milk in the fridge. "What are you so happy about?" he asked, eyebrows raised, and that got me laughing all over again.

His reaction, when I told him what had happened, was understandably different from my own. "Oh, Tawny. I'm so sorry. I can't believe she did that to you." I tried to hold in another giggle and failed. He put down his tools and stared at me. "Seriously, why are you laughing? It's not funny."

"You're right, it's not," I said, finally containing my euphoria. "But it's just...so...so *stupid*." His eyes widened. "I mean, can you believe that? The gall of that woman, to make an accusation against me—against *us*—when she's the one...it's nuts."

"*She's* nuts," he said. "I'm sorry. If you want me to talk to her—"

"No, no—I'm okay." I didn't want to say it out loud, but I thought he should stay far away from Keri. If she acted like that with someone she didn't even know, what would she be capable of with an ex? I didn't want Jesse getting stabbed trying to defend my honor.

He walked over to the back door. "I at least want to see what she did to your car. I'll pay for the damage."

I shook my head. "No. I don't want you cleaning up her mess." He'd suffered enough with her penchant for destructive behavior. There was no way I'd make him pay more. It wasn't his fault she was mental.

He set his jaw and looked at me. "I want to see it, Tawny."

I sighed. "Fine. But I won't accept your money." He didn't reply, but there was a stubborn look in his eyes. That was okay—I could be just as stubborn.

We went out back to inspect the car. The driver's side door had a series of long, vertical scratches, like someone was writing a capital letter W over and over. Along the same side was the original gash, complimenting Keri's latest artistic endeavor.

Jesse shook his head slowly, taking in the damage. "I want to fix this, Tawny." He looked at me, his eyes pleading. "I need to. Not for her sake, but for mine."

I relented a little. "Do you think we could patch it with touch up paint? Mark thought we could when the car first got keyed."

"I don't." He crouched down and brushed the vertical scratches with the tips of his fingers. "She sure worked hard on this, didn't she?" he said, more to himself than me. "These are so deep, I think they'd still be visible if you tried to touch them up. This is the kind of thing a paint shop needs to fix."

"Yeah, and that sounds pricey," I said, crossing my arms. "No offense, Jesse, but I think your money would be better spent taking care of *you*." I couldn't imagine how he'd be able to pay for the damage to my car as well as first and last month's rent on an apartment. Anyway, it wasn't fair he should be punished for what the ex-wife had done. "If you have to pay for this, she wins."

He stood and met my gaze. He looked wounded by what I'd said, but there was also an expression on his face that was hard to read— maybe surprise? Gratitude? "You're too good to me, Tawny. I don't deserve your kindness."

I stared at him, confused. "What are you talking about? Of course you do. What you don't deserve is to be treated like trash by that witch."

"You won't file a police report? You should, you know."

I gave him a bitter smile. "You're right. I should've called them instead of driving off. But I didn't, and I don't have anyone to corroborate my story, so I doubt it would do much good now." I shook my head and sighed. "Lesson learned." I traced one of the scratches with my finger. It was deep, like he'd said, and our moist weather would probably invite rust. I'd have to get it fixed sometime. But my car was ten years old, and it didn't make sense to spend money on something aesthetic, not when we were sinking so much money into the house. "Maybe I'll just think of these scratches as battle scars. I bested the enemy, but didn't come away unscathed."

Keri had branded me as an adulteress with my very own scarlet letter. A "W" for whore. It didn't matter that it wasn't true. I'd think about what she said every time I saw the scratch marks.

Jesse raised his eyebrows. "You have an odd way of looking at things."

I shrugged. "Perpetual optimist. Mark finds it pretty annoying, actually."

He gave me a smile. "After what I've been through, I find it refreshing."

I grinned at him and started for the house, and then remembered something. "Oh! I forgot my plant." I hurried back to the car to retrieve the pitcher plant from the floor of the front seat.

"What the heck is that?" he asked.

I explained why I'd bought the plant and how it captured prey, lifting the leafy trap door on one of the pitchers so he could see inside.

"Wow. That sounds like my marriage," he said. "Everything was peachy at first, luring me in just like one of those flies. Then I was trapped with no way out."

I laughed. "Sometimes I feel that way about this house. It seemed like such a good deal, but it's been a pit we've dumped money into. Thank goodness we've got you to help us. Otherwise, we'd never make it."

"You'll make it," he assured me, squeezing my shoulder.

I gave him a grateful smile, but neither of us knew how bad things would get before they got better.

Chapter Twelve

I didn't tell Mark the whole truth about what happened to the car. I couldn't. If I had, he would've made Jesse pay for it one way or another.

Even if I'd filed a police report, it was doubtful Keri would've paid for the damage, and if I filed an insurance claim, our rates would go up. I knew my husband. He'd either guilt Jesse into paying for the damage directly or negotiate another deal on the work for the house. Either way, that wasn't fair.

I called him at work and told him someone keyed the car again. He was understandably upset about the car and annoyed about the interruption at work, but he said he'd take a look when he got home. He didn't though. He came home late, had a quick supper, and went straight to bed. I could tell something, besides the car, was bothering him. I wondered if he'd heard anything about budget cuts. It was a scary thought.

In the middle of the night, I woke to the sound of someone singing. After Mark's rough day, I didn't dare disturb him. I got up and quietly pulled the door shut behind me as I left our bedroom. Sara's bedside lamp was on. I went in her room to find her sitting on the floor next to her doll, singing and coloring. "Sara, honey? What're you doing?"

She looked up at me. "Playing with Tara."

I didn't realize she'd named her doll. "Well, it's two in the morning. You and Tara need to go back to bed." I felt grumpy about having to leave the warmth of my bed to tell her that, but I tried to temper my annoyance. "There's school tomorrow, sweetie."

She nodded and started picking up her crayons. I knelt down to help her. The drawing was of her and another little girl, holding hands. The girl had hair in braids. "Aw, were you drawing a picture of you and Sophie?"

Sara shook her head. "No. That's Tara. She comes to play with me at night."

A chill ran down my spine, though I wasn't sure why—not right then. I tucked my daughter and her doll back in bed, and gave Sara a kiss on her forehead.

I moved to turn off the lamp when Sara whispered, "Tara wants a goodnight kiss too." I smiled and kissed the doll's forehead. Then Sara said, "No, not the doll, Mom. *Tara.*"

I stared at her, puzzled. It occurred to me Tara might be the name of an imaginary friend. It wouldn't be the first time Sara had one. "Okay…where's Tara?"

"Don't be silly, Mom. She's right here." Sara patted the place next to her—there was a slight indentation on the pillow next to her head. "Can't you see her?"

I shook my head. "I'm sorry, honey. I can't." Sara's brow furrowed in disappointment, so I added, "How 'bout I blow her a kiss? Think that would be okay?"

Sara smiled, nodding. I puckered up, kissed my own hand, and blew it at the spot next to my daughter. Then I turned off the light. "Sweet dreams."

"Sweet dreams, Mama," Sara said. I couldn't see her in the dark, but the blankets rustled as she burrowed into them.

It wasn't until I was back in my own bed that I remembered the photo we'd found before we moved in. The little girl who'd lived here before—Tara.

**

I ransacked the house the next morning, trying to find that photo. I was sure we hadn't thrown it away, even though we'd discarded some of the other things the former tenants left behind. I remembered collecting a few things—sentimental items—and tucking them away somewhere. They weren't in the trunk in the basement, or in the garbage bag beside it.

Jesse's eyes bored into me as I tore through the secretary desk in the living room and the junk drawer in the kitchen. He had been working on the living room windows, but stopped to ask, "What are you looking for?"

"A photo," I said, rummaging through the closet in the kitchen. "There was a little girl who lived in the house before us." If I hadn't stashed the photograph in the kitchen, there was only one other place I could think of. I checked the side table by the couch. It had a drawer—too small for practical use, really—but I couldn't think of anywhere else I'd put a stray photo. I slid open the drawer, and sure enough, there it was, sitting on top of several drawings. Tara's drawings. They'd been tacked to the walls of the room Sara now occupied.

Jesse looked over my shoulder as I held up the photo. Nose dotted with freckles, two front teeth missing, light brown hair in braids, and on the back of the photo—*Tara, 2nd grade*. I shivered. The Tara in the photo looked a whole lot like the Tara in the picture my daughter drew.

"I know that kid," Jesse said softly.

I turned to him, my mouth gaping. "You do?"

"Well, I know her mom. We went to high school together. Ashley Chambers. What a mess." I raised an eyebrow, and he said, "Sounds mean, but it's true. Ashley had a baby junior year and gave the kid up for adoption. Dropped out of school and had two more kids, but she was heavy into drugs, and those two were taken by the state, put in foster care."

"Wow. That's rough."

"Yeah. May I?" He gestured to the photo, and I handed it to him. He studied the writing on the back, a sad look in his eyes. "My mom used to stay in touch with her folks—they went to the same church. Ash was in and out of rehab a few times. By the time this little one came along, she was finally getting her act together. She was staying clean, keeping a job. She seemed really happy." He flipped the photo back over, looking at Tara. "She had a lot of anger at her dad. I kinda always wondered if that first baby was his."

I stared at him in horror. "That's awful. I can't imagine."

"Yep. Pretty terrible." He gave the photo back to me. "She sure loved that last little girl though. Tara. Saw them around town a few times over the years, and they were like two peas in a pod. Ashley said having Tara saved her life."

"I think they were squatting here." I told him about all the things we'd found—the stroller, the sleeping bags. "What happened to them?"

Jesse shook his head. "No idea. Must've left town, I guess."

"They left so much behind; they must've been in a hurry."

"Wouldn't surprise me—seemed like Ash was always running."

"They're still alive though, aren't they?" I asked him. "As far as you know."

He was quiet, giving me a questioning look. After a moment, he said, "I haven't heard anything to the contrary. Why do you ask?"

Legs trembling, I sank down on the couch. He hesitated a second and then walked around the coffee table to sit next to me. Remembering the night before made me feel cold and frightened all over again. I grabbed the throw from the back of the couch and wrapped it around my shoulders, drawing my knees to my chest so my legs could be under the blanket too. Then I told him what had happened.

"Where's Sara's drawing?" he asked.

I nodded to the secretary desk. He rose and picked up the paper lying on top of it. He stiffened, but didn't say anything. He didn't have to, because I'd had the same reaction, seeing those braids in Sara's drawing and remembering how the Tara in the photo was sporting the same hairstyle. It could be coincidence—that was possible, of course. Lots of little girls wore braids, and I thought Tara might be a popular name. But it sure didn't feel like a coincidence.

He brought the drawing over and studied the photo again. "She really called her Tara? And said she could see her?"

I nodded. "I'm starting to wonder if that little girl died…in this house."

"If she did, that would explain why Ash ran away again." With a long, low whistle, he sat back down on the couch. "I can't imagine what that would be like, losing a kid. I think that would break me."

"Me too." We sat there in silence for a while, each of us pondering the horror of losing a child. How had it happened? An accident? An abusive boyfriend? I remembered the shape the house had been in when we bought it. There hadn't been any heat. The kid could've died of hypothermia for all we knew. A thought occurred to me. "Do you still have the doll?"

He shook his head. "I tossed it."

I felt a mixture of guilt and relief. "I wonder if it was hers."

"You think maybe she was the one gaslighting you? Putting the doll in different places?"

I looked at him. "I don't know. It seems crazy, but I don't know how the doll got out of the garbage and the trunk. It's weird that it showed up in Sara's room, twice that I can remember, and then she was drawing a picture of the kid."

"Maybe you should ask her."

"What?" I shook my head. "No. I'm not doing a séance. That's too creepy."

"No, not the ghost," he said. "Ask Sara about it. Ask if the doll was Tara's and see what she says. Then show her the photo."

I gave him a shaky laugh, which did nothing to mask how unnerved I felt. "If she says the girl in the photo is *her* Tara, I might lose my mind."

He chuckled. "You might. But at least you'll have an answer."
**

By the time my daughters got off the bus, I still hadn't made up my mind about talking to Sara. She came in and hung up her backpack, and we chatted about how the school day had gone and what homework she had. Jesse turned his gaze to us from time to time as he worked on the last window in the living room. At one point, I met his eyes, and he gave me a meaningful nod. I returned that with a weak smile and led Sara over to the couch.

I had a number of conflicting feelings—fear over what she'd say, guilt over manipulating her into talking about a girl who might be dead, and hope that we'd finally get some answers. It wasn't my best parenting moment, but Jesse was right—I didn't have a whole lot of options if I wanted to figure out what was going on in our house.

"Sara, honey, do you remember the friend you were talking about last night?"

She smiled brightly and nodded. "Tara."

"Right. Is Tara a friend from school? Someone in your class?" When she shook her head, I asked, "Did you know her before we moved to this house?"

She shook her head again. "No."

I frowned. That ruled out the idea she could be one of the kids from our old neighborhood. "And she only comes to play with you at night?"

"No. Sometimes we play in the daytime."

Okay. I wasn't expecting that, but then again, I wasn't sure what I'd been expecting. "But she was with you last night." More nodding from my daughter. "Sara, is Tara real? Or imaginary?"

Sara's brows knitted together. "She's real, Mom."

I brushed Sara's hair off her face. "How come I've never seen her, honey?"

Sara shrugged. "She gets scared sometimes and hides. She hides under my bed."

I shivered involuntarily and tried to cover my reaction by crossing my arms. The idea of a dead girl lurking under my daughter's bed was not one I wanted to entertain. Somehow I managed to appear composed even though on the inside I was curled up in the fetal position and screaming. It wouldn't help for Sara to become as freaked out as I was. I took a deep breath and said, "Okay, so she hides from me. How about Sophie? Does Tara hide from her too?"

Sara nodded. "She hides from everybody but me. Because we're friends and we have the same room."

The hair on the back of my neck stood up. I was frightened, but also angry at myself for letting Jesse talk me into having this conversation. I wished I'd never asked about Tara—ignorance was bliss.

Jesse seemed to sense my angst because he came over and knelt near Sara. He held out the school photo. "Sara, do you recognize the girl in this picture?"

Sara nodded, beaming at him. "That's Tara." She looked at me. "See—told you she was real."

I gave her a nervous laugh, like, *Ha-ha, yes, your mother is a dingbat for not believing you about the dead girl. Silly me.* But my eyes were on Jesse's.

He held my gaze for a moment and then turned to my daughter. "That doll that kept showing up around the house—was that Tara's?"

Sara nodded, frowning. "But you threw it away."

"Yes, I did, and I'm sorry," he told her, as he laid the photo on top of the coffee table in front of us. "We didn't realize it belonged to someone."

Sara patted his hand like she was an adult comforting a small child, instead of the other way around. "It's okay. She can share mine." She looked at me. "Mom said that doll was too old and dirty anyway."

I gave her an apologetic smile, and then felt annoyed, because honestly, what did I have to feel sorry about? So I got rid of something that once belonged to a girl who'd lived here—and might still be here if what Sara said was true. Was I supposed to keep everything from the people who'd lived here before us? I ground my teeth, but I knew my anger was just a flimsy cover for fear and guilt.

Fear there might actually be a ghost getting chummy with my daughter, and guilt I was being insensitive. Something awful must've happened to that little girl. No matter how creepy the doll had been, I felt bad about tossing out something that brought her comfort. Scared too—what if she punished Sara for my actions? I didn't know what a spirit was capable of, and I didn't want to find out.

"Sara," Jesse said gently, "I have one more question for you. Did Tara die in this house?"

I shook my head at him, not wanting to hear the answer, even though part of me did want to know. This was too much—he was pushing my daughter too far.

Sara ignored me, her eyes on Jesse's. "Yes."

Apparently, he was intent on ignoring me too, because he kept his eyes on hers and asked, "How did she die?"

"No," I said, pulling Sara close to me. "No more, Jesse."

He looked at me. "I thought you wanted to know."

"I do, but this is too much. She's just a kid. We shouldn't be talking about this stuff."

Jesse raised his hands in surrender, ready to back off. But then Sara said, "It was the bad man. That's why Tara hides."

Chapter Thirteen

The bad man. Who was the bad man? I had a guess, but I didn't want to bias Sara by sharing my theory in front of her. She'd already had one brush with Nick Stroud, and I didn't want to upset her further with the idea he'd hurt a kid.

As it was, she had nothing else to share—her phantom friend hadn't revealed a name or modus operandi. Just a moniker—the bad man. I could only guess at what he'd done to that little girl. No wonder Ashley Chambers left in a hurry—I couldn't imagine the anguish she must've felt.

Before I sent Sara off to play, I made her promise to keep Tara a secret. Another stellar parenting move on my part, but I didn't want Sara to frighten Sophie by telling her there was a ghost who lived under her bed. I should probably share what I'd learned with Mark, but I was hesitant to do that too. I could see him dismissing her, and being angry with me for putting ideas in her head. He'd probably say I was turning into my mother, or worse, Sara was. I didn't think I was seeing or hearing things that didn't exist and I didn't want to entertain the idea that my daughter could be having a psychotic break either. It was all too possible considering our family history and that wasn't a conversation I was keen to have. I leaned against the back of the couch and sighed, shaking my head at Jesse.

"At least you know *something* now," he said, his tone defensive.

I frowned. "And I wish I didn't." He looked hurt at that. I reached over and put my hand on his arm. "Sorry—I'm not mad. Just freaked out."

He stared at my hand, and then looked at me. I started to move my hand away, but he placed his hand over mine and gave it an affectionate squeeze before letting go. "No, I'm sorry. You're right—I shouldn't have pushed her. I overstepped my bounds."

I gave him a small smile and withdrew my hand. "A little. But it's okay. I mean, we do know something now. More than we knew a half hour ago."

He nodded, and returned my smile. "So. You've got a ghost. And it's not Stroud's mother."

"Hey, we haven't ruled that one out." I threw up my hands and laughed, a sense of helplessness settling over me. "What am I supposed to do with this, Jesse?"

He shrugged. "Who says you have to do anything?"

"This ghost said there's a bad man. Someone who is probably responsible for her death. I'm pretty sure that means I'm supposed to do something. That's what happened in *Hamlet*."

He shifted in his seat. "Not necessarily—you're not living in a Shakespearian tragedy."

"Wow. My handyman is well-read."

He laughed. "Yes. I am. Part of my charm." His finger traced the lines on Sara's drawing of Tara. "Maybe your ghost is some kind of residual effect, you know, a psychic afterimage of some kind."

I crossed my arms. "She doesn't sound residual. She sounds like she's actively communicating with my daughter." That scared me. How did I know this Tara entity was who she said she was? What guarantee did I have she wouldn't hurt my girls? All I knew was what Sara had told me.

"Maybe Tara just needs to find her way to the light or where ever it is we go when we die," Jesse said. "Maybe she somehow got trapped in the house after she died and needs help moving on."

"Maybe." I felt skeptical about that. "What if she wants us to find her killer and bring him to justice? What if it was Stroud who did it?"

"I think you're getting ahead of yourself," Jesse answered. I cocked an eyebrow at him, and he continued. "You don't know she was killed. Yes, she said there was a bad man, but we know nothing about how she died. And what happened to Ash? She didn't stick around. Maybe she had a boyfriend who hurt her daughter, and then she took off so she wouldn't be held for child abuse." He frowned. "I hate to say it, but I wouldn't put it past her. Ashley wasn't exactly stable."

So much for my image of a grieving mother. Jesse's line of reasoning opened up a whole new batch of questions. Where did Ashley go? Did she leave Tara for her parents to bury or did she at least stay for the funeral? If her boyfriend was the bad man, who was he, and where was he now? "What am I supposed to do with all this?" I asked again, feeling overwhelmed.

"I don't know," Jesse said, sounding resigned. We both sat there, quiet, thinking. Then he said, "I could talk to my mom."

"What?"

He nodded, more to himself than me. "Yeah. I could just ask her—casually—if she'd heard anything new about how Ashley's doing. She still talks to Ashley's mom sometimes." He looked at me. "And you—you could look at news articles—like you did when you were looking up Stroud. See if there's any stories about Tara Chambers."

I brightened at the thought. "I could."

"Whatever happened to Tara had to have happened within the last couple of years. I think the last time I saw Ash was about two years ago." He picked up the photo again, staring at Tara's sweet smile. "Probably around the time this picture was taken."

"Okay. But then what? What do we do if we actually find something?"

He smiled, looking excited at that prospect. "Then we go to the police. With hard evidence, not with the ghost stuff."

"Okay. Yes." I couldn't help but feel a little excited myself. At the risk of sounding macabre, who doesn't like a mystery? I wanted to find out what had happened and help Tara find peace.

**

My online search of the local papers netted me exactly zero information. No mentions of a little girl murdered or missing within the last five years. Jesse did a little better. His mother stayed in touch with the Chambers, and reported that Ashley's mom believed she left town around two years before. Ashley hadn't been in touch since, and though she worried about her granddaughter, Mrs. Chambers assumed Tara left with her mother.

"You have to understand, Ashley has done this to Miriam before. The drugs, you know," Jesse's mom had told him. His impression of his mother was comical—a little like the church lady from *Saturday Night Live*, condescending and self-righteous. Clearly, Jesse's mom was of the opinion that Ashley was to blame.

Jesse said he didn't share our theory with her, but it explained why no one had filed a missing persons report on either of them. Who would look for a homeless addict squatting in a house with her daughter? No one, apparently. Not even her parents. That said a lot about the state of the relationship with the elder Chambers, and I felt a wave of sympathy for Ashley and her daughter. I could see why Ashley would skip town after her daughter died.

I did feel some sadness for the grandparents. Tara was dead, and they had no idea. There was no way we could tell them though, not without proof. I was starting to understand why Tara wasn't resting in peace.

That begged another question—where, exactly, was she resting? Surely, if Ashley had to deal with her daughter's remains, there would be something—a news story, an investigation into the child's death. But there wasn't. It was as if they'd both just vanished.

Had Ashley taken the body with her? It was a morbid thought, but maybe, if you were a mother crazy with grief, drowning your sorrows by getting high, you might just do that. Skip town and bury your kid in the forest where no one would find her. After that, you'd simply disappear. That'd certainly keep people from asking questions.

I couldn't see myself doing that, but I'd never done anything more than smoke a cigarette in high school. Mark and I drank wine occasionally, but that was it. I had no idea what I might be like strung out and homeless. Then there was the abuse issue. Had Ashley's dad abused her? There was no way to know, but what if he had? What would that do to someone's psyche? Maybe you wouldn't react to loss like other people—maybe you'd just want to run away, start over. Or maybe, and this made the most sense to my mind, maybe there had been no word from Ashley because she was dead too.

It wasn't uncommon for people to commit suicide on the coast. With our dark, rainy winters, a lot of people suffered from seasonal affective disorder. What if you lost your kid—maybe through some terrible accident, maybe because of something more sinister—and you were on your own, with no support system and few resources? Suicide might look appealing, especially if you were already struggling with addiction.

She could've hitchhiked out to the jetty and let the waves take her, or climbed to the top of one of our rocky cliffs and leaped to her death. If she did, no one would ever know, unless her body washed to shore. With our coastal storms, it was just as likely she'd be washed out to sea, never to be seen again.

Chapter Fourteen

One week until Christmas, and we still didn't have a tree. Mark promised me and the girls we'd go shopping for one as soon as finals were done and he'd turned in his grades. Then he reneged, saying he needed time to prepare for the upcoming term before the college closed for winter break. There was always something, it seemed. At least with the college closed for a week, we'd finally get some time as a family.

Mark had a shorter temper these days. I tried to be patient with him, understanding the stress he was under at work, but it wasn't easy. I found myself thinking about what Jesse said about his own marriage—how he'd gotten lured and trapped like those flies in my pitcher plant. Did Mark feel trapped? I know I did sometimes, between the marital tension and our money worries. It didn't help that Mark kept breaking promises.

Worried there wouldn't be any trees left to buy, I asked Jesse if he'd help me pick one up. I was nervous about getting it loaded and strapped to the roof of my car. He agreed, and we decided to make the trip after I picked up the girls from school. It was their last day before winter vacation, and I was volunteering, helping with a school-wide holiday party.

The holidays always put me in a good mood. I loved the smell of baking cookies, decorating the tree, and the way people seemed to be kinder to one another, exchanging pleasantries around town. That was why the incident at the gas station threw me for a loop.

I pulled into the station on my way to Seaside Elementary, rolled down my window, and shut off the car. The gas station attendant made his way over and said, "Happy holidays, ma'am. I'll be right with you."

"Thanks. Happy holidays," I said, giving him a smile. He nodded and crossed over the fuel island to finish filling up the gas tank for the customer on the other side. The small station was busy—a truck pulled in behind me, and someone else was jockeying for the space on the other side. People hurrying to do last minute shopping, I supposed.

I felt thankful I'd already finished mine. It turned out Jesse liked to read science-fiction, just like my mom and sister, so I had his gift wrapped and hidden under my bed, and my family's gifts shipped. I'd already wrapped gifts for Mark and the girls too, so all I lacked was stuffing the girls' stockings come Christmas Eve.

Caught up in my thoughts, I was startled to see a man standing at my shoulder, just outside the car. "Sorry!" I said, holding out my credit card. "Can you fill it up with regular, please?"

"You never brought the girls by," the man said.

"Pardon?" Confused by this odd statement, I leaned out the window. The man standing there wasn't the gas station attendant. It was Richard Olheiser. Seeing him standing next to my car, out of context, it took me a second to recognize him. "Oh—hi Richard."

He ignored my greeting. "You said you were going to bring them to see me playing Santa, but you didn't."

I thought back to bumping into Richard in Joe's, right before I'd left the store and been confronted by Keri. It felt like our conversation had been weeks ago, and it was no wonder I'd forgotten, after all the stress of dealing with Jesse's nightmare of an ex. "Oh. I'm sorry. There was a problem with my car and I couldn't g—"

He cut me off. "You shouldn't make a promise and not keep it. You shouldn't lie." Anger burned in his eyes as he leaned down, his head and shoulders filling up the open car window. I found myself leaning away from him.

I hadn't promised him anything, had I? I couldn't remember my exact words, but I thought I'd said I'd *try* to bring the girls to see him. I didn't remember committing to anything. I was about to say so, when the station attendant approached us.

"Excuse me, sir," he said. "Is there a problem here?"

Richard eyed me, and then turned to the attendant, giving him the kind of smile he usually reserved for me. "No problem."

The attendant nodded. "Okay, sir. I'll have to ask you to return to your vehicle. Company policy."

That last part sounded flimsy. I doubted such a policy existed, but I appreciated the intervention nevertheless. I watched as Richard returned to the silver truck parked behind me and got behind the wheel.

"Thanks," I told the attendant, handing him my credit card.

"It's nothing, ma'am. You let me know if he bothers you again," the station attendant said in a low voice. "Fill 'er up?"

"Yes, please. Regular."

"You got it, ma'am." He swiped my card, returned it to me, and got to work filling my tank. I stole a glance in my rearview mirror to look at Richard. I wasn't surprised to find him looking back at me, his gaze trained on the back of my head.

What did surprise me was his anger. I guess I could understand how he might feel disappointed or even jilted if he'd misunderstood and thought I broke a promise. What I didn't understand was the sense I owed him something. I mean, we'd talked a few times, sure, and they'd been pleasant exchanges. There was camaraderie over our issues with Nick Stroud, and I appreciated the information Richard had given me, as well as his kindness toward my daughters. His reaction over us not visiting him when he played Santa, though? That was odd. He'd looked so angry, and then, just like that, had given the station attendant one of those trademark Richard Olheiser smiles. It made me rethink my first impressions of him.

The attendant put the gas nozzle back in its cradle, replaced the cap on my tank, and handed me my receipt. "You have a good day, ma'am. Merry Christmas."

"Thank you. Have a Merry Christmas." I started the car, rolled up my window, and drove forward, daring a glance back as the attendant approached Richard's window. The exchange seemed polite, nothing like how he'd been with me.

Maybe I was reading too much into this whole thing. Maybe he was just a lonely, older man, and he'd felt an attachment to me because of our interactions. If I truly had hurt his feelings, I was sorry for it.

**

I didn't give Richard more thought after that. Volunteering at the school took all my focus, handing out cookies to children and helping them with holiday crafts. Sara joined me at my table with three of her friends, and we made snowmen ornaments using foam circles, beads, and liberal amounts of glitter. Before long, the final bell rang, and it was time to collect backpacks and head home.

Jesse was ready for us, work gloves in hand. The rope he'd use to tie down the tree sat on the kitchen counter. We piled back in the car and headed to the tree lot.

Sophie, of course, wanted the daintiest tree available, and Sara wanted the largest. We compromised, going for a middle-sized one that would fit on the roof of the car. I paid the dealer while the girls chattered at Jesse about how to secure the tree. I chuckled to myself, watching the three of them. He endured their instructions while keeping them occupied with silly jokes so he could tie the knots without interference. Then we headed home once again, with promises of hot chocolate for little girls who helped put ornaments on the tree.

It took us a while to get the tree in position. The dealer at the tree lot cut the trunk at a slight angle, so no matter how we turned the tree, it threatened to tip over. We laid the tree on the floor of the living room, and Jesse assessed the situation. "I'm going to have to slice some off the bottom," he said, pointing out the problem with the trunk.

While he ran out to grab a saw from his truck, I laid out dinner. It took some time for him to get the tree stable, and then, after dinner, we brought down boxes of ornaments from the attic. By the time we were ready to decorate, it was nearly bedtime for the girls. Since they didn't have school the next day, they were thrilled to stay up late and help out.

I showed Jesse which ornaments went on the tree first, and then made hot chocolate for all of us, stirring warm milk on the stove. Jesse managed to keep the girls on task, patiently listening as they showed off their favorite ornaments.

Stacking our drinks on a tray, I brought them into the living room, handing Jesse his before giving mugs to the girls.

"Hey," Sara said, "how come he gets his first?"

"Because he's been super nice, helping us with our tree," I told her.

"Jesse *is* nice," Sophie agreed, giving Sara a condescending look.

Jesse put an arm around Sophie and gave her a squeeze. "Thanks, Soph." She beamed up at him and went back to hanging ornaments.

"I think someone's got a little crush on you," I whispered to him.

He laughed. "I'm pretty crazy about her, too." Dune came over and bumped his leg with her head, and he laughed some more. "I'm crazy about you too, Dune, but I'm not sharing my hot chocolate." She looked up at him, wagged her tail back and forth, and then went over to the couch to curl up and watch us work on the tree.

We were almost done with it when Mark came home, and so caught up in decorating we didn't notice him at first. But he noticed us. Arms crossed over his chest, he came into the living room. "Well, this is cozy."

I looked up at him, noting the dark look in his eyes. From the way Jesse stiffened next to me, he was wary of Mark too. "Hey, Mark," I said, giving him a diplomatic smile. "We made hot chocolate. There's some on the stove for you." I scooted past him as I went into the kitchen to pour him a mug.

"No thanks," he said, following me in.

I opened the fridge. "There's dinner too—we made ham and turkey sandwiches."

"I thought you were going to wait to get the tree until I was available."

I pulled my head out of the fridge, platter of sandwiches in hand. "We did wait until you turned in grades." I kept my voice low so Jesse and the girls wouldn't overhear. "But then it was something else, and something else, and there weren't going to be any trees left by the time you were available."

"Sure there were. They always have a bunch left over."

I set the platter down on the table. "Not this year—there were only five to choose from." I could tell he was angry about us moving forward with the tree without him, but I was angry we always had to do things on his terms. "Look, I'm sorry if you feel like we excluded you. I didn't want the girls to miss out."

He waved me off and grabbed a sandwich, taking it and his briefcase upstairs to his office. I watched him go and then turned to find Jesse watching me.

"Everything okay?" he asked.

I nodded, looking at my feet so he wouldn't see my face. It wasn't okay, but I didn't trust myself not to cry. I did feel bad about leaving Mark out, but it was his own fault. We'd tried to be accommodating, hadn't we? I appreciated he was working so hard to support our family, but he'd become increasingly moody, ever since he'd learned about the pending budget cuts. I understood his fears and appreciated the amount of stress he must be under, but he didn't have to take out his frustrations on us. It was nearly Christmas, for goodness sakes. He could make an effort to be civil, for the girls, if not for me.

Jesse sat down on the couch next to Dune, scratching her ears and under her collar. Dune grunted and rolled onto her back so he'd rub her belly. "Hey, I've been thinking, with the holidays coming up…" I glanced up at him. "It's just that, I can see you need family time here, and I was planning on visiting my family anyway."

"What are you saying?"

"I know Mark and the girls have a week off, so I was thinking of taking a break on the house, stay with my folks instead," Jesse said.

"Oh." I looked from him to the stairs, where Mark had skulked off. "Yeah, I guess that makes sense." I hadn't given it much thought. I mean, I hadn't figured Jesse would be a part of our Christmas because he had his own family to be with, but I had only thought about Christmas day, not the entire winter break. I envisioned us continuing to work on the house.

"I don't have to take time off if you need me here," he said, his tone uncertain. "I'm open to working during that time. If both you and Mark want me around."

Ah, Jesse had witnessed tension between me and Mark on several occasions, and he felt uncomfortable about it. He peered up at me, looking guilty, and I wondered if he blamed himself. I couldn't imagine why he would. All this stuff between me and my husband wasn't his fault.

"About what just happened," I said, "please don't take offense to Mark. I know he's been grumpy lately, but we *do* want you here. You've been a huge help."

Jesse nodded, gently rubbing the underside of Dune's neck. The dog stretched, clearly enjoying his attention. "Thanks, but I don't want to wear out my welcome. I, uh—" He paused, looking uneasy. "Well, I found an apartment. Soon as I cough up first and last month's rent, I can get out of your hair."

"You're not in our hair, Jesse. We love having you here."

"Maybe, but I get that you and Mark need space," he said. I started to object, but he held up his hands. "Maybe you don't see it, but he does. And so do I."

"Okay." What else could I say? He was right. I adored having him with us, but Mark was big on privacy, and it'd been a stretch for him to invite someone to live with us, even on a temporary basis. How he was going to deal with guests when we opened the B & B, I had no idea.

**

Jesse moving out was for the best. In spite of the prior conflict between me and Mark, and aside from the annoyed look he gave me when I called my mom on Christmas day and chatted with her and my sister for an hour, we had a good, peaceful holiday with our daughters. It was uneventful with our resident ghost as well. Sara hadn't mentioned her phantom friend again, and nothing odd happened over winter break with the girls and Mark around.

All that changed when the girls went back to school and Mark returned to work. It started the Sunday before school resumed. I woke up to one of the girls screaming. Grabbing my robe off the bedpost, I slipped it on and rushed across the common area upstairs to figure out what was going on.

I expected it to be Sara having a nightmare, but it wasn't. I found Sophie clutching her covers to her chin, shrieking. She stopped as soon as I turned on the light, but she was still trembling. "Sophie, sweetie, what's going on? Did you have a bad dream?"

She shook her head, but tears trailed down her cheeks. Her little shoulders were quaking with fear. She stared at me with wild eyes and whispered, "There's something under my bed."

A chill ran down my spine as I belted my robe, not so much to feel warmth, but to take a second to slow my racing heart and appear calm for Sophie's sake. "Why do you say that? Did you see something?"

"I heard something," she said. "I heard it growling under my bed."

"Okay," I said slowly, biting back a small scream. I was going to have to look, and I didn't want to. I didn't want to get on my hands and knees, lift the bed skirt, and peer into the eyes of a dead child. But I had to, because if the ghost did exist and had taken up residence under Sophie's bed with the intent of terrorizing her, I wasn't going to leave my daughter alone in her room. I had to because that's what you do at three in the morning when you're a parent. You hunt down whatever is frightening your child, whether it's a windstorm shaking the entire house or a demon from the depths of hell.

I got down on my knees and bent to look under the bed. I lifted the bed skirt, and then I did scream, recoiling when I saw a pair of eyes looking back at me.

"What?" Sophie asked, her voice frantic. "What is it, Mama?"

I realized what I was looking at and let out a shaky laugh. "It's the dog," I told her, raising my head to meet her gaze. "Your silly dog is cowering under your bed."

I bent down again to coax Dune out. She was huddled against the headboard, staring at me with wide eyes. "Come on, Dune. Come on out, you silly goose." The dog just looked at me. She was trembling like Sophie had been.

I rose to my feet and sat on the edge of Sophie's bed. "I don't think she's gonna come out 'til she's ready, Soph."

"Can I sleep with you, Mama?" Sophie asked. She looked so scared, I was tempted to scoop her up and take her back to bed with me. Mark needed his sleep though, and I knew he'd be grouchy if we woke him. Sophie needed her sleep too, so she'd make it through school the next day.

"Tell you what," I said, "I'll lay down next to you for a while, okay? Just until you fall back asleep."

Sophie nodded and patted the space next to her. I pulled back the covers and got in, enveloping her small body in my arms. I hadn't planned on falling asleep like that, but I did. We both did, and sometime during the night Dune came out from under the bed. When we woke, she was asleep on the floor next to us.

**

After the weird incident with our dog, things escalated. I thought our pitcher plant was making a dent in the insect problem, but the flies came back in earnest. Daily temperatures were unusually high for those first weeks in January, and the unexpected sunshine provided a welcome respite from rainy winter days. Jesse finished our roof, and I got a crash course by helping him. He thought the warmer weather might be contributing to the flies' increased activity. He brought me a fly swatter as a gift after several days of shooing flies as we worked on the kitchen floor, scraping it clean of broken tiles and grout. The kitchen still looked as hideous as it had when Mark and I bought the house, but other projects had taken precedence. Now that the roof was staying on, the windows weren't leaking, the heating system was installed, and the wiring wouldn't burn down the house, Jesse and I could get to the fun projects.

Or so I thought. I hadn't planned on having a plumbing problem. Right after we got the kitchen floor sanded, the drain in the kitchen sink started backing up. So did the drains in the bathroom sink and tub. The toilet seemed to be having issues as well, clogging for no reason, and draining slowly even after I'd used a plunger on it.

"Pretty sure you've got a clog somewhere in your system," Jesse told me.

I groaned. A clog sounded bad, like the kind of problem that might be expensive to fix. It would have to be fixed though, because we couldn't live in the house if the plumbing wasn't working.

"Don't worry, drain cleaner will probably take care of it," Jesse assured me, his hand on my shoulder. His touch surprised me. Since he'd moved out, he'd been careful not to appear too familiar with me, especially if Mark was around. I guess he knew what it was like to have a jealous spouse, and didn't want to give Mark the wrong impression.

I glanced at his hand, and he removed it quickly like he was worried about offending me. I wasn't offended, so I gave him a smile.

"You don't think we've got a more serious issue with our plumbing?"

He looked at me soberly. "Well, I hope not. If that doesn't work, we should bring in a professional."

I nodded, crossing my fingers the drain cleaner would do the trick. I knew Jesse had contacts who might give us a cheaper rate, but ever since Mark had returned to work, he'd been obsessed about saving money. He said the college announced potential budget cuts, and although Mark hoped the cuts would be minor for personnel, he still feared he might lose his job since he had less seniority than other faculty in his department. The rumors flying rampant around campus didn't ease his mind.

I hoped to have enough money to install new cabinets in the kitchen, but it looked like that wasn't going to happen. Jesse thought we might be able to salvage the old ones, reinforcing them. I wasn't opposed to the vintage look, as long as they didn't fall off the walls. I worried that a plumbing project would suck up what little money I'd managed to set aside for kitchen repairs.

Then there was our resident ghost. Sara still hadn't mentioned her since before Christmas, but I started having strange dreams, the kind that were so vivid, I thought I was awake. For several nights, I thought I woke up to find a tall, dark figure standing at the foot of my bed. I lay there, frozen in fear, as the figure reached for me with grasping hands. Then I'd wake for real, gasping for air like I'd been drowning, heart racing in my chest.

I could never distinguish the person's features. I only got a sense the person wanted to hurt me, and I felt cornered in my own bed. Once, after waking, I thought I heard the rustle of fabric, as though someone else was in the bedroom with Mark and me, moving near my side of the bed. I didn't see anyone, and my sudden waking didn't disturb his sleep.

One night, I was so restless, I couldn't go back to sleep. It was four in the morning, but my nightmare seemed even more real than past dreams. I realized the figure standing at the end of my bed was a man, and when he came closer and reached for me, I felt his breath on my skin. When I woke, I lay there panting, trying to convince myself it had been a dream.

I couldn't relax enough to stay in bed. I shifted, rolling from one side to the other, trying to get comfortable, but my mind was focused on that feeling from the dream—warm breath on my shoulders from a man looming over me, his hands winding around my neck. The thought of it made my skin crawl.

I knew if I stayed in bed, my inability to rest would wake my husband. I went downstairs for a glass of milk. Looking out the window, through a gap in the sheers, a white car was parked outside our house. I ducked down, and took a closer look, trying to figure out if the driver was a man or a woman.

The car Keri Hayes drove the day she assaulted my vehicle looked similar to the one Nick Stroud drove. But Keri wasn't the person sitting in the driver's seat, staring at my house. In the light of the streetlamp, I could see that the driver was male, and looked an awful lot like Stroud.

He's back, I thought angrily. He let us live in peace for a while, but now he's back. Why couldn't he just leave us alone? I didn't get an answer until the next time it rained.

Chapter Fifteen

I needn't have worried about the plumbing issues. They resolved themselves after Jesse poured cleaner down the drains. A few backed up pipes were nothing compared to the problems in our basement when the next storm hit.

High wind advisories were issued along the coast, as well as warnings about areal flooding. I felt snug in our house, knowing we had a new roof and leak-free windows. We were a few blocks from the beach, so I wasn't worried about rogue waves hitting us either. What I hadn't planned on was the river overflowing.

In late January, after a week of no rain, the skies opened up and dumped buckets of water on the north coast of Oregon. Gale-force winds pummeled the shoreline, the gusts breaking trees like twigs, knocking them over on powerlines and blocking roads and waterways.

All that rain turned Seaside into one giant mud puddle. Our front yard became a pond. A pair of ducks gathered there, seeking refuge. The girls loved kneeling on the couch and looking out the living room window to watch the ducks as they paddled along the surface of the water.

I had to keep Dune inside for most of the day. The wind terrified her, and then, once I finally coaxed her outside to pee, she wanted to chase the ducks. Even though I was wearing a rain-resistant jacket with a hood, I was soaked by the time she finished her business, and I finally got her back inside the house. The wind blew my hood back and sent my hair flying in my face. My sneakers and jeans were sopping, and I had to wring my hair out over the sink. Jesse and my daughters thought it was funny, having witnessed my ill-fated adventure from the safety of the warm, dry house.

"Will you be okay?" Jesse asked, when it was time for him to quit work for the day and head back to his place.

"I'm sure we'll be fine," I said, hanging up my newly dried coat. After getting soaked, I'd had to change my clothes and throw the wet ones in the dryer so they wouldn't drip on the floor. "Mark will be home soon, and anyway, this isn't our first storm."

"Yeah, but it's the worst I've seen this winter," he said. "I wish I could lend you my gennie again, but that's one of the things Keri kept."

"We'll be all right," I told him. "We've got candles and flashlights. Worst case scenario, maybe this will finally get Mark to buy us a generator of our own."

"If you need anything, call me," Jesse said. "I'll come right over."

"Thanks," I said, giving him a smile and a brief hug. He looked at me, surprised, but didn't say anything. He just returned my smile and hurried out to brave the storm, no doubt soaked by the time he got to his truck.

**

Not long after Jesse left, I noticed the street outside our house looked as though it were starting to flood. Water seeped up from the manhole in the middle of the street, and the gutters lining Holladay looked like they'd reached capacity. Leaves and garbage piled up in mounds along the street, no longer directed to the drains. That was worrisome, but our house was positioned above street level, so I didn't give it much thought. When you got as much rain as we did on the coast, you learned not to freak out until water hit your door.

We lost power soon after dark, and the girls and I lit candles. Mark still wasn't home, so we gathered blankets in the living room and had a picnic of cold pizza. I didn't start to worry until it was time to take Dune out again. That was when I noticed high water around the foundation of our house.

Realizing the water was higher than the level of our basement, I grabbed the dog and rushed back into the house. "Stay here!" I told the girls. Flashlight in hand, I scrambled down the steps of our basement, feeling dismay at several inches of water in the hallway at the bottom of the stairs.

Grateful I'd worn my rubber boots, I ventured into the basement. It was worse where the wood floor dropped off and the dirt floor began. Water seeped through cracks around the basement door, and plastic bags, paper, and garbage floated in the dark water. I tried not to think about all the filth I was walking in, as my boots sank several inches into the muck. The antique trunk was still down here, likely ruined now.

I walked a little further in, shining my light over everything, trying to assess the damage and wondering how we could possibly pay for repairs. I was still too shocked by what I was seeing to feel weighed down by the thought the storm might've damaged the house enough to bankrupt us. That kind of despair would come later.

One of my boots stuck fast, suddenly sinking two feet into the floor. I was nearly knocked off balance, but recovered, throwing out my arms to steady myself. Frigid water rushed over the top of my boot, soaking my pants leg and sock.

Setting my flashlight on the top of the trunk, I worked to free myself. Balancing on one foot, I pulled my other free, but the boot didn't come with me. The force of yanking my foot from the boot caused me to careen to one side, and I would've fallen into the water if I hadn't latched onto the edge of the trunk.

I let out a long breath to calm down, and then I hopped closer to the trunk, trying to keep my bootless foot out of the water. I swiveled my hips to perch on the trunk. With that to ground me, I reached down and tried to retrieve my boot.

The boot was stuck, like the toe had lodged under something. A root, perhaps. I grunted, yanking on the boot. With a wet, sucking sound, the boot gave, and I pulled harder to free it. There was a pop as the mud released its hold, and then water flowed over the place the boot had been. As it did, something floated to the surface.

I caught a flash of white, and put my boot back on before grabbing my flashlight to see what was in the dank water next to me. When the beam hit the surface and gave me a clear view of what trapped my boot, I started screaming. Bobbing on the surface of the water was a skeletal hand—a child's hand.

The worst part was when I realized the hand was still attached to something…and that something was buried under my feet.

**

When I finally regained my composure enough to stop freaking out and think rationally, I realized I'd left my two small daughters alone upstairs in a dark house. They were probably scared to death after hearing a blood-curdling scream come from the basement. With that thought in mind, I carefully stepped over the body, terrified I'd sink in the mud again as I inched my way across the flooded floor. I made it to the wood floor and turned, directing the beam of my flashlight over to where I'd seen the hand. Part of me hoped I'd imagined the whole thing, but I knew I hadn't. I also knew *who* I'd found—Tara.

To my horror, the hand was still there, floating. It was all too easy to imagine what lay beneath the surface of the water, and suddenly, I couldn't get out of the basement fast enough. I half stumbled, half clawed my way up the stairs and down the hallway into the living room.

When the girls saw me burst through the doorway, breathless, heart thudding in my chest, they both jumped up from the blankets and wrapped their arms around me.

"Mommy!" Sophie cried, burying her face in my thigh. "I thought you died!"

Someone died, but it wasn't me, I thought. I stroked her hair, trying to soothe her and myself. My pulse slowed, and the panic faded as my breathing returned to normal. Sara didn't say anything—she just wrapped her arms around my waist and squeezed me tight, like she was terrified to let go. I disentangled myself enough that I could kneel down and hold them both close.

"Everything's okay," I lied. "I just got spooked is all." There was no way I was telling them about my grisly discovery. I looked them over. "Are you guys okay?"

Sara nodded. "We heard a scream, and we got scared."

I forced a laugh. "Yeah, that was just your big scaredy-cat mom. Sorry I frightened you."

Sara grinned. "A big scaredy-cat like our dog." She turned her head toward the kitchen, and I followed her gaze. Dune was cowering under the table. Some protector she was. One little puff of wind and she was a goner. I was surprised she waited this long to find a hiding place.

I kissed Sara on the head and then nuzzled Sophie's cheek. "Okay girls—you two snuggle under those blankets again. I need to call your dad." I rose and walked over to the kitchen to grab my cell off the counter. I had to step over Dune's tail, which stuck out from under the table and thumped twice on the floor in greeting. "Hi, puppy. Sorry about the storm."

I dialed Mark's number and then waited. It rang several times before going to voicemail. Did he have class tonight? I couldn't remember his new teaching schedule. As I waited for the beep so I could leave a message, I looked at the clock. Just after seven. I hoped he wasn't planning on working until nine again, and would actually check his messages for once. "Hey, it's me. Call me back as soon as you can. We have a flooded basement, and I...I found something. Something *really* bad. Okay. Call me." I'd have to try him again later if he didn't call me back.

After I hung up, I thought about waiting until eight to call him again, and then decided that was too long a wait. Maybe he didn't hear his phone ring—he'd have it on silent if he was in class. But maybe he heard it and was ignoring it, wrapped up in some project. He didn't like being interrupted while he was working.

In that case, he wouldn't check the message right away, and I wasn't sure I'd conveyed the gravity of the situation. There was a *dead body* in our basement, for goodness sakes. I didn't want to say that in front of the girls, but this was urgent. I dialed his number again, hoping he'd pick up if he got two calls in a row. He didn't, so I left another message. "Mark, we've got an emergency, so please call me back." I realized he might interpret that as something bad happening to one of our kids, so I added, "The girls and I are okay, but I *really* need to talk to you." Frustrated, I hung up.

Now what? Call the police? I didn't want to talk to them without talking to my husband first—what if they thought we killed that little girl? *Jesse.* He'd said to call him if I needed him, and I did.

I dialed his number, and he answered right away. "This is Jesse."

"Jesse," I said. "Can you come over? I need you."

"What's wrong?"

"Our basement flooded, and—" I glanced at the girls. They were playing a board game by candlelight, oblivious to my dilemma. I lowered my voice to a whisper, "And I think I found Tara."

"What?" It took him a second to process what I was saying, and then he said, "Okay, yeah. I'm on my way."

I hung up and joined the girls on the floor, trying to pass the time by watching them play Candyland. I wasn't sure how many minutes passed before Jesse pulled into our driveway. I jumped up and ran to answer the door.

He wiped off his feet and set his Maglite on the kitchen counter. "Sorry I took so long. The streets are flooded 'cause the river's overflowing. Water's over the bridge."

"The Necanicum?"

He nodded. "Neawanna Creek too, I'm sure. Hopefully it'll recede when the tide goes out." He looked at me. "Were you serious? About what you found?"

"Yes, but don't say anything. The girls don't know."

He looked at the girls and grabbed his flashlight. "You want to show me, or you want to stay here with them, and I'll go look?"

I didn't want to look at the body again, but I wasn't sure he'd find it without me. I worried the water had risen and covered it up. "I'll go with you." I knelt down between Sophie and Sara. "Hey, girls? Jesse and I need to go down to the basement, okay? You stay here. Promise?"

"Yeah, Mom," Sara said, not even looking at me. She and Sophie were engrossed in the game. That was a good thing.

"Okay. We'll be right back. If you need us, just yell—don't come down there." I stood up and led the way.

**

I was right. The water was higher, but it didn't seem to be flowing in as quickly. I hoped Jesse was right and the outgoing tide would make the level of the river go down. That could take hours if we were currently at high tide, and it wouldn't help with the flooding in our basement. We'd have to pump the water out.

Jesse scanned the surface of the dark water. "Where is she?"

"By the trunk," I said, directing the beam of my flashlight to the area where I'd lost my boot. I told him what happened.

He listened, staying surprisingly calm as he took it all in. Then he reached for a garden hoe propped against the wall before making his way toward the body.

I grabbed his arm before he had a chance to get far. "You can't dig her up. This is a crime scene."

He shook his head. "I wasn't gonna. You said the ground is soft, and I don't want to sink in the mud." He flipped the hoe upside down, so the metal part was up, and used the handle as a guide, sticking it into the mud to test how deep it was before he took each step, treading carefully in his boots. He was smarter than I'd been about it. When the handle sank several feet, he stopped. "This is where you found her?"

I nodded, wrapping my arms around myself to ward off the chill. It was cold in the basement, but what I felt had nothing to do with that.

He lifted the hoe up, out of the mud, and then used it to gently probe the area I'd indicated. He frowned. "I feel something down there, but…." He leaned the hoe against the trunk, placed his flashlight on the trunk's lid, and rolled up his sleeves before crouching down.

"Oh, you're not going to—" I couldn't even finish that sentence, but he understood.

"Yeah. I am." Holding onto the trunk with one hand to steady himself, he slipped his other arm into the muddy water, feeling blindly for a corpse.

I cringed—you couldn't pay me a million bucks to do that. "Why are you doing that? I told you she was there."

He grunted, leaning forward to reach deeper into the water. "You did. And I believe you, but—" He froze in a crouch, a look of horror on his face. He stood up, not saying a word, grabbed the hoe, and crossed the room to where I was standing.

"Jesse?"

"Yeah. I believe you." He leaned the hoe back against the wall, started to wipe his hand on his pants, and then changed his mind, shaking it dry instead. "I had to know for sure before we called the police." His eyes were wild, and his tan skin drained of color, uncharacteristically pale. "Now I know for sure." He stared at me and shuddered. "I touched her hair. I think it was still in a braid."

Chapter Sixteen

I tried to get a hold of Mark once more before calling the police. He still wasn't answering. Typical, but of all the times not to answer or check his messages…I stuffed down my anger. Frustration at my husband was not helpful. I needed a clear head to deal with this.

I forced myself to calm down and made the call, dialing the police station instead of 911. We had our own emergency, yes, but between the storm and the rivers overflowing, I imagined our crisis wouldn't have priority. Tara wasn't going anywhere, but if someone drove into the estuary because the road was flooded, they couldn't wait for help.

I gave the dispatcher our details, and she said she would send an officer over. While we waited, I collected Tara's drawings and photo and set them on top of my desk. Jesse kept the girls busy with their games, looking up occasionally as I passed by, pacing from the kitchen to the living room, looking out the windows.

At one point, he got up, took my arm, and made me sit at the table while he made coffee for me. "What if they think we did it?" I asked him.

"They won't," he assured me. "How could they? She's been here much longer than you've lived here."

I nodded, but I wasn't convinced. It looked bad. How do you live in a house for months and not know there's a body buried under your feet? Tara's grave couldn't be more than two feet deep. Surely we would've found her eventually, if we'd done work in the basement. But we hadn't. We'd been preoccupied with other projects, and the basement had been the least of my concerns.

No, that wasn't true. Truth was, I'd avoided the basement all this time, only going down there when I absolutely needed to. Because I *had* known something was wrong with this house. I'd known it from the start, from the first time I went down to the basement and felt uneasy. I just didn't want to believe it. If the basement hadn't flooded, I never would've found that poor child. If there was guilt to be borne, it was for that, at least. I didn't *want* to know.

I knew my guilt was irrational—I hadn't killed her, and I hadn't buried her in a shallow grave in an abandoned house. Someone else was to blame. Still, I'd been content to pick out paint colors and fantasize about my dream kitchen while a little kid rotted in my basement. I had to wonder—what kind of person did that make me?

Finally, sitting there across from Jesse as we quietly sipped coffee, I saw red and blue lights flashing outside the kitchen window as an officer pulled up to the house. Jesse reached over and squeezed my hand, and then I rose to answer the door.

After that, time seemed to speed up. I sent the girls upstairs to play in their rooms. Then Jesse and I showed Officer Billings the basement, and he got in touch with dispatch. I tried not to eavesdrop, but I heard a few things anyway—words like forensics, coroner, and investigation. Soon after, our house turned into a hive of activity. Jesse and I took refuge on the couch in the living room, trying to stay out of the way. People in white hazmat suits came in toting cases filled with forensics equipment. An officer hung crime scene tape around the borders of our property, and the coroner brought in a black body bag and a gurney. Then there was the detective, who had a whole lot of questions for me.

Jesse seemed to know her, because before she had a chance to introduce herself, he rose from his seat and said, "Angie. It's been a long time." He held out his hand to shake hers.

The petite, dark-skinned woman looked him up and down and smiled as she accepted his hand with a firm grip. "Jesse Hayes. Haven't seen you for over a year, at least. How are you?"

He gave her a sheepish look. "I've been better. I guess you heard about me and Keri."

She nodded. "I heard rumors. I assume it's true then, about the divorce?"

"'Fraid so."

She patted his shoulder. "That's too bad. It's tough, but it gets better. I'm better without Steven, and you'll be better without her."

She turned to me and held out her hand for me to shake. "Detective Angela Ramirez. You're the homeowner?"

I nodded, and then stood and shook her hand, making sure my grip was firm, confident. "Tawny Ellis. My husband Mark and I bought the house back in October. Jesse's been helping us fix it up."

"Ah—I wondered what his connection was," she said, her gaze turning back to Jesse.

"Angie and I went to high school together," Jesse explained.

"Angela, please," she told him. "No one's called me Angie since we graduated."

"Sorry," he said. "I didn't realize—"

"That's all right." She took a seat in the armchair across from me, perching on the edge and leaning forward. I followed her lead, sitting back down on the couch, and Jesse resumed his post beside me. "Mrs. Ellis, I know you related all this to Officer Billings, but I'd like you to walk me through it again," the detective said. "You found the body?"

Her abrupt tone with Jesse threw me off, but I nodded and told my story. How I'd seen the rising water, worried about my basement flooding, and discovered Tara when my boot sank into the muddy floor.

"You keep calling her Tara," Angela remarked, looking up from her notepad, her gaze sharp. "Why is that?"

I hadn't realized I'd been calling Tara by name. "We found some things. When we moved in." I rose from the couch and retrieved the photo and drawings from my desk. "I think a mother and daughter lived here before we did, and they might've been homeless." I told her about the sleeping bags, the stroller, the cast-off clothing, the trash. "I wanted to return their belongings to them, and asked around, but they seemed to have disappeared. So when I saw the body and realized it was a kid, I thought it might be the little girl who lived here. Tara."

"Tara Chambers. As in Ashley Chamber's kid," Jesse said. The detective's eyes widened in recognition at the name. Of course they all knew each other—Seaside was a small town with one high school. Everybody knew everybody. "I recognized Tara from the photo. Used to see them playing at the park together."

"When did you see them last?" Angela asked him.

"About two years ago," he said. "After Tawny showed me the photo, I was curious and asked my mom if she'd heard anything. She and Ashley's mom stay in touch, you know?" Angela nodded, and he continued. "Mrs. Chambers thought Ashley had skipped town and took the kid with her. She never called or anything, but that was par for the course with Ash, with her history and all."

Angela nodded. "In and out of rehab, yes. No surprise there." She held up the photo, studying it. "We'll need to hold on to this and the drawings."

"Of course. I can show you where I put the other things they left too, if that would help," I offered. I chanced a look at Jesse, hoping he wouldn't mention the doll we'd thrown away. I started thinking about those weird brown stains on the doll's dress. What if they'd been blood? What if we'd tossed out a crucial piece of evidence? He met my gaze, but didn't say anything.

Angela seemed to notice the look we shared, but she didn't comment on it. I worried she knew we were hiding something, but I couldn't tell her about the doll. I couldn't begin to explain the strange things that had happened. Trying would make me look crazy or guilty.

"That would help," Angela said. "I'd also like to speak with your husband, Mrs. Ellis." She checked her notes, circling something with her pen.

Me too, I thought. "Mark's at work—he teaches business courses at the college. I left him a message to call, but he hasn't called me back yet. I'm sure he'll be home soon though."

"All right." She started to say something else, but then Officer Billings came over and tapped her on the shoulder. She turned to him. "Yes?"

He leaned down and whispered something in her ear. She raised her eyebrows and then nodded. He retreated back toward the basement, and she rose from her chair. "Excuse me. I'll have more questions for you, but I'm needed downstairs."

"Is it okay if I go upstairs?" I asked. "I sent my daughters up there to play, so they wouldn't be in your way, but it's been a while since I checked on them."

"Of course, Mrs. Ellis. I'll come up and see you when we're done down here," she said.

"I'll go with you," Jesse said to me.

I gave him a grateful smile. "Thanks." To Angela, I said, "I'll try to call Mark again too."

"Please do," she said.

**

Once we were out of earshot, I turned to Jesse in the stairwell. "I don't think we should mention that doll."

"I don't think there's a need to—we dumped a bunch of trash, and we already owned up to that. How were we supposed to know it might be evidence?"

"Exactly. And if we mentioned it we'd just look guilty," I said.

"Yeah. Agreed." He took my hand. "Are you okay with all this?"

I shook my head. "Not really, no. But I'm managing."

"That's all you can do."

I pulled him into a hug, and it occurred to me I was clinging to him like a life preserver, desperate for some sort of anchor in a life that was spinning out of control. "Thanks for being here," I whispered.

He held me tight. "Of course."

I pulled back and looked at him. "I'm scared, Jesse. What if this ruins us? The basement's a mess. There's no way people are going to want to stay here now, and what if we have to end up selling, but no one wants to buy our house? I mean, would you buy a house where someone had been murdered?"

"One thing at a time, Tawny. We can pump the basement, and repair the damage. And I think you'd be surprised at the number of folks who'd be interested in a haunted house." He gave me a sad smile. "Not to be callous about a kid being murdered, but it might actually increase interest for the B & B."

I shook my head, not because I didn't believe him, but because I did. I could see people seeking out our establishment for just that reason. Morbid curiosity, like when people gawk at a car wreck. We'd probably have no problem filling our guest room at Halloween. As much as that idea turned my stomach, I felt a sense of relief that we might be okay financially. My sense of guilt deepened. What a selfish thought. "That's society for you. I can't decide if you're an optimist or a pessimist."

He grimaced. "Maybe a little of both."

We went upstairs to check on the girls. They both had their faces glued to the window in Sara's room, watching the police activity outside. It was macabre, but I couldn't blame them for being curious. I sat down on the bed and drew them away from the window, beckoning for them to sit next to me. "Do you know what's going on, girls?"

Sara looked at me, uncharacteristically somber. "They found Tara."

I gaped at her. Had she been eavesdropping on my conversation with the detective? "Who told you that?"

She shook her head. "Nobody. I just know."

I was scared to ask how she knew, so I turned to Sophie. What's the right thing to do in a situation like this? Lie, sugarcoat it, or tell the truth? I decided it was best to be honest. "Yes. The police are here because I found a little girl who died. We don't know what happened to her, but she was buried in our basement. I know most people who die are buried in a graveyard…" I watched Sophie's reaction. She looked frightened. "Did what I said scare you, Sophie?"

She hesitated and then shook her head. "Like Papa. He got buried in a grave."

"Yes. Like Papa." I would've thought she was too young to remember my father's passing a year before, but it seemed she remembered something. "So now the police are going to take the little girl's body and bury her in a nicer place, so her family can know what happened to her, and maybe that'll help them to not be so sad."

Sophie nodded sagely, and then scooted off the edge of the bed to return to the window, her little arms resting on the sill. I wondered if I should tell her to come away from the window, to not look, but what was she going to see? If they brought out the body, it'd be in a bag, and I didn't think she'd know what it was. I doubted I could keep her from looking anyway. I put my arm around Sara. "Are you okay, honey?"

She looked up at me. "Yes, Mama."

"You said Tara was your friend. Did she tell you anything about the basement?" I asked.

She thought about it. "She said it was a bad place."

I exchanged a look with Jesse and then asked, "But did she say why? Did she tell you what happened to her?"

Sara shook her head. "She said there was a bad man."

"That's all she said?" I asked. Sara nodded. "Okay." I gave her a hug, and then she pulled away, in a hurry to take up her post at the window. She didn't want to miss anything, especially if Sophie got to look and she was forced to talk to me. I turned to Jesse, and he shrugged, as befuddled by her statement as I was.

I opened my mouth to say something more, but then someone knocked on the doorframe of Sara's room, and I saw Angela Ramirez standing there. "Mrs. Ellis, if you could join us downstairs again."

"Yes. No problem." I got up and went over to the window, putting my hands on my daughters' shoulders. "You girls stay here, okay?"

"Okay, Mom," Sara said, not taking her eyes off the action outside. Among the police vehicles was a van I hadn't noticed. On the side, I could just make out the words *Water Damage*.

"Are they pumping out the basement?" I asked the detective.

"Yes. That's why I need to talk to you. We found something else."
**

Angela waited until Jesse and I were seated on the couch to tell us. "There's a second body. An adult female, it seems."

It took a moment for that to sink in, and when I responded, my voice was as shaky as I felt. I had a pretty good idea of who the woman could be. "The mom?" I asked.

Angela nodded. "Possibly. We won't know until forensics runs tests."

Jesse leaned forward in his seat, staring at his hands. "That would explain why Ash hasn't been in touch with her folks." His expression was pained. He looked up at Angela. "What happened to them?"

"That's what we intend to find out." She turned in her seat, taking in the activity behind her, as people came in and out of our house, disappearing into the basement and reappearing a while later. She turned back to me. "This place is going to be a circus for a while. We're still pumping the basement, and we'll probably be here all night collecting evidence. Is there some place you can stay tonight?"

"I—I don't know. I really need to get a hold of Mark, and—" I hadn't thought about my house being full of people when I called the police. That my girls would be upstairs, staring out the window when they should be sleeping.

"You can stay at my place," Jesse offered. "I'll drive you to the college so you can tell Mark." He glanced at the phone I was clenching in my hand. "Maybe the cell towers are down, and that's why Mark's not answering."

I thought about it and nodded. "Okay. Yes—we'll stay with you. I'll grab some things for me and the girls."

"I'll need your number and address," Angela told Jesse. "We may need to contact her later this evening with more questions." She flipped to a fresh page in her notebook and had Jesse write down his information. I added Mark's cell number and mine. "Who owned the property before you?" she asked me.

"We bought it from a man in Portland. Bob Peterson." I rose from the couch and went over to my desk. "I have his number. He got the house at auction and didn't own it for long. I think it sat empty for a long time during the foreclosure. Before that, it belonged to Nick Stroud." I remembered what Sara said about the bad man. "Do you think he had something to do with this?"

"We'll follow up on all leads," Angela said. "It sounds like you think he might've had something to do with it."

I looked at Jesse, and he nodded encouragingly. "I've had a couple of strange encounters with the guy," I said.

Angela looked at me, her pen poised over her notebook. "Strange how?"

"Well, the girls and I went into his store once. Trinkets, down at the Carousel Mall?" She nodded in recognition, and I continued. "He was really rude to us—for no reason. Then I heard he'd owned the house and ended up losing it, and I wondered if he might be mad about us living here."

"Tell her about his car," Jesse prompted.

"I've seen his car parked across the street on several occasions. Like he was watching us," I said. The detective was listening intently, taking notes, her reaction completely different from what my husband's had been. It felt good to be taken seriously. "Once, I thought Mr. Stroud broke into the basement. There were footprints—Jesse took a photo."

Angela looked at Jesse. "Still got the photo?"

He nodded and pulled up the picture on his phone to show her. "The one on the right is mine. We were trying to compare for size. I wear an eleven, so I'd guess Stroud wears a thirteen."

Angela retrieved a business card from her jacket pocket and handed it to him, tapping her contact information on the card. "Email that to me." Then she looked at me. "You didn't report the break-in?" When I shook my head, she asked, "Why not?"

"Nothing was stolen, so I thought he just wanted to scare us. It seemed like changing the locks would put a stop to it," I answered.

"If he was harassing you, you should've filed a report," she said.

"I thought about it." And I had, but then Mark thought I was blowing the whole thing out of proportion and brushed it off. Thinking about the fight we'd had made me cringe. Part of it had been about Stroud, but part of it had been because Mark thought money spent changing locks had been unnecessary—maybe even indulgent on my part. I remembered how angry I'd been that he hadn't taken the safety issue seriously. Saying all that out loud felt like a betrayal though, so I simply said, "After we changed the locks, things settled down, so I thought…" What had I thought? That he'd gone away? That he'd let go of whatever issue he had with us? No, I'd still been scared, and now it appeared I had good reason.

Angela looked at me, waiting for me to finish. When I didn't, she said, "Okay. We'll look into it. You're free to go, but I'm going to want to follow up with you and your husband tomorrow." She took out a second card and handed it to me. "I'll be in touch."

I pocketed the card. "All right. Thanks."

**

It was a good thing the four of us could fit in the truck because even with the tide going out and the water receding, I don't think my car would've made the trip to the college. Jesse's vehicle had four-wheel drive, and he needed it, plowing through puddles at least six inches deep. He took his time, but even so, I could feel the water gripping at the wheels.

The girls loved watching the water splash up on the sidewalks as we drove past. It's funny how resilient kids can be. As we packed up, I worried about them being traumatized from the police finding not one, but two bodies in the house we shared. I needn't have worried. They were much more interested in the emergency vehicles and high water. To them, death was abstract, something far off and not quite real. The funeral for my father had been closed-casket, so they'd never seen a dead body. I wish I could say the same.

I worried about Dune too. She'd been excited about all the activity and would've gotten in the way with all the officers coming in and out of our house. I'd put her in her dog crate in the house for most of the night but had to let her out before we left. Jesse thought she'd be okay in our yard and wouldn't get in the way of the investigation. I hoped he was right. I worried the wind might scare her, and she'd jump the fence and run off, but there just wasn't room for her in the cab of his truck, and I figured she'd jump out of the back as we were driving. We couldn't take her to his apartment either, so the yard was the best we could do.

It was after nine when we got to the college. I'd been watching the road for Mark's car during the drive, thinking he might pass us on his way home. I could imagine his shock, pulling up to our house to see all those emergency vehicles. I'd tried to warn him though—it wasn't my fault if he got a surprise. He should check his messages more often.

The college hadn't lost power like we had. The light in Mark's third story office window was still on, but the shades were drawn. I knew which window was his from the times I'd brought the girls to see him at work. We hadn't done it much—a handful of lunches in the time since we first moved to the coast and he'd started working there. That stopped several months ago when he'd felt the need to buckle down in the face of budget cut rumors. Now that the cuts had been confirmed, I'd been careful not to interrupt him here. If he was staying late every night and working hard, it was doubtful my presence would've been detrimental, but if he ended up losing his job, I didn't want him to blame me.

I wasn't worried about interrupting him tonight though. That's why, instead of having the girls stay in the truck with Jesse, we all went in. We took the elevator to the third floor, the girls proudly showing Jesse how they knew which buttons to push. They did a silly little dance once the doors closed, and we all laughed. I felt relieved they hadn't been scarred for life by the events of the evening.

When the doors opened, Sara and Sophie raced down to their dad's office near the end of the hall. Jesse and I hurried after them, me half-whispering for them to be quiet, in case other faculty were still around. I thought Dr. Whitfield was. Her light was on, and her office door stood ajar. I promised myself I'd apologize if the girls' antics disturbed her. She was probably under the same pressure Mark was. He had mentioned working on a grant with her and some other colleagues.

I looked up to see Sara push open Mark's office door, and then she and Sophie stood there, staring inside. "Dad?" Sara asked. "Why are you kissing that lady?"

After everything that happened that night, I thought I was done being shocked. I wasn't. Not by a long shot.

I reached the door and heard a woman's voice. "I thought you locked the door!"

I found Cynthia Whitfield straddling my husband, who was sitting in his office chair. Her gray pencil skirt was hiked up, and both of them were hastily buttoning their shirts—his white, hers blue. His jacket had been discarded on top of his cluttered desk, and her heels were strewn across the floor. He stood when he saw me, pushing her off his lap. For a second, it looked like she might go sprawling, but she managed to keep her feet, if not her dignity.

I didn't say a word. What was there to say? I certainly wasn't going to make that apology for my children disturbing people at work. I grabbed the girls' hands, turned, and marched back to the elevator, Jesse close behind. To his credit, he didn't say anything either. He just looked from Mark to me, and left with us.

Behind us, I could hear Mark calling after me. "Tawny! Wait!"

I wasn't going to wait. I'd seen everything I needed to see, and there was nothing he could say to make it right.

Chapter Seventeen

Jesse helped me buckle the girls in the small back seat of his truck, and then we both got inside wordlessly. Before he turned the key, he reached for my hand.

"Don't ask if I'm okay, because I'm not," I told him.

"I know," he said. "Believe me, I know." He did know, didn't he? I'd never asked how he found out about Keri and her new man. I hadn't wanted to pry. I hoped he hadn't found out like I had.

"Mom?" Sara asked.

I took a breath, trying to hide my hurt, and turned to her. "Yes, honey?"

"Are you and dad gonna get a divorce like Jesse did?"

Wow, kid, don't hold back. I felt like she'd sucker-punched me. Jesse looked like he felt the same. For the second time that night, I wondered if parents were supposed to lie or tell the truth in a bad situation. "I don't know, sweetheart. We're going to talk, but right now I'm too mad at him."

"I'm mad too," Sophie said, and I couldn't help but laugh. The situation was ridiculous, just so completely ludicrous, laughing was the only thing that made sense. I felt like my life was careening toward the edge of a cliff, and there was nothing left to do but laugh and ride it out, or fall helplessly while I sobbed my eyes out.

"Know what we need?" Jesse asked. "Ice cream. I've got a whole tub of it back at my place. Plus fixin's for sundaes."

Sara loved that idea. "Let's go stuff our faces!"

I looked at him and nodded my head as I gave him a smile, grateful for the intervention and not about to protest. "Let's go stuff our faces."

**

I figured all that sugar would keep the girls up for hours, but it wasn't like they were going to school the next day. With all that was going on at our house, it wasn't going to happen. I knew the murder story would be all over the news, and I wanted to isolate them from that as long as I could. They didn't need people asking questions, however well-meaning they might be. After that last bite of ice cream, Sophie looked like she was about to fall asleep in her bowl, so I wiped her face and got her settled in Jesse's bed. Sara joined her soon after, and I didn't even make them brush their teeth. After a night like tonight, good parenting was taking a time out. What a rebel I was.

The bed was big enough for me to join them, but I couldn't sleep. Neither could Jesse, apparently, though he had laid out his sleeping bag on the floor of his small studio apartment. It was strange seeing him here. He didn't have much—a kitchenette, a bathroom with a shower, a tiny closet, the bed—which was a mattress set on a metal frame, no headboard—a small TV sitting on a cardboard moving box, and his surfboard. But he was close to the beach, and that's what mattered to him.

He gestured for me to come out on the balcony, and I closed the door behind us so we wouldn't disturb my sleeping daughters. There was a lawn chair there, and he grabbed another, leaned up against the wall, and unfolded it so we'd both have a place to sit. The rain and wind had stopped, finally, and the night was dark. In the absence of the storm, waves echoed, and every now and again, the chirp of a Pacific tree frog joined in. Those sounds gave me a sense of peace on a night when there hadn't been any.

"Thanks for letting us stay here," I said to Jesse. "Even if things weren't crazy at our house with the police, they'd still be crazy because of Mark." There was no way I could've stayed there waiting for Mark to come home, not after what I'd witnessed between him and that woman. I wasn't sure if I could ever look at him again.

"I'm sorry he did that to you," Jesse said quietly.

"How did you find out about Keri? Like that?"

He shook his head. "No. Which is good, because I don't know if I would've killed the guy or congratulated him. I'm just glad that part of my life is done. She's his problem now."

I wasn't there yet, but I thought I could understand how he felt. "I feel so stupid. How could I have not known?"

He shrugged. "Because you're a trusting person. Because you'd never do that to him, and you thought he'd never do it to you either." He scooted his chair to face me and leaned forward, looking into my eyes. "No matter how dumb you feel for not seeing this coming, it's not your fault. You didn't do this."

I knew that, but I could see his point. My default position was to blame myself for things, to apologize so I could avoid conflict. It was something I'd learned to do growing up with a mentally ill parent, but it had to stop. "You're right. This is his fault. But it seems so obvious now—I should've known something was wrong. All those nights he said he was working late, and instead he was with her."

"How long do you think it's been going on?"

I shrugged, and then leaned back in my chair, listening to the rhythmic sound of the waves in the darkness. If I squinted, I could just make out the white crests of the waves. Maybe in the morning I'd have a better view, and I'd have more answers, but for now, I thought about Jesse's question. When had Mark started working late? When fall term started? Before that? I couldn't remember. I knew he started talking about the budget after we bought the house in October, and that was when he began stressing over money and telling me he needed to work late so he wouldn't lose his job.

What would his department head think about the affair? Would Mark lose his job if his boss knew? I had mixed feelings about that. My practical side argued that we still needed Mark's income to pay for our house, but another part of me, an uglier side, admittedly, felt tempted to expose him. I didn't think college administrators would take kindly to faculty using their offices for those kinds of extracurricular activities.

Of course, maybe all the drama about budget cuts had been a lie—a diversion to keep me from questioning him. The budget cuts hadn't made the papers, not yet anyway. Everything I thought I knew had come straight from Mark's mouth. Clearly, I could no longer trust him as a source. It seemed insane to think he'd lie about something big, like the college planning to cut jobs, but a few hours ago I would've said it was crazy to think he'd cheat on me too.

I didn't know when the affair had begun, but I wasn't sure it mattered. I looked at Jesse. "Would it have made a difference if it had been a one-time fling for Keri? Would you be able to forgive her? Even if it was something that had gone on for a while?"

He stared out toward the ocean, considering my question. "I don't know." Well, at least that was an honest answer. He sighed. "I think I could've forgiven her for anything, if she hadn't been so hell-bent on ending the marriage."

"You loved her that much?"

When he turned to look at me, I could see pain in his eyes. "I did. Part of me still does, but we were never going to work. I see that now."

I felt a wave of guilt wash over me. Guilt over my train wreck of a relationship and all the things I should've done to make it work. I found I couldn't hold Jesse's gaze. The strength of his love for his ex-wife surprised me. Did I love Mark that much? I honestly wasn't sure. It was hard to know what I felt for him, other than the anger and hurt presently clouding my judgment.

Living with Mark hadn't been easy, especially over the past several months. It was as though a dark cloud settled over our home. There were times when I felt I walked on eggshells around him, trying not to set him off. How many times had I tried to keep the girls entertained so they wouldn't bother him? He'd been angry with them too, provoked by the slightest things. Sara being too loud, Sophie being overly clingy, both of them wanting his attention.

It wasn't fair—not to them, not to me. I thought about all the times I'd made dinner, hoping he'd join us, only to have him come home late or grab food and retreat to his desk upstairs. I thought about the incident with the Christmas tree, when he'd sulked after finding Jesse helping us decorate. It seemed like no matter what I did, I was wrong, and I couldn't make our marriage work. Even if he hadn't been having an affair, our relationship was in trouble. Maybe it had only been a matter of time before our marriage was going to end. Learning about his dalliance with Cynthia Whitfield just made that happen more quickly.

I must not have hidden my emotions well, because it seemed like Jesse could read my thoughts. Or maybe he knew what I was feeling because he'd stood where I was not that long ago. "What are you going to do?" he asked. "Leave him?"

"I don't know. I don't think I can stay with him."

He nodded. "Yeah. I get that." He laughed bitterly. "Course, for me, leaving wasn't too hard. For you, it might be more complicated."

I stared at him. "What do you mean?"

Jesse spread his hands, backpedaling at my defensive tone. "I mean I was on my own. No kids. No custody issues. Except over the dog."

He was right about that. He packed up his surfboard and his clothes, and he left. He lived on a shoestring budget, but he was surviving, building a new life for himself. My life was a little more complex. I sighed. "You're right. I've got kids *and* a dog. And a mortgage. And no job." I ran my hands through my hair in frustration. "I'm stuck. I can't live with him anymore. I can't. But I can't make it without his income either."

"You're stuck in a pitcher plant." He reached over and put his hand on my arm. "But you don't have to be, if you don't want to be. Far as I can see, you've done everything you can to make this marriage work. He's the one who threw it away. So you take him to court, get alimony, make him pay child support. You get your B & B going, and you find a way to make it without him."

"What if I can't?"

He gave me a smile. "You can. I'll help you."

I returned his smile. "Not to sound depressing, but you might be the first person to ever say that to me. Mark never believed in me, and neither did my family." I hated the bitterness in my voice, but it felt good to talk about things I'd stuffed deep inside. I laughed. "He *hates* my mom and sister. He says they're toxic. He kept me and the girls away from them, like he worried crazy was catching. Turns out he's the one who's toxic."

Jesse didn't say anything in reply, but he held my hand in both of his and nodded, so I continued. I told him things I'd never shared with anyone, aside from my husband. "My mother is mentally ill. Paranoid schizophrenia. It made it hard to live with her, which is why she and my dad got divorced a long time ago. It's also one of the reasons we moved here. She lives with my sister, Marcia, and there's a lot of conflict between them. Marci takes care of my mom, but with all the drama she causes, it's almost as tough as dealing with someone who is actually mentally ill. That kind of bled over into my marriage. Mark couldn't take it.

"When he got the offer to teach at the college, it was an opportunity for us to have some distance from my family. It helped, but my mom and sister thought he was being controlling, isolating me from them." I laughed again, shaking my head. "I guess they were right. But he was right, too—they're just as messed up as he is, and I ended up torn between them and him." I looked at Jesse. "Living away from them has been a good thing for me."

"So I guess moving back isn't an option."

I shook my head. "I think that would be a mistake. I love them, I do. But being around them…it's like they drain me. Like they're psychic vampires. I don't want to live like that again." I looked down at my hand in Jesse's, grateful to be here with him. Grateful for the chance to unload. "Guess my dad couldn't live like that either. He left before I was born, but he was there for me later."

"That's good he came back and helped you."

I nodded. "It was. He passed last year."

"I'm so sorry, Tawny," Jesse said quietly.

I made the mistake of looking into his eyes, and his emotion filled me with warmth and made me want to weep at the same time. He cared for me, maybe more than I realized. There was openness and acceptance in him I'd never seen in anyone before, genuine empathy I'd lacked in other relationships.

I lowered my gaze, blinking back tears. He'd been an amazing friend to me, and I adored him, but I wasn't sure how I felt about being so vulnerable with him, about this new intimacy between us. Thinking about my dad would make me feel like crying even more, and I didn't want to cry in front of Jesse. Instead, I said, "Want to hear something funny?"

He released my hand and leaned back in his chair, as if sensing I needed distance. "Yeah. I do."

"When I was born, Mom hadn't thought of a name for me yet, so she let my sister pick." I smiled, thinking about my mother sharing the story with me, how lucid she'd been when she sat me down to tell it. I remembered the good-natured humor in her eyes, a rare glimpse of who she could be when she was on her meds. "Marci was eight, and at school, they'd read this book about a lion and its tawny mane. I guess my hair was sticking up all over, and it was the same color as that lion's mane, so she wanted to call me Tawny." I laughed. "I mean, who does that? Who lets a kid name an infant?" Jesse shrugged and shook his head, smiling. "I let Sara name our dog Sand Dune, in honor of the beach, but I would never let her name a baby."

"Ah, so that explains it. Little did I know Dune was a nickname. I thought you were a hardcore sci-fi fan."

I smiled. "I am." I'd given him Frank Herbert's book for Christmas.

He grinned and reached over to playfully tug one of my curls. "Tawny suits you though."

"Thanks." I smirked. "I suppose it could've been worse."

"I suppose so. Imagine if she'd been reading Dr. Seuss."

I groaned. I'm as big a fan of Dr. Seuss as anyone, but I didn't fancy being named Horton or Yertle the Turtle, as much as I loved those stories. It felt good to laugh with Jesse though, after having such an awful night. I put my hands over my eyes, and let out a breath. "Well, if there's one good thing about what happened between Mark and me, it's this. No matter how crazy my family is, and no matter how much he thinks their crazy rubbed off on me, he can never fault me again. Not after what he did." I took my hands off my eyes and looked at Jesse. "Remember the meltdown over the Christmas tree?"

He nodded, cringing at the memory, an awkward smile on his face.

"He's been cheating on me all this time, but he had the gall to insinuate something was going on between me and you." I laughed—I still couldn't believe we'd had that conversation. "He said I was spending too much time with you. That you had a thing for me. Can you believe it?"

Jesse got quiet and stared at his hands folded in his lap. He wasn't smiling anymore. "That's not exactly untrue." My eyes widened, and he looked up at me.

Just like that, I knew exactly how I felt about him. I guess Mark had been right after all. I leaned forward, placed my hands on his cheeks, and kissed him.

Jesse kissed me back, pulling me to him as though he needed me as much as I wanted him. Then he stopped, gently pushing me away. "No." I wrapped my arms tighter around his neck, and he reached up and disentangled himself. "No, Tawny. We have to stop."

I sat back in my chair, feeling hurt and ashamed, unable to look at him.

He reached over and ran his thumb over my cheekbone. "It's not that I don't want this. I do." He laughed to himself. "Believe me, I do. But we can't. Not like this." He leaned back in his chair and took a breath. "You're hurt and you're angry, and I don't want this to be some kind of revenge thing against Mark."

I braved a look at him. "That's not what this is." I thought about my first impression of him when we'd met. I'd thought he was cute and I liked him flirting with me. I'd tried really hard to keep some distance, even though we'd grown closer over the months we'd known each other. My girls—and even my dog—loved him. Being around him was easy, uncomplicated. I needed uncomplicated in my life. I needed him.

He held my gaze, studying my face. "Maybe. But you just found out about him tonight, and you haven't had a chance to work through things yet. If you end up leaving him, and you still want this, then yes, I'm absolutely for it. But I don't want you to feel like I've pushed you into anything, not while you're still feeling raw over what he did. You need time."

I stared out toward the waves. I knew he was right, but him pushing me away hurt just the same.

He took my hand again. "I like you, Tawny. I like you enough that I want to wait, and I'll be here for whatever you need." He sighed. "And, like it or not, there's a practical reason for waiting. I don't want him to have anything he can use against you. If he saw us like this—if he could prove there was something going on between us—he could say you cheated first, that you pushed him toward that woman. As it is, he's got nothing, and you have the advantage. He'll have to help you financially, and he won't be able to demand custody of the girls."

"But I don't have any proof he had an affair."

Jesse gave me a sly smile. "Actually, you do. The girls got an eyeful, and I might have taken a photo of your husband in a compromising situation."

My mouth dropped open. "You didn't."

He laughed. "Oh, I did." When he pulled out his phone and showed me the photograph he'd snapped, I couldn't help feeling giddy myself, in spite of seeing a half-naked woman locking lips with my soon-to-be ex-husband.

I think that was the moment I fell in love with Jesse Hayes.

When I checked my phone the next morning, I had several messages. Three from Mark, and one from that detective I'd spoken with the night before. Mark's first message was apologetic. He sounded awfully repentant, and a little bit sniffly. He might've been crying.

He must've just arrived home when leaving the second one because he wanted to know where we were and why the police were at the house. I guess he found out about the bodies by the time he left the third message. In that one he was mad, demanding to know where I'd taken the girls and why I wasn't calling him back. His angry tone gave me absolutely no motivation to call him, and besides, he knew very well why I wouldn't want to return his calls.

I saved his messages in case I needed them later, and called Angela Ramirez instead. She answered on the second ring. After asking how we were doing, she gave me an update on the case. "I spoke with your husband, Mrs. Ellis. He was unaware of the situation when he arrived at your residence last night. I take it you weren't able to get in touch with him?"

"I tried," I told her, wondering how much detail I needed to share. "I left several messages, and then went to see him at his office. But he was occupied, and we didn't get a chance to talk."

"I see. Well, I briefed him on the situation and informed him we would need you to make a formal statement. Can you come in to do that today?"

"Of course. Whatever you need me to do," I said.

"Good. We appreciate your cooperation," Angela replied.

"Are we able to return to the house?" I asked.

"Yes, though we've cordoned off your basement until the investigation is complete," she said. "We pumped out the water and removed the bodies, but we may need to return to collect more evidence."

I wondered how badly the water damaged our house, and when I'd have a chance to see the basement for myself. I imagined my neighbors had suffered similar damage. I guess the upside of living in a crime scene was our basement got pumped for free, though I wouldn't call myself an optimist for finding a silver lining in such a nightmarish situation. "I understand. We have no problem with that."

"I'm not so sure about that," Angela said. "Your husband took issue with our being there."

Well then, he should've checked his messages, I thought angrily. Not to mention the things he *shouldn't* have been doing. "Detective Ramirez, I need to be honest with you," I said, raking my hand through my hair. I started to pace around Jesse's small apartment. He'd been kind enough to take the girls for a walk on the beach so I could make the call. "Mark and I have been having some marital issues. That's unrelated to your investigation, but as far as I'm concerned, you have full access to our property."

"Good," she said. "I'd hate to have to get a search warrant. I will though, if he's unwilling to consent. You should know that even if he doesn't, we can fall back on probable cause since there's evidence of a crime."

"I see. May I ask where things stand with the investigation? Were you able to identify the victims?"

"Not definitely, but we have contacted the Chambers family. I can't disclose details, but I can give you an update when our office issues a press release," she said.

"Thank you. I want to know what happened to them, and help their family, if I can," I told her.

"I *can* tell you that I spoke with Mr. Peterson. He bought the house about six months after Ms. Chambers and her daughter disappeared, so we've ruled him out as a suspect."

That was a relief. Bob Peterson was a nice man—I hated to think he'd been involved. If the police didn't consider him a suspect, we must be cleared as well, since we'd only been in possession of the house for a few months. "What about Nick Stroud?"

"We're looking into that. I can't tell you anything right now."

No, I wouldn't have guessed she could. But maybe I knew something that might help. "I remembered something else about him. I was looking into the history of our house, partly because I was worried about him stalking us, but also because we were hoping to open a bed and breakfast, and I thought people would find the history interesting."

"Okay. What did you find out?"

"His mother died in the house. She fell down the basement stairs." I almost told her where I'd gotten my information, but that felt like a betrayal of Richard Olheiser. I didn't know how much of the story was true, so I just said, "There was a rumor that Stroud pushed her."

"A rumor?"

I laughed nervously. "Yeah—just one of those small town things. But I thought it might be important."

"It might be," she said. "But we didn't find a third body."

"No, you wouldn't, and thank goodness for that," I said. Two bodies in our basement were two too many. "The mother was buried at Ocean View Cemetery."

"You've certainly done some research," she said. She sounded skeptical. I could only guess what she was thinking, but if I were in her shoes, I'd be thinking a certain homeowner had become obsessed with a pretty morbid topic.

"Yeah, well—I was trying to get some history on the house. It wasn't because of Nick Stroud so much as it was because his family built the house and lived there so long," I assured her. "He had a sister who died too, when she was ten. Under strange circumstances."

"Oh?" It sounded like I'd piqued the detective's interest.

"It's probably unrelated, but she disappeared from the house in the middle of the night. She was found drowned in the Necanicum."

"Hmm." There was a pause, and then Angela said, "Well, as I said, we're looking into Mr. Stroud. I appreciate you sharing, but we'll take it from here."

Ah. She was brushing me off. Okay, I could take a hint. "Duly noted. I'll stay out of it."

"Good. I'm glad we understand each other," she said. "Make sure you stop by the station today. We'll need that statement."

I promised I would and finished the call. I wasn't sure if she was taking my concerns about Stroud seriously, but I hoped she would. Who else would've had access to the house to bury the bodies? I couldn't imagine it was a long list.

I wasn't sure what Stroud's motive might've been, but I thought the sequence of events went something like this—his house went into foreclosure, and he was upset about losing it. He stopped by the house before he'd have to turn in his keys, only to discover it was occupied by a couple of squatters. Enraged, he killed Ashley Chambers and her little girl. Then he panicked. He buried the bodies in the basement, thinking he'd get the house back and find a better way to dispose of the evidence—except he never got the house back.

That scenario made a lot of sense to me. It explained why he'd kept an eye on the house, and why he'd broken into the basement. I hoped the detective had enough evidence to arrest him, because if I was right, I had good reason to be scared of him. As long as he was free, he could come after us as well. After all, he knew where we lived.

**

It took me two cups of coffee to work up my courage to call Mark. As I sat on Jesse's balcony, I wrote a few notes for myself, things I wanted to say to Mark. As I'd suspected, Jesse's view was spectacular, even if his studio apartment lacked space and charm. I could see him out on the beach with Sara and Sophie, looking for sand dollars, and I felt gratitude for him. If Jesse hadn't been in my life, I'm not sure how I would've survived the night before. I think finding out about Mark would've devastated me.

As it was, I was still standing, not even close to feeling destroyed. I felt angry and hurt, yes, and frightened about the future, but not as much as I'd feel without Jesse's support. I would have thought the photo he showed me would have crushed me. Instead, I felt empowered, ready to do some crushing.

With that thought in mind, I dialed Mark's number. He answered right away, which was pretty funny considering how many times I'd tried to reach him the night before, without success. I didn't feel like laughing though. "Hi, Mark."

"Tawny? Where are you? Are you okay?" he asked.

Oh, now *he's concerned about my well-being?* "I'm fine. The girls are fine."

"You left your car here. Where are you? I'll come pick you up."

I assumed *here* meant he was at our house. Had he stayed there last night? Probably. We'd left so the girls could get some decent sleep, but Mark could sleep through anything. I could see him doing just that as the investigation continued downstairs. I bet even the roar of the pump sucking out water didn't faze him. I felt annoyed at the thought of him sleeping, when I'd stayed up half the night fretting over a marriage in shambles. Then I thought about that first tearful message he'd left, and realized my assumptions might be wrong. Maybe he hadn't slept well either. "We're in a safe place, but I don't want to see you."

"We need to talk, Tawny. About the police being at our house and about—"

"About what, Mark? About what you were doing with Cynthia Whitfield? Yes, Mark. Let's talk." My anger eclipsed my sadness as I started pacing again, clutching the phone to my ear.

"Tawny, I—" He sighed, as though he'd expected my anger and already had a speech prepared.

"Save it, Mark." I knew how he'd want this to go. He'd say sorry, it was a mistake, it would never happen again, and couldn't I just forgive him and forget about it? Yeah, I could forgive him, in time. But what he wouldn't understand, what I had to *make* him understand, was I was done. I looked at my notes, clenched in my other hand. "Here's what's going to happen. You're going to pack your bags and find somewhere else to live. I want the kids. I'm open to sharing custody, but I'm not willing to shake up our girls' lives more than necessary because of what you did. The three of us will stay in the house, and I expect you to pay child support."

"Stay in the house? Tawny, if you really want to do this, we're going to have to *sell* the house. I don't know why you'd want to stay there anyway, after what was in our basement."

"Maybe we will have to sell it, but I still want to give the B & B a try. You can at least give me that chance. If it gets off the ground, I'll take over the mortgage. If it doesn't, we'll sell and split the profits."

He was quiet for a while. I was tempted to ask if he was still there, but thought it prudent to let him stew. Finally, he cleared his throat and said, "Okay. If that's what you really want."

That surprised me. It scared me a little too—I hadn't been prepared for him to accept my terms so easily, and it left me feeling uneasy, like I was missing something crucial. But maybe he realized, like I did, that we'd been headed this direction for a long time. "It *is* what I want. I'll take care of the divorce papers, you just have to sign them."

"Tawny, I am sorry. If I could take it back…"

No—I wasn't going there with him. I'd said my piece, and I needed to get off the phone before he convinced me to renege. "I know, Mark. We'll come back to the house after three. That should give you enough time to pack what you'll need, initially. We can discuss furniture and anything else later, but I don't want to see you today."

"Okay. Fine. But we *will* talk soon."

"I'll be in touch." With that, I hung up. There was nothing else to say. I couldn't risk him trying to change my mind, and I sure didn't want to know where he was going to stay. Maybe he'd convince Cynthia to take pity on him and let him move in.

What I needed was to not think about him anymore. I needed time at the beach with my beautiful daughters and the kind-hearted man who'd been there for me during the worst night of my life. I didn't know what would happen with Jesse, but I looked forward to finding out.

**

Mark was true to his word and gone by the time we came home. So were one of the suitcases we stored in the closet under the stairs and most of his clothes. With the police gone as well, the house felt eerily quiet. I wondered if Tara was gone too—if she could finally rest peacefully, now that she and her mother had been found. Although Angela Ramirez hadn't confirmed the identities of the victims, I felt sure about who they were, if for no other reason because of the things Sara had told me about her ghostly friend.

I hadn't mentioned any of that to Angela, nor did I plan to. Maybe, a long time from now, Tara's story would become part of the lore of the house, something we might share with B & B guests, so long as we did it respectfully. If Jesse was right, people wouldn't be deterred by the idea that bodies had been buried here. I couldn't see us sharing what happened anytime soon though. Thinking about the horrors Ashley and Tara must've experienced felt raw, like a wound. Talking about it to strangers felt like a violation, like we'd be turning them into victims again.

That was one reason I didn't return calls to our local newspapers. The other reason was I'd promised the detective I'd stay out of it, and that meant letting her office handle the press. I intended to keep my promise. It's funny how fate has other plans.

Chapter Nineteen

W e got access to the basement several days after the investigation began. Angela called and told me she believed her department had collected all the evidence from our house they were able to find, but we should be prepared to cooperate again, should there be new developments in the case. She was careful not to give me too many details. It was frustrating, because I was curious to know what was going on, but I understood.

She did confirm that Ashley and Tara had been identified, based on dental records. I asked her if there was anything I could do for the Chambers family. "Will they be having a memorial service? Should we attend?"

"I can understand why you'd want to, but I have to recommend against that. The family has requested privacy. They're not speaking to the press, and it wouldn't be a bad idea for you to keep a low profile as well," she said. "If you'd like to send them a card or flowers, I think that would be appropriate."

"All right. I'll do that." The least I could do was express my sympathy.

"Mrs. Ellis, this may sound odd, but in your interactions with Mr. Stroud, did he ever say anything about hair?"

"Hair?" The nonsequitur threw me off. Nick Stroud and I hadn't had too many conversations, but I couldn't ever recall him talking about hair. "No, I don't believe so. Why?"

"I followed up on that hunch you had about the Stroud girl. Foul play was never ruled out, so she's in our cold case files. It's been over fifty years, so I was surprised we still had a file on her." She lowered her voice. "Small towns are notorious for bad record keeping, but it seems like Seaside has done okay."

"That's good to hear," I said. She was usually so formal with me, it was odd to hear her letting down her guard.

"What was strange about the Stroud case was a section of the girl's hair had been clipped. She could've done it herself, of course, but it was just one of those odd things that stood out," Angela said. "It even made the papers."

"Hmm." I couldn't remember reading about that in my research, but I might've glossed over a detail like that. "How does that connect to Tara and her mom?"

"It seems the Chambers girl liked to wear her hair in braids."

"Yes, she did," I agreed, remembering how Tara had looked in the school picture.

"When we recovered her body, one of her braids was still intact. The other was clipped," Angela told me.

I felt a chill thinking about it. A tiny connection, but what if it represented some sort of fetish Stroud had, one he'd indulged with his sister in the '60s and more recently with Tara? "Do you think he killed them and kept the hair? Like some sort of trophy?"

"That's what we're wondering," Angela said.

If Stroud was twisted enough to keep something from his victims, what else was he capable of? "Does he sexually assault his victims?"

"We didn't find any evidence of that. After several years in the ground, bodies undergo various stages of decay, so it's difficult to know for sure. I apologize for being graphic, Mrs. Ellis, but I'm trying to answer your question," she said.

"I appreciate it, but after what I saw in my basement, that's hardly graphic," I told her. "How did they die?"

"We suspect he strangled them. The mother first, we believe, then the daughter—though the girl also had several deep wounds, like he'd cut her to the bone," she said.

I thought about the dream I'd had several weeks prior and shivered. The dark figure of a man, leaning over my bed, wrapping his hands around my neck.

"In the sister's case, she drowned," Angela continued, unaware of my growing horror. "The fact that the M.O. was different leaves some doubt as to whether the cases are related."

"But if she was his first victim," I said, "and he was young, he might've done things differently. Maybe he cornered Ashley and

Tara in the house, and strangling them was, I don't know, more efficient."

"Maybe. We're planning to search his house," she said. "We don't have enough evidence to arrest him yet, but if we find Tara's hair in his home, I'm confident we'll have a case the DA would pursue."

"No offense, but why are you telling me this? I thought you couldn't disclose certain details," I said.

"That's still the case, but given your experiences with him, I thought you might have insight into his behavior," Angela explained.

"Are you saying I should be worried about him? That he might come after me and my daughters?"

"No," she said. "I'm asking if you have any other information about his habits, if there's anywhere else we should search for a lock of hair."

The only place I could think of was his toy store, and that's when it hit me. I remembered seeing those antique dolls he'd been so protective of, and how I had been certain they'd had real hair. They'd been in a glass case right near the register, perhaps hidden out in the open, where no one would think to look. They'd had sales tags on them, but that might've been part of the camouflage. He'd been sure to price them high enough that only select customers would inquire about them, and if they did, he could always change his mind about selling them. The dolls had been old, with cracked porcelain and aged clothing. The hair though, had that been old? There was only one way to find out. I shared my theory with the detective, urging her to get a search warrant for Trinkets. She sounded intrigued by the idea and promised to let me know what happened.

**

"Tell me the truth. Is the house toast?" I asked Jesse. We were standing in the basement, surveying the damage. The pump from the clean-up crew was gone, but they'd left industrial fans for us to use for the week. We kept them running night and day to dry out the basement and keep mildew from gaining a foothold. My power bill for the month was going to be sky-high, but at least we hadn't had to pay for pumping.

Jesse inspected the brick walls for damage, running his fingers along fine cracks. Once we'd gotten the okay to use the basement, we'd spent two days cleaning it out, tossing trash, scrap wood, and wilted sheets of paper. Even the antique trunk hadn't been salvageable—the water had soaked right through the cracks in the wood.

Now the space looked empty, void of everything, including the bodies of two murder victims. For the first time since we'd been in the house, the basement felt clean. Not just cleared of filth and garbage, but free of whatever psychic residue had taken hold of this place in the wake of a horrific crime. No longer did I feel the urge to glance over my shoulder, or sense a dark presence out of the corner of my eye. Even the flies that pestered us for months seemed to have vanished. Not for the first time, I found myself wondering if we'd hear from Tara again, or if she was finally at peace.

"Now that I'm able to get a good look at the foundation, I think you might be all right," Jesse said. "I was worried, with all that wet junk stacked against the walls, but the fans seem to be doing the trick. I don't see any major cracks that would indicate your foundation is settling."

"I'm glad we finally cleared this place out," I said. "We probably should've addressed the basement when we first moved in."

"Probably," he agreed, "but you had other priorities."

"Yeah. Not just that though—I hated coming down here. It felt *bad*. Like some part of me knew something was wrong. You know?"

He nodded. "I got that same feeling. But I've felt something like that in other houses too, and I guess I just learned to shrug it off. I've never felt it as strong as I did down here though. Now we know why."

"Yes." I suppressed a shiver and slipped my hand into his. He gave me a small smile in return. We were being careful, taking things slow. No kisses since that first one, but we were more free about casual touches—sitting shoulder to shoulder on the couch, hands brushing when we passed each other in the kitchen. We were still careful to keep distance from each other around the girls though. We both agreed it was for the best until my divorce was finalized.

My daughters knew about the divorce and had taken it as well as could be expected. Sara didn't seem too surprised, but then, she'd been the one to vocalize her objections to seeing her dad kissing someone who wasn't her mom. She seemed angrier with Mark than sad about the separation. Sophie seemed more sensitive than usual, clinging to me at bedtime, asking to sleep in my bed. She missed Mark and had been happy when I'd agreed to let the girls spend the weekend at his new apartment. He hadn't moved in with his lover after all, but I didn't care to ask for details.

Jesse let go of my hand to kneel down and inspect the wooden floorboards leading to the basement's stairway. "I think we're going to have to replace these," he said. "Anything wood is going to show damage, like those first risers on the stairs." He rose and ran his hand over the wall separating the entrance to the basement from the larger room. "Wouldn't be a bad idea to replace this too, though the fans have helped."

I glanced over at the door that led to the yard, remembering the way water had poured through small gaps at the sides and bottom. "What about the basement door?"

Jesse followed my gaze. "Yeah. It's probably okay for now, but eventually, you'll need a new one. It doesn't look warped, so it'll open and close just fine, but I'm sure the water weakened it."

Seemed like there were a lot of things to repair. I hoped that wouldn't delay opening the B & B. "Do you think all that could wait until we finish the kitchen and guest bath?"

He nodded. "I think so. None of what I'm seeing is going to affect your home's structure." He rapped on the wall with his knuckles. "I don't even know why this wall is here. It's not load-bearing. We could tear it down." He looked at the floor again. "Really, you could get rid of this floor and not replace it, unless you want to. Have the whole basement be dirt. It's not that different from what you'd find in a crawlspace, it's just the ceiling is higher." He glanced back at the stairs. "I might put a security door there though. It wouldn't hurt to have a second door that locked, since the outside door has damage and you'll be living here alone."

"I wish you'd move back in with us. You could save on rent." I flashed him a grin. "I wouldn't mind having you around, and I'd feel safer."

He slipped his arms around my waist and kissed my forehead. "Tempting, but we need to be careful. Once Mark signs the papers, we can do whatever we want."

"Yeah. I know." Jesse was right. The last thing I wanted was to give Mark leverage to change our deal.

**

I got a surprise the next morning. A few of them, actually. The first came at 7:30, right after I'd put the girls on the bus and come back inside. I was filling my mug with coffee when there was a knock on the door. Thinking it was Jesse, I didn't even check. I swung the door wide open, a smile on my face. "Well, good morning."

Richard Olheiser was standing at my back door. He looked nervous but brightened when he saw my smile. Shocked as I was to see him, the smile now felt frozen on my face, more of a grimace than a grin. The last time we'd seen each other had been before Christmas, at that gas station when he'd confronted me about not bringing the girls to see Santa. With all that happened since, Richard had been the last thing on my mind. Seeing him now, the memory came rushing back, but I resisted the urge to shut the door in his face. For a second I wondered how he knew where I lived, but then I realized I'd told him. Of course he knew—how could he not, after we'd talked about Mark and I buying Nick Stroud's old house?

"Good morning," he said, his eyes watchful. "I'm sure I'm not who you were expecting." He stood awkwardly, his large form filling the doorframe, one hand tucked behind his back. In the other was a gift bag. I recognized it as the kind he sold in his store.

I wasn't sure what Richard wanted, but he stepped back from the doorway, holding the gift bag out like some kind of peace offering. He seemed to be making an effort to appear nonthreatening. I wasn't too worried, knowing Jesse would be along any moment. I felt secure in the knowledge that if Richard gave me any trouble, Jesse *would* intervene. Still, it seemed prudent to let my visitor know I wouldn't be alone for long. "I was expecting my handyman. He's helping me with my kitchen this morning. He'll be here soon."

"Ah," Richard said, nodding. "I don't want to intrude, but I brought you something." He gave me a careful smile and handed me the gift bag. "The candy is for the girls, and this is for you." From behind his back, he drew out the hand he had been hiding, presenting me with a mercury glass pot filled with paperwhites.

Feeling guarded, I set the bag on the table behind me and accepted the flowers. They were a lovely, clean white against the wreck that was my kitchen. "Thank you. What's the occasion?"

"No occasion, just an apology." He ran his hands through his thick white hair. "I wanted to say I'm sorry for the way I behaved when I last saw you." He sighed heavily. "I meant to apologize sooner, but I've been taking care of my father. He's been ill and, well, he passed away this week."

That melted the icy hold on my heart. I felt my guard slipping away. "Oh, Richard. I'm so sorry."

"Thank you. The funeral was yesterday."

I stared at the man at my door. He was clearly distraught, wringing his hands, looking as though he were fighting to keep his grief in check. There was something boyish about his face, even though I knew he had to be in his sixties. He looked lost. I felt awful for the things I'd thought about him. "Would you like to come in? I just made coffee."

He hesitated and glanced at his watch. "Perhaps just for a moment. My shop has been closed since he passed, and I need to re-open today."

"You don't have anyone else who can do it?" I asked.

He shook his head. "I'm a one-man band with bills to pay, and with Valentine's Day coming, I've got to make up for lost time. That's a bigger holiday than Christmas for those of us in the candy biz."

I'd never thought about that before, but it made sense. It also made sense a small business owner wouldn't have the luxury of taking time off whenever he wanted. Creditors and customers wouldn't care that someone had died. "I'm sorry," I said again. I grabbed another mug and filled it with coffee for him.

He accepted it with a grateful smile. "It's all right." He took a sip. "Tell the truth, it's a relief to be getting back to work. My mind's no good being idle."

I gestured to the living room, offering him the couch. He sat down gingerly, taking up almost two of the cushions. He set his cup on a coaster just as carefully, as though he were aware of how huge he was and took pains to be graceful. I curled up in the armchair across from him, remembering how delicately he'd selected candy when I'd shopped in his store. You wouldn't expect such a large person to move so carefully, but thinking about how much time he invested in his store, the pride he took in making candy, how he'd lovingly embroidered the faces of the Lolly Dollies—he was a man of contrasts.

"I was under a great deal of stress when I saw you last," he said. "No excuse for how I treated you, but there it is."

"Richard, you don't have to say—"

He held up his hand, stopping me, and gave me a sad smile. "I do though—I need to say sorry. My mother always said a real man owns up to his mistakes." He took another sip of his coffee, and then said, "My father had been living with me, but then he starting having lapses in his memory and episodes where he'd wander while I was at work, and I couldn't keep him at home. I moved him into assisted living. I should've known that was a bad idea."

"What happened?"

"Respiratory issues." He gave me a level look. "You know how those places are—filled with germs. His immune system wasn't strong, and I knew it. Sending him there was a death sentence."

"I'm sure you did the best you could for him." I couldn't imagine the guilt he must be carrying, second-guessing his decisions. I reached over and patted his hand. "Caring for parents isn't easy, and sometimes you have to make tough decisions so you can care for yourself too." I knew all about that. Growing up with my mother, trying to help my sister when things got bad because Mom was paranoid and refused to take her meds…it took a toll on my own sanity. Moving away from her was one of the toughest decisions I'd ever made, but it was for the best. My mental health was better for it, and my girls deserved a nicer childhood than I'd had.

Richard gave me a bitter smile. "That's kind of you to say, Tawny." He barked out a hoarse laugh. "The worst thing is I feel more relief than sadness over his death. Isn't that awful?"

I shook my head, thinking about what I'd felt after Mark moved out. There was grief over the dissolution of my marriage, but the relief overshadowed the sense of loss. "Maybe, but it's also understandable. It doesn't make you a bad person." I truly believed that. I had to, or I'd drown in my own guilt—over Mark, and over my mom and sister. I looked up to find Richard watching me carefully, and wondered if he could see some of that guilt on my face.

"My father was a hard man to live with," he told me. "My mother could've attested to that fact—if she'd stuck around."

I stared at him, remembering the obituary I'd found for his mother. "What do you mean?"

"She left my dad when I was ten. But that was in 1960, and divorce simply wasn't done. There was a lot of shame over it—people ostracized us, refusing to shop at the store." He frowned, wringing his hands again. "I remember a man from our church stopping by the house. He told my father it was a sin what my mother had done, and it was Dad's godly duty to get his wife under control."

I put my hand over my mouth, holding in my shock. I knew gender roles were different back then, and that women were expected to be submissive to their husbands, but hearing Richard speak about it was jarring. Things had changed by the time I was born. Divorce was more prevalent, and as far as I knew, no one delivered a speech about morality to my parents when they separated.

"She promised she'd come back for me, but she never did," Richard said, staring into his cup. He looked lost again, and I could see that ten-year-old boy in his face.

"What happened to her?"

He looked at me. "She died. The cops found her car at South Jetty. They figured she stood on the rocks, then slipped into the ocean and drowned. You know how the waves are unforgiving in that area."

I nodded. We'd only lived on the coast a few years, but it seemed like someone drowned every year. It didn't just happen in places like the jetty, where the waves were rough. Sometimes, sneaker waves swept onto a deceptively peaceful-looking shore, taking people out to sea in the grip of the undertow.

"Dad said it was suicide. That she abandoned us," Richard said. "Of course, he never told anyone else that. Suicide was frowned upon more than divorce in those days, and we had enough shame on our heads. But after that, I guess people felt sorry for us, because they started frequenting the shop again."

"I'm so sorry, Richard. I can't imagine what that must've been like." I wanted to say more to comfort him, but there was a knock on the door. "Excuse me," I said, reluctant to leave my chair to answer it. "That would be my handyman." I hated to cut Richard short, in the middle of his story, but I couldn't leave Jesse waiting outside.

I opened the door to see Jesse grinning, holding up a gallon of paint in either hand. "Hello, beautiful. I brought you a present."

I glanced over at Richard, who was rising from his seat and shot Jesse a meaningful look. "Hi, come on in. I've got company."

"Oh," he said, giving Richard an awkward smile as he set the paint cans on the kitchen counter.

I could tell by the color rising to his cheeks Jesse regretted his overly friendly greeting, since we'd agreed to be discreet about our relationship. I felt a little self-conscious myself, realizing I hadn't told Richard about kicking Mark out. Then I thought it was silly to feel embarrassed when Richard had just been so open with me. "Uh, Jesse, this is my friend Richard Olheiser. He owns the Confection Cottage at the Carousel Mall. Richard, meet my friend Jesse Hayes. He's been helping me fix up the house."

Richard approached Jesse, looking at the two of us appraisingly, as if our big secret was blindingly obvious. I suppose it was. He didn't call us out though. Instead, he held out a hand to Jesse. "How do you do?"

Jesse shook with him. "Fine, thanks. Pleased to meet you." He nodded toward the gift bag on the table. "So you're the candy man. Best seafoam I've ever tasted."

Richard smiled. "Thank you. That's one of my favorites to make." He turned to me. "Well, I've got to get to the shop. It was nice to talk with you, Tawny."

I put my hand on his arm. "Take care of yourself, Richard. I'm sorry about your father."

He gave me a smile, nodded to Jesse, and let himself out, closing the door behind him. Once he was gone, Jesse gave me an apologetic smile. "Sorry about that."

I shrugged. "I think it's fine."

"Did you tell him about us?"

I shook my head. "I think he figured it out, but it's nothing to worry about. I didn't tell him about Mark either, but Richard seems to keep to himself." After hearing the story about his family being judged, I doubted he'd go around spreading gossip about mine. "I don't think he'll say anything to anyone."

"That's good." Jesse lifted the paint off the counter and set it on the floor.

"What's that for?"

He smiled. "A present. You said you wanted white kitchen cabinets, and that's what you're going to get." He eyed the paperwhites on the kitchen table. "Course, maybe I should have gone with flowers."

I gave him a grin. "Jealous? Worried about an older man stealing my heart?"

He gave me a smoldering look before kissing me. When he pulled back, he said, "Not at all. Flowers die. Kitchen cabinets are forever."

I laughed, looking at the way the cabinets were hung askew over the countertop. They looked so precarious, I didn't dare put anything in them, only using the lower cabinets to hold dishes and canned food. "Or at least until they fall off the walls."

"Yeah, we're going to fix that before we paint," Jesse said.

Chapter Twenty

I wouldn't say I missed Mark. The longer he was gone, the more I realized how much I'd lived under his thumb and how liberating it felt to be on my own. What I missed was having another adult around, someone to talk with about grown-up things, someone to snuggle up with at night. But it wasn't that I simply wanted Jesse around as a replacement. I was eager to see what would happen with our relationship, but we were friends first, and I truly missed his company when he left work for the day and went back to his place.

The nights were the hardest, when the girls were tucked into their beds and the house was too quiet. I had trouble sleeping. Sometimes it felt like someone was watching me, standing over me while I slept. I would drift off to sleep, doze for a while, and then suddenly wake, sure someone else was in my bedroom. I thought it could be Tara—maybe she hadn't left us after all, but Sara had stopped talking about her. What I felt seemed more foreboding, more sinister. I had more dreams about the shadow man—when his grip tightened, shutting off my airway, I'd wake in a panic.

The worst scare came one night when I woke thinking someone was screaming in my ear. I sat up, heart racing, and looked around my dark bedroom. After a slight rustling sound, I listened intently, scanning the room for signs of movement. Nothing, but then a loud bang from downstairs. Already wide awake, I knew I wasn't dreaming.

I slipped out from the covers and grabbed the baseball bat I'd placed between my bed and the nightstand. After glancing in on the girls, I flipped on the light for the stairwell and padded downstairs, barefoot. Claws clicked on the hardwood behind me, and Dune followed me into the downstairs hallway. Knowing she was there buoyed my courage. Flipping on lights, I checked out the house, searching for an intruder.

I saw no one. The doors were still locked, and no windows were broken. That left the basement. I felt more frightened about going down there than I'd been before, when I thought our house was haunted, but it wasn't a ghost I was afraid of this time.

I stuffed my feet into my sneakers, grabbed a flashlight from the kitchen junk drawer, and clutched my bat before starting down the steps. Dune didn't follow. Instead, she remained on the top step and whined. That did nothing to ease my mind.

When I got to the doorway of the basement, I waited, listening. The only sounds were Dune shifting nervously on the step and my own breathing. I crossed the threshold into the darkness, shining my light around, looking for whoever or whatever had made the noise. The basement wasn't as scary now that it had been cleared out—there was nowhere for someone to hide, and I quickly determined it was empty. Then the beam of my light swept the dirt floor, and I saw that it hadn't been void of an intruder after all.

I clamped my hand over my mouth, holding in a scream. The floor was covered in boot prints—large boot prints—as though someone had been down here, walking around. It hadn't been me or Jesse. I knew what the bottom of my own sneakers looked like, and I was familiar with the tread pattern on Jesse's work boots. How could I not be, after working with him for so long? We'd left footprints all over the place when we cleaned out the basement, and on several occasions, he'd had to work on his knees to repair something, providing a clear view of the bottom of his shoes. The main reason I knew the prints weren't his, though, was the photo he had taken, comparing his footprints to the larger prints. The prints I saw in my basement looked just like those.

I thought about walking upstairs to grab my phone from my desk in the living room so I could snap photos, documenting the footprints. Then the basement door that led to our front yard swung open on its hinges, creaking as a cool breeze swept into the room, stirring the dust. That spooked me and sent me running.

I leaped up the stairs, snatched my phone, and punched in 911. I didn't dare turn my back on the doorway leading to the basement, especially since Dune had planted herself in front of me and was staring at that same spot as she growled, hackles raised. The dispatcher answered, and I asked her to send an officer over. Then I waited, baseball bat poised to strike.

**

Thomas George, the officer who responded, calmly listened to my story. I thought he was too calm, considering someone had been in my house at two a.m., and felt like he brushed off my concerns. I guess I'd envisioned him coming in gun drawn, and then camping out in my driveway for the rest of the night. Without an intruder to arrest, there was little for him to do besides check out the house and then go downstairs to photograph the boot prints. I felt patronized when he advised me to change the lock on the basement door.

"I already did that," I informed him.

"Wouldn't be a bad idea to do it again," he said. "Goodnight, ma'am."

That was why I went downstairs again, to take my own photos, and then sat on the couch the rest of the night, armed with coffee and my baseball bat. I called Detective Ramirez once the rest of the world was awake.

**

"You're sure the prints aren't your husband's?" Angela Ramirez asked me.

"I'm sure. He doesn't own boots like that."

Angela eyed me from her seat in my armchair, her hand gripping a ballpoint pen, her slim notepad balanced on her knee. "But he moved out a few weeks ago?" I nodded, and she made a note. "So he could've bought boots since then."

I stared at her from the couch, holding my coffee mug in both hands, warming them. I was fully dressed, finally getting the courage to go back upstairs and change out of my pajamas once the sun came up. I couldn't seem to warm up though, even wearing my hoodie indoors. I'd felt chilled ever since I'd woken up and realized we weren't alone in the house. "The prints aren't Mark's. Frankly, I don't understand why you're asking about him. Why would he be sneaking into our basement in the middle of the night?"

Angela held my gaze. "You'd be surprised what estranged spouses will do." Her eyes were hard, her jaw tight. I wondered if she was speaking from experience.

I swallowed. "I hear what you're saying, but Mark's not like that. He'd never raise a hand to me or the girls. Besides, there's no reason for him to sneak around. I asked him to leave, but he still has a key, and he's been respectful about the boundaries I set, calling before coming to visit the girls."

The detective nodded and made another note, though she didn't look convinced that Mark wasn't a threat. "You think it was Nick Stroud, then."

I nodded vigorously, relieved she was finally listening to me. "*Yes.* I'm sure it was him. Like I told you on the phone, the prints exactly match the ones we found earlier." I placed my mug on the coffee table and held out my phone, showing her the photos I'd taken. "But now he knows the bodies have been found, so he must be searching for some other evidence, trying to destroy any links back to him."

I was certain Stroud knew the cops were onto him. The grisly discovery of the remains two weeks before had been all over the media—covered by the local papers and even by the television news stations in Portland. Once the bodies had been identified and the Chambers family was notified, the police had held a press conference, and the mystery of what happened to Ashley and Tara was all anyone could talk about.

Luckily, Detective Ramirez kept my family's name out of the press. I heard the grocery store gossip—people in town speculating it was our house where the bodies were found, rumors no doubt fueled by what our neighbors witnessed the night of the storm— but since the police department would neither confirm nor deny the location, it remained just that, speculation. Angela Ramirez hadn't released much information about the case to the press and swore me to secrecy about the details. She felt the department had a better chance of catching the person responsible if they kept confidential certain facts about the crime, things only the killer would know.

"You said Officer George took photos?" she asked. I nodded. "Good. Send me your copies as well."

"Okay," I said. "What happens now? Are you going to arrest Nick Stroud for murder?"

The detective studied my face and then shook her head. "We may have enough to get him on breaking and entering, but not for murder."

I stared at her in disbelief. "You've got to be kidding me. This was *his* house! What other evidence do you need to arrest him?"

"It *was* his house," Angela said. "Technically he didn't own it at the time the murders occurred. Just because he once owned the house, doesn't mean he killed that woman and her daughter."

"But he had access to it," I insisted. I couldn't understand her reluctance to accept his guilt. "I believe Nick Stroud not only had a place to hide the bodies, but motive. I could see him coming back to the house, angry about losing it, and then becoming enraged to find squatters living here. I could see him taking out his anger by killing Ashley and Tara Chambers, and then dragging them down to the basement to hide what he did. Surely you're going to at least question him."

She gave me a level look. "I understand your concern, but I'd appreciate you leaving the investigation to me. For your information, we do intend to question him, and with this new evidence you've provided, we'll be getting a search warrant for his residence." Her eyes narrowed, pinning me in place. "I'm trusting you to keep that confidential. I share it only to allay your obvious fear that I'm not doing my job." The anger in her voice was tightly reined, but I could sense it simmering, building a wall between us.

"I'm sorry," I said, holding up my hands. "It's not that I don't think you're doing your job. I do." I sighed. "But he was here, in the middle of the night, doing who knows what while my daughters and I were asleep upstairs." I reached over and grabbed her hand, trying to tear down that wall. She seemed taken aback, but didn't pull away. "I'm scared, Angela. I'm scared he'll hurt my little girls like he hurt Tara. You can understand that, can't you?"

A dark look crossed over her face and was gone in a flash, hidden by a carefully composed expression of neutrality. I wondered what this woman had been through, if the reason she hid behind a mask of calm professionalism was because of something in her past. I made a mental note to ask Jesse about her divorce. "I recommend you get a restraining order against Nicholas Stroud," she said. I started to object, but she shook her head, stopping me. "I know you don't think it will do any good, but it will set a precedent, documenting that he's been harassing you. That may come in handy. For you, and for our investigation."

I studied her face, waiting for her to say more. She didn't. She just looked back at me with that same neutral expression, and I could see I wasn't going to get any more information out of her. "Okay," I said. "I'll do that. But please keep me posted. I know you can't tell me all the details of the investigation, but please warn me if there's something that could put my girls in danger."

"Of course," she said. I suspected I'd offended her since she flipped her notebook closed and rose from her chair, ready to leave. "I have no intention of letting harm come to your family. You're going to have to trust me, Mrs. Ellis. We're doing all we can to protect you and find justice for the victims."

**

Jesse wasn't happy when he heard what happened. I'd never seen him so angry. I told him as soon as he arrived that morning, and he stood there in my kitchen, listening, clenching and opening his fists, a dark look on his face. "I wish I'd been here," he said. "I would've made sure he never bothers you again."

"That sounds ominous, but thank you."

Jesse shook his head. "It ticks me off, the thought of him coming here. Even if Stroud had no intention of hurting you, even if he was just trying to scare you." He clenched his fists again. "I never thought I'd want to deck an old guy, but I could punch Nick Stroud. I could punch his lights out." He unclenched his fists and looked at me. "Why didn't you call me?"

"It was too early," I said. "This happened at two a.m."

Jesse crossed over to me and placed his hand on my cheek. "It's never too early. You call, I'll come." He wrapped his arms around me, cradling my head against his chest.

We stayed like that for a while, and I found myself wishing I'd called him instead of the police. He would've believed me, and maybe

Officer George would've considered me more credible if someone else had been with me. "Okay," I said. "If it happens again, I'll call."

Jesse drew back, lifting my chin to look into my eyes. "Good. It would kill me if something happened to you or the girls."

I hadn't expected such a strong reaction from him. I knew he cared for me, and there were times when I thought he might even love me. He hadn't said the words, but standing there in my kitchen, looking into his eyes, he didn't have to. I could see he did.

It scared me, even though I was falling for him too. It hadn't been that long since Mark left. Before that, I couldn't have imagined being with anyone else. I adored Jesse, but I still didn't know if I was ready for someone else, and I wasn't sure it was fair to the girls to start a new relationship. I thought about Jesse a lot at night, when the house was too quiet, when I worried about being there alone.

It was during the day, facing stark reality, that I had my doubts, as much as I loved having him there with me, working on the house. It felt like we already had a partnership, something good that made me feel warm, but I was terrified of screwing it up. What if the problem hadn't been Mark, but me? What if my relationship with Jesse turned out exactly the way my marriage had?

I gave Jesse a smile, hoping he couldn't see the doubt in my eyes. "I'm glad you're here with me now. It helps." I yawned. "What should we work on today?"

He laughed, running his fingers down one of my curls. He led me over to the couch, gesturing for me to sit. "I'm going to finish your kitchen cabinets. You're going to take a nap, Miss Woke-up-at-two-a.m."

I did feel exhausted. "That sounds great, actually." I lay down, resting my head on a decorative pillow.

Jesse grabbed the throw off the back of the armchair, and covered me with it. Then he knelt down and kissed my forehead. "Sleep for a few hours, and then I'll take you to look at tile. You can decide what you want to do about the countertop and backsplash, okay?"

"Okay."

He rose to get to work. As I watched him paint the outsides of the cabinets he'd repaired, I smiled to myself. Why was I doubting this thing between us? Jesse was great. Jesse was *more* than great. It was complicated, sure, dealing with the divorce and trying to move on, and Jesse and I were still tiptoeing around being together at the same time I was paying him to fix up my house. But it was good, and it was working. Maybe I didn't need to have all the answers right at the moment.

He woke me a few hours later, sitting on the couch next to me, running his fingers through my hair. "I'm done," he whispered.

I opened my eyes and glanced toward the kitchen. The doors on the upper cabinets had been in such bad shape, we'd had to toss them, but Jesse assured me the open cabinets would look okay. They looked better than okay. The outsides were white, but he painted the insides a dark teal, giving them a fresh, beachy look that worked well, contrasted against the muted gray floorboards below. It was something extra I never would've thought of, but it was perfect. I stared at him, marveling. "You're a genius. They look beautiful."

He grinned. "Glad you like them. I was nervous about the color."

"It's perfect. The color reminds me of the ocean." The shade he picked was the exact color of our local waves, backlit by sunlight. I held his face in my hands and kissed him.

When I let him go, he chuckled. "Time well spent." He stood and held out his hand to pull me to my feet. "Want to go tile shopping?"

"I do. But I'm scared about the budget. Do you really think we can find something inexpensive that will look good? I don't want to cheapen what you just did."

He nodded. "I think we can. How about subway tiles? They don't have to be stone. White ceramic would look great, and what we save could be put toward your counter top."

"I think I'm going to trust you. You know what you're doing." I kissed his cheek. "Give me ten minutes to freshen up, then we'll go."

**

Out in public, at River & Sea Hardware, we kept our distance from each other. Even so, it felt like a date, walking down the lighting aisle as we made our way to the tile department, cracking jokes over hideous-looking lamp shades. Jesse spotted a flush mount pendant made of art glass the exact color and texture of vomit, if it had been immortalized in glass.

"How about this one? It would really improve the lighting in your kitchen." He managed to keep a straight face.

I started laughing. "I have enough trouble getting Sophie to eat her veggies without triggering her gag reflex. Somehow I don't think a barf-colored light would help."

He laughed too. "Barf-colored? Nice description."

"Oh sure, make fun of the way I describe things." I grinned. "Forget what I said about the cabinets. You have terrible taste."

Jesse gave me a mischievous smile, like he wanted to kiss me again, but then one of the store's employees spotted us.

"Can I help you?" The man pushed his glasses up on his nose, and then his eyes widened in recognition. "Oh, Jesse. Hi, how are you?"

Jesse turned. "Oh hey, John. I'm good. How have things been?"

"Can't complain. Looking for a new light?" the man asked. He eyed the vomit light appreciatively.

I nearly started laughing again, but Jesse shot me a look of warning. "No, actually. We came in to look at tile."

"Ah, right this way." John led us over to Flooring and then showed us several tile samples after Jesse explained what we were after. "You have your measurements?" When Jesse nodded, John said, "Let me know when you're ready, and we can place your order." Then he excused himself so we could talk it over.

Jesse was right—the ceramic tile would work with my style, and the price was much better than marble or travertine. I held up two samples of white subway tile—one with beveled edges, one without. "Which one? I can't decide."

Jesse stepped back, eyeing them from a distance. "Beveled, I think. It has that something extra."

"I agree." I put the samples back and wrote down the item number for the one he liked. Jesse seemed more serious than in the lighting department. I guess he had a professional relationship with the store employee he wanted to maintain. That figured—it was a small town where everyone knew everyone. I remembered he knew Detective Ramirez too, that they'd gone to high school together. "What do you know about Angela Ramirez?"

Jesse looked at me, surprised. He'd been looking at other samples. He held up one of them, featuring small, iridescent blue tiles arranged in a mosaic. "Sorry—I was thinking of this for your guest bath. What were you saying?"

"When I talked with Angela this morning, she said some things that made me wonder about her. She worried about Mark being abusive, but the way she said it, I thought maybe she was speaking from personal experience."

Jesse set the tile sample down carefully before answering. "She might've been." He stared at the tile, tracing the pattern of the mosaic with his finger. "I don't know the whole story, but when she left Steven, it wasn't pretty. He beat her up bad. My guess is he did that a lot, and that's why she left."

I'd suspected as much, but it still shocked me. Detective Ramirez seemed like such a strong woman—intimidating even. I couldn't see her as a victim.

"I know," he said. "The way she carries herself, you'd think she'd be the one doing the beating. She's tough. Always has been."

"But she's a cop. Wouldn't she have reported him? Wouldn't they have believed her?"

Jesse shrugged. "I don't know. I'd hope so, but thing is, I don't think she did report him. I think she just lived with it for a long time."

I couldn't understand that at all. "Why?"

"Embarrassment would be my guess. She's never told me, but based on other things she's said…I think she was ashamed of being a victim in her own home. As a cop, she's supposed to be the one protecting people, not needing protection."

"So she toughed it out," I said.

"Even tough people can get in bad situations. People can trick you—you think they're a certain way, and they sucker you in. You fall in love with them. By the time you realize you were wrong, it's too late."

I nodded, remembering what he'd said about the pitcher plant. Both of us had been trapped in our marriages, but he'd gotten free, and I was working on it. "I guess we both know about that."

He squeezed my hand briefly and let go. "Yeah. We do."

Chapter Twenty-one

L ater that week I got a call from Angela Ramirez. "We've arrested Nicholas Stroud. Can you come in this afternoon to do a lineup?"

"You want me to point him out in a lineup? I don't understand. I've already identified him."

"It's another way to gather evidence," the detective explained. "If you can correctly identify him in a lineup, it gives credibility to your account of him trespassing."

"I don't have to talk to him though, do I?" The thought of being in close proximity with Stroud, knowing he'd been in my house that night, sent fear crawling up my spine.

"No. You'll stand behind mirrored glass. He won't be able to see you," she answered.

"Okay. I'll do it."

At one-thirty, I found myself in a small, dark room, safely hidden behind a one-way mirror, looking into a white room with black lines to indicate height painted on the wall. The detective and another female officer stood with me, which made me feel more secure.

At Angela's signal, pushing a lighted button next to the intercom, five men filed in. They looked remarkably similar in height and age, some with receding hairlines, one with a full head of white hair. I had no trouble identifying Stroud though—I'd caught him staring at my house enough times to know his features. "Second from the left," I told her. "That's Nick Stroud. The guy who broke into my house."

Angela nodded. "All right." She leaned in close to the intercom and pushed another button. "We're done. Thank you."

An officer ushered the men out of the room, and Angela turned to me. "I'd like to speak with you further. Why don't you wait for me while I finish up here?" She looked at the officer. "Haley, would you escort Mrs. Ellis to my office?"

"Yes, ma'am." Haley turned to me. "Right this way, Mrs. Ellis." The young woman led me down a narrow hallway to an office that looked neat but dated. "Can I get you anything?" she asked. "Water? Coffee?"

"A glass of water would be great," I said. "Thank you."

"Sure thing," Haley said, and left to retrieve my drink.

As I sat there waiting, I glanced around the office. If I had to guess, Angela's metal desk had been new thirty-something years ago, probably around the time she was born. Her chair had seen better days too—the fabric threadbare, the cushion visible in some places. The top of her desk was organized though—every form neatly filed in trays, a desk calendar covering the surface. Lying on that was her closed laptop. A sculptural modern vase held pens. No photographs, no other decoration. Spartan, but efficient, not unlike the detective.

I heard a noise behind me and turned. There was some kind of commotion going on down the hallway. I should've stayed in my chair, but my curiosity got the best of me. I rose and stuck my head out of the office, peering down the hallway into the main room of the station, where an officer stood, trying to wrestle a man to the ground.

"She's lying!" the man cried. He turned his head and spotted me, and I realized he was talking about me. "Liar!" Nick Stroud screamed at me. "I never set foot in that house!"

Terrified he'd break free of the officer's grip, I fled into the office, backing up against the desk. Angela Ramirez ran past, giving me a look of warning as she did. *Stay out of this.* Not a problem, Detective. I had no intention of leaving the office until Stroud was back in his cell.

"You got him, George?" Angela asked, and I found the courage to peek out again. Stroud was now cuffed, his hands behind him, and flanked by two officers, Haley and the officer who'd been on call the night of the break-in, Thomas George.

"I got him," Officer George said.

"Good. You and Christina get him in a cell," Angela said. I hadn't realized Haley wasn't a first name, but it fit what I knew about the detective, that she'd call everybody by their last names.

"Yes, ma'am," Officer Haley said, nudging Stroud toward a different hallway, presumably where the cells were housed.

I stepped back from the door as Angela came back down the hall, settling into my chair just before she walked in. She gave me a knowing look but didn't call me out. Instead, she went around her desk and sank into her chair with a heavy sigh. "Sorry about that. That's the third time I've told George to take suspects down the back hall instead of through the front office. Guy's been here six months, and he thinks he knows better than me because he's a man." She rolled her eyes. "Maybe this time he'll finally get why we have these procedures in place."

I felt like I owed her an apology for exacerbating the situation. "I was nosy. I shouldn't have been." She waved me off and retrieved a manila file from her desk drawer, studying it for a moment. "What was he saying about me lying?" I asked.

She laughed, and pulled something from the file, sliding it toward me. It was a photograph of brown hiking boots, covered in dirt. "He's accusing you of planting evidence. He says he never broke into your house, and in fact, you put these boots in *his* house. Tell me that's crazy."

I sucked in a breath. "That's crazy." I shook my head, trying to digest this new information. "How could I do that? I don't know where he lives. Even if I did, *why* would I do that?"

She shrugged. "That's the question, isn't it? What's your motive for framing him?"

"I don't have one. That's insane." I studied her face. She wasn't accusing me, but I wasn't sure if she believed me. "So, he's saying I bought a pair of men's boots, walked around my basement to make footprints, snuck over to his house, and left the boots there, all to accuse him? That I made up all those times he was standing outside, watching our house? That's ridiculous."

She gave me a level look. "I agree. The treads on the boots match the prints from your basement. I bet the dirt on them will match the samples we gathered from your house as well."

I nodded enthusiastically, feeling triumphant. "See? That proves it. He was there, even though he denies it."

Angela frowned, leaning back in her chair. "Maybe. Maybe not. It proves the boots were there, and that evidence was found in his house, linking him to your place. There's a possible case for breaking and entering if the prosecuting attorney chooses to pursue it. But if Stroud makes bail, we won't be able to hold him."

"You can't charge him for murder? I thought that was the whole point behind the search warrant. To find evidence he killed that woman and her daughter."

Angela nodded, lacing her fingers together on top of her desk. "It was. Unfortunately, we haven't found any evidence at his home or business. We followed up on your lead and had the hair on his porcelain dolls tested, trying to find a match to Ashley or Tara Chambers. There wasn't one. That's not to say we won't find something linking him to the murders, but for now, we're back at square one." She held my gaze. "Can you think of anything else that might connect him? Something he's said?"

I thought about it, then shook my head. I never actually saw him in our basement, just loitering outside the house, staring at our windows. There was the knocking on the basement door, but I hadn't caught him doing it. I just saw him driving off in a hurry. What else did I have to offer? That he was a grumpy old man who was angry about losing his house? That didn't make him a murderer.

If he didn't kill Ashley and Tara Chambers, who did? But what if he did kill them, and managed to get away with it because there wasn't enough evidence to convict him? Was he going to come after me and my daughters next? "There's nothing else I can tell you." I clenched my hands in my lap, watching my knuckles turn white. "Isn't there anything that can keep him in jail? A criminal record? Something that shows he's dangerous?"

Angela leaned forward, scanning the details of the file. "He does have a record, but that's still not enough to keep him here."

"Great. For what?"

Her eyebrows furrowed. "You know I can't give you those kinds of details."

That made me angry. "Come on, Detective. You said you would protect me and my family. If you know something that could put us in danger, we deserve to know. Besides, isn't that a public record? I'm sure I could request the information."

She looked from me to the file, as if trying to decide. I figured she'd tell me to go ahead, make a formal request for the information, and then kick me out of her office. She sighed again. "Assault. Several years ago, he and another man were arrested at a bar for fighting and for drunk and disorderly conduct."

"Who was the other man?" I asked.

"Harold Olheiser. Does the name ring a bell?"

I thought about it. "Maybe. I know a Richard Olheiser. Are they related?"

She nodded. "Richard's father. Apparently, Stroud made a disparaging comment about Mr. Olheiser's son."

I was reminded of something Richard had once told me. "Nick Stroud took issue with Richard selling his Lolly Dollies." Angela's eyebrows quirked up in question, so I clarified. "He sells these cute little rag dolls holding lollipops. They were a big hit, and Stroud didn't like the competition with his toy store. Richard said it got heated. Stroud tried to get the property manager to boot Richard from the mall, but luckily, the manager refused."

"And was there any further conflict between Richard Olheiser and Stroud?"

"I don't know," I said. "All I know is Richard said Stroud treated him badly. You could ask him. I'm sure Richard wouldn't mind answering your questions. He's a kind man. He was nice to my girls when Stroud wasn't." I told her about the day in the mall when Stroud chastised Sara, making her cry, and how Richard had cheered her up.

Angela shook her head. "Somehow I can see Stroud yelling at a kid. Why is a guy like that running a toy store?"

"I don't know, but you see what I'm saying. He doesn't like children," I said. Angela started to object, but I held up my hands, stopping her. "I'm not saying he murdered Tara Chambers, but I've seen the low tolerance he has for kids, and I've seen him outside my house." I could feel my control over my anger slipping. "You can't tell me he's not a danger to my family. How am I supposed to protect my girls if he's not in jail?"

"Have you filed a restraining order yet?" she asked.

"No." I still didn't see how a piece of paper was supposed to help.

"Do it," she ordered, pulling a form from her desk drawer. "That's step one. Step two is to call me if he shows up at your house again. In the meantime, I'll talk with your friend, see what he knows about Mr. Stroud. Maybe Mr. Olheiser holds the key to keeping him locked up."

**

Nicholas Stroud didn't stay locked up.

He made bail. I found out when I ran into him at the grocery store. I'd been so scared of encountering him, but we lived in a small town, and I couldn't avoid him indefinitely. Turns out I'd been right to be afraid.

I was standing in the meat department, reaching up for a plastic bag for my hamburger when I sensed someone behind me. "Sorry," I said, shifting my cart to the side to get out of the way. "I can never get these darn bags open." The meat was sealed in plastic, but the hamburger packaging had a tendency to leak, and I hated the thought of blood oozing onto the other items in my cart.

As I thumbed the bag open and slipped the hamburger inside, a man said, "Liar."

I looked up to see Nick Stroud standing in front of me. He'd been drinking—his breath reeked of booze. I backed up into my cart, and my hip sent it banging into the refrigerated meat case.

"Liar," he repeated. "Filthy little liar." He reached out, slapping the bag from my hands. The hamburger hit the tile floor, bursting open. Blood spurted onto my shoes and the side of the meat case.

"I filed a restraining order against you," I told him. "You have to stay away from me." He just smiled and moved closer, towering over me. In the periphery of my vision, I saw someone in a green smock—a Josephson's staff member. "Help me," I called out, afraid to take my eyes off the man in front of me.

The clerk came over, and I felt a sense of relief thinking she'd intervene. Then I saw the smirk on her face and realized she had no intention of helping me.

"She's not just a liar," Jesse's ex-wife said, crossing her arms over her chest. "She's a whore. She's been sleeping with my husband."

"I'm not. And you're the one who left Jesse," I said, knowing full-well that arguing was futile. Keri wouldn't listen to anything I had to say. Never mind the fact that she kicked her husband out so *she* could sleep with someone else, or that Jesse was no longer her husband. The divorce had been finalized a month ago. She was as crazy as Nick Stroud.

I looked around frantically, searching for someone to help me—another staff member, a customer, someone. The store was usually busy, the aisles blocked by elderly people gabbing as I navigated my cart past them as politely as I could. Today there was no one. Surely someone at the checkout would come running if I screamed.

Stroud laughed bitterly. "A liar and a whore. Figures. She's been telling everyone I killed the Chambers kid. But the cops got nothin' on me, little liar." He cocked his fist and drove it into my face. The force of the punch rocked my head back, throwing me against the grocery cart. I managed to grab the handle, but then my feet slipped in the blood on the floor, and I went sprawling.

Keri raised her foot like she was going to kick me in the stomach. I clenched my muscles, and she lowered her foot, laughing.

"Hey! What's going on here?"

I looked up to see someone running toward us. My head was swimming with pain, and the vision in my left eye was blurry. A gangly man in a green smock looked from me to Stroud to Jesse's ex. "What's going on here, Keri?" he asked. His name tag was a shiny gold color and read, '*Brad, Assistant Manager.*' He had one of those thin faces that look youthful, making him seem a few years younger than Keri.

She feigned innocence. "I don't know, sir. These people were arguing, so I came over to see if I could help."

I raised myself up on one elbow. "That's not true. He hit me, and she stood by and watched."

"Tawny?" I glanced up to see a large man striding toward us, shopping basket slung over one arm. Richard. Thank goodness. He pushed past Keri and knelt down beside me, helping me to my knees.

He glowered up at Nick Stroud. "You better get out of here, Stroud. I'm calling the cops."

"Go ahead," Stroud spat. "They'll get a mouthful about you." A crowd was gathering around us, and he glared at Richard first, then the onlookers.

"Idle threat," Richard said, his face full of fury. "I'm not a drunk who punches women." He clenched his fists. "I should punch you."

I grabbed Richard's sleeve. "Don't. He's not worth it. Let's just call the police."

Stroud gave me a dirty look and then turned and shoved past several middle-aged women on his way out.

"Ma'am, why don't we take you into the office," Brad suggested, helping Richard lift me to my feet. He stared at my face. "We should put some ice on that."

"Take a picture," an elderly woman said.

Brad turned to her. "Thank you, ma'am, but I think we've got it under control now."

"Like hell you do," the woman replied. She looked frail, as though her shopping cart were the only thing propping her up. "You didn't see what happened. That guy clobbered her, and your girl there egged him on."

"I did not," Keri snapped. She turned to her manager. "What was I supposed to do? I wanted to help, but I was scared he'd hit me too." She sounded awfully convincing.

"Save it, girl," the old woman said to Keri. She took out her phone and held it up to my face, snapping a picture. I stared at her, and she smiled. "Surprised to see some old lady with one of these? Birthday present from my granddaughter."

"Thank you," I said. I pulled Angela's business card out of my purse. "Can you email that to Detective Ramirez?"

"Yes, I can," the woman said, taking the card. She typed in the address and hit send, and then gave the card back to me. "You get some ice on that now, honey. I'll talk to the police when they come."

Brad took my arm to lead me away, Richard by my side, protective. Keri started to follow, but Brad stopped her, shaking his head. "Ms. Hayes, if what this woman said is true, I'm afraid I'm going to have to ask you to turn in your sales apron. We don't tolerate that kind of behavior at Joe's."

"It is true," the old woman said.

Keri scowled at her, and then lifted her smock over her head, handing it over to Brad. He nodded. "Your last check will be mailed to you."

As Keri left, people applauded. Richard gave me a smile. "Can you get that woman's name and address?" I asked him, pointing to the woman who spoke up on my behalf. "I'm going to send her a gift basket."

He chuckled and left me in Brad's care, walking back to where the old woman was standing.

↑↑

Richard came back and stayed with me to talk to the police. Officer Haley took our statements and snapped another photo of my face, advising me to have my doctor look at it.

"Are you going to arrest Nick Stroud?" I asked her, holding the ice pack up to my cheek.

"Yep. And hopefully this time we can keep him in jail," she said.

"I hope so." I turned to Richard. "Has Detective Ramirez talked to you?"

He nodded. "Yes. I'm afraid I wasn't much help though. I told her what happened between Stroud and me, but it doesn't shed light on the murders."

"It shows what he's capable of," I said, wincing at the cold. The ice was helping take down the swelling, but my cheek still felt like it was on fire. I hoped nothing was broken. My nose wasn't bleeding at least, but I wouldn't be surprised if I ended up with a black eye.

I still had to get groceries—I wondered if my cart was where I left it, and how warm the food was getting sitting there. I texted Jesse, to see if he could pick the girls up at school. I didn't want them riding the bus, getting off at a stop where Stroud could intercept them. I wanted them home, safe with me and Jesse. I looked up to see Richard watching me.

"Are the girls going to be okay? Do you need me to get them for you?"

My phone pinged with a text from Jesse. *Will do. Everything ok?* "Thanks, but I've got it covered," I told Richard. I took his hand. "Thank you for staying with me. If you hadn't stepped in…"

He gave me a sad smile and squeezed my hand gently. "It was nothing. I'm just sorry I couldn't keep him from harming you."

**

After I paid for my groceries—Brad the Assistant Manager gave me a generous discount, probably fearing I'd sue—I drove myself home. Richard offered to drive me, but then he'd have had to come back to the store for his car. "Too much trouble," I said. "Thank you, but I'm okay to drive." The tissue around my eye felt puffy but hadn't swollen shut, and my vision had cleared. I ached, but I could see.

"I'll at least follow you in my car," he said. "I'll feel better knowing you got home all right."

I did, and gave him a friendly wave before I let myself in the house.

Jesse was making a snack for the girls when I came in, slicing apples and spreading peanut butter on saltines while they watched cartoons on TV. When I pulled the door closed, he looked up to see me holding the ice pack against my cheek.

The butter knife clattered on the table as he dropped it and came rushing over. "Oh, Tawny, what happened?"

Sara and Sophie looked up from the TV, concern on their faces. Sophie jumped up from the couch to wrap her arms around my waist. "I'm okay," I told her. "Go on back and sit down, sweetheart. You don't want to miss your show."

Jesse set the snacks on the coffee table and then pulled me into the guest room so we could speak without having to talk over the sound of the television. He gently pried the ice pack away from my face and winced. It looked bad, I knew, a raised purple lump on my left cheekbone. "What happened?" he repeated.

"Got punched by an old man."

Jesse's mouth dropped open. "What?"

I told him the story, how Nick Stroud attacked me, how Keri encouraged him, and how Harriet Neale, the elderly lady with the hip new phone from her granddaughter, had saved the day.

When I finished, Jesse shook his head, disgusted. "Keri. I can't believe her." He looked at me. "I do believe it, but I'm sorry to hear she stooped to that level. Seems low even for her." His eyebrows knit together. "And Stroud..." His eyes hardened. "If he ever touches you again—"

"Officer Haley assured me they're going to arrest him for it."

"They didn't arrest him right then and there?" he asked.

"Stroud left before the police arrived," I explained.

"Oh," Jesse said. He frowned, shaking his head. "Oh no. I'm so glad you had me pick up the girls."

"Why?"

His frown deepened, and he took my hand. "Come on. There's something I need to show you." He led me out the front door, which was odd, since we rarely used it. Anybody who parked in our driveway used the back door.

He closed the aqua-colored door he'd only recently painted so I could see what he wanted to show me. Carved into the surface of the wood were the words, *LYING WHORE.*

The trauma of the last few hours came thudding back. I felt like weeping.

"I'm so sorry, Tawny," he said, watching my reaction. "I'll sand it down and paint over it."

"No," I said, wiping my eyes. "We need to take a photo, send it to Detective Ramirez." Suddenly I felt like screaming instead of crying. "I'm so tired of this. Every time I turn around, there's one more nasty surprise waiting."

"He must've driven straight here after leaving Joe's," Jesse said. "I guess I just missed him doing it because I'd left to get the girls." He clenched his jaw. "He's lucky I didn't catch him in the act."

"You keep saying *him,* but Keri's the one who called me a whore first. How do we know this isn't her doing?"

Jesse looked at the ugly words scrawled across my front door. "It could've been. It's her style, isn't it?"

Considering what she'd done to the paint on my car, I couldn't disagree. "At this point, I wouldn't put anything past her."

He sighed. "I saw it when I drove the girls home. Usually, I take

Broadway to get here, but today Seventh was faster. If I hadn't gone that way, I wouldn't have seen it. Now I wish I hadn't. I'm sorry."

I gave him a weak smile. "Only one thing to do about it now." Holding up my phone, I snapped a photo. "Good thing I've got Detective Angie on speed dial."

Jesse gave me a humorless smile of his own. "She hates it when people call her that."

Detective Angie was not amused. There was cursing on the other end and then she said, "Again? I can't believe it. You're sending me the photo?"

"Already sent."

"Good. One more thing we can hold against him when we arrest him," she said.

"I'm not entirely sure it was him," I reminded her. "It might have been Keri Hayes."

"Regardless, we've issued an APB for Stroud."

"A what?" I asked.

"All points bulletin," she explained. "I've sent it to the neighboring counties as well. We'll catch him, even if he leaves town."

"And how soon before you catch him?"

"If things go as I'd like, he'll be in jail tonight," she assured me.

Chapter Twenty-two

Two days later and Stroud wasn't in jail yet, but my face was still swollen. I'd been having trouble sleeping because of the pain. I was almost asleep when the sound of breaking glass came from somewhere downstairs. I leaped out of bed, grabbing the baseball bat next to my nightstand. I found Dune standing at the top of the stairs, her hackles raised as she stared and growled at something hidden in the darkness of the stairwell. Heart hammering in my chest, I reached for the light switch with one trembling hand. I had the bat gripped in the other, ready to swing at anything that moved.

I flipped the switch, flooding the stairs with light, and I saw someone standing at the bottom, his hand on the banister. Nick Stroud. He stared back at me, scowling for a moment, before starting up the stairs. My swollen cheek began to throb, in synch with my rapidly beating heart.

"Don't come any closer!" I yelled, gripping the bat in both hands now, ready to bring it down on his head. I didn't want to kill him, but there was no way I was letting him past me to prey on my daughters. I'd die first.

"Liar," he said, his voice a low growl. He had a slight limp and used the banister to pull himself up the stairs. "It wasn't enough that you moved into my house. You had to slander me too. Now no one—" He paused to glare at me. "*No one* comes to my store."

"What do you want?" I demanded. He didn't answer, just shook his head and took another step toward me. "Stop—just stop and tell me what you want." I brandished the bat, trying to look menacing. "I don't want to hurt you, but I will."

At that, he laughed, doubling his efforts to get up the stairs. Dune went from growling to barking. "Oh shush, dog," Stroud said. "All I ever wanted was to run my store. To make children happy. But you soiled that with your lies. You told people I was a monster." He shook his head, laughing bitterly. "I never touched the Chambers woman or her kid, but nobody listens to the old man, do they? No, a woman like you makes a fuss, and everybody comes running. But nobody's coming this time."

There was a shadow in the hallway behind him, and then a second man appeared. Richard. I felt relieved seeing him, realizing I wasn't alone with Stroud. Richard looked up at me with my bat, and then at the older man halfway up the stairs. His eyes narrowed, furious, and he charged up the stairs after Stroud. I thought Richard was about to plow into the man, tackling him, but instead, he wrapped one beefy arm around his neck and squeezed. Stroud's hands went to his throat, trying in vain to claw at Richard's arm, but Richard held tight in spite of getting scratched by the man's yellowed nails. After half a minute of struggling, Stroud's eyes fluttered closed, and he grew limp in Richard's arms.

"Is he dead?" I asked as Richard lowered Stroud's body to the stairs.

Richard looked up, meeting my gaze. "No. Just out cold." I let out a breath I didn't realize I'd been holding. "You okay? He hurt you?" he asked.

"I'm fine," I told him. "But if you hadn't come…" I stopped mid-sentence, thinking. "How did you know I was in trouble?"

"I was driving by," Richard said, climbing the stairs. "Saw the dirty old rat peeping in your windows. Then he broke one and climbed in. Pervert."

That explained the sound of breaking glass. I nodded. "We've got to call the police." I turned to go back to my room, to grab my cell, when Richard gently grabbed my hand. I looked down at my hand in his large one and then up at his face.

"Wait," he said.

"For what?"

He gave me a sad smile and reached up, brushing a stray curl out of my eyes. "You're shaking. Here." He guided me over to Mark's desk and pulled out the chair. "Just sit down for a second, catch your breath." I sat down, and he studied my face. "You look so pale, Tawny. He must have given you quite a fright. I'm worried you're going to pass out on me."

I shook my head. "I'm okay. I really think we should call the police before he wakes up."

"We will. Just take a second, gather your thoughts so you can tell the police what happened. Is your phone in your room?" he asked. When I nodded, he said, "Okay, good. I'll grab it and get you a glass of water too."

"Thank you," I called after him. Dune trotted over and put her head in my lap. As I stroked her ears, trying to calm myself down, I saw Sophie peering out of her room. Her eyes were wide with fear. "Everything's okay, Soph."

Richard came out of the bathroom, carrying my cell phone and a glass of water. "Here," he said, handing me the glass. "Drink this. You'll feel better."

I obediently took a swig. It tasted slightly salty, but the water was refreshingly cool, and he was right—I did feel better. I took another drink, trying to figure out what to say when I called the police. I'd probably have to get them to send the paramedics for Stroud, tempted as I was to leave him crumpled in the stairwell, the peeping tom.

Richard turned and saw Sophie. He chuckled, slipping my cell phone in his jacket pocket, as he knelt down on one knee. "Come on out, little one. Everything's all right. Your mom just had a fright, is all."

Sophie nodded at him and then ran over to me, pushing past Dune to hug me. Then Richard patted his knee, and she went over to him to perch there.

"Did all that racket scare you?" he asked her, petting her light blond curls. She nodded. "And your sister slept through it, didn't she?"

"Did not," Sara said. She stood in her doorway, rubbing her eyes. It looked like she'd been crying. She walked up to Richard. "I hid under my bed so the bad man wouldn't find me."

"That was smart," he told her. He looked at me. "How are you feeling now?"

I thought about it. My heart wasn't thundering in my chest anymore, and I felt surprisingly calm, if not a little woozy. I opened my mouth to say so, but found I didn't have the words. My thoughts felt fuzzy, like they were slipping out of reach. And there was an odd buzzing in my ears. "Kinda funny." My mouth felt like it was stuffed full of gauze, slurring my speech.

Richard gave me a smile and then turned to Sophie. "I've been working on a present for you, little one. Would you like to know what it is?" She still hadn't said a word, but she nodded. His smile grew wider. "Do you remember the fairy dolls in my store? The ones in the front window?"

Sophie smiled back at him and nodded again, this time more enthusiastically.

Richard grinned. "I've been making one just for you. She's got the most beautiful wings in the world. Beautiful wings for a beautiful girl."

"Did you make one for me too?" Sara asked. As I looked at her, her image blurred before my eyes, creating two Saras. I blinked, trying to clear my vision.

Richard turned to her. "I did indeed. And one for your mom too. Three dolls for three beautiful girls." His smile faded as he gave Sara a serious look. "They're almost done, but I need one more thing." His voice sounded far away, and I strained to hear him over the growing sound of buzzing.

"What's that?" Sophie asked, her curiosity finally eclipsing her fear of speaking up.

"They still need hair." Richard gave her a small smile and reached inside his coat to retrieve something shiny. A pair of scissors. The light overhead glinted off long, silvery blades. "I can't use yarn for these dolls. They're much too special for that." He glanced from Sophie to the scissors and back again. "It's got to be real hair for the magic to work. Would you mind terribly if I borrowed some of yours?"

Sophie stared at Richard, rendered speechless once again. The buzzing in my ears had grown so loud, I could barely make out what he was saying to her, but between the scissors and the way he was holding my daughter, possessive, just out of my reach, my gut filled with dread.

"It won't hurt, I promise," Richard assured her. "I don't need much—just a lock or two." I could see that the flies had returned. They circled his head in a dark, swirling cloud. That must be where the buzzing was coming from.

"You can cut my hair," Sara piped up. "I don't mind."

Richard turned to her. "Can I? That's very brave, my dear." He motioned her forward with the scissors, and Sophie slid off his knee so her sister could take her place. Sara held out a length of her long, light brown hair, and Richard raised the scissors.

Under the buzzing, someone moaned. It took me a second to realize it was me. "Nnnnn…nooo. Nooo."

Richard chuckled and looked over at me, slumped in my chair, dangerously close to sliding to the floor. "Now, Tawny, you'll have to wait your turn." He looked at Sara and gave her a wink. "I'll have to get a sample from your mother too, of course. I did say there were three dolls, didn't I? Here we go, dear—don't let go of the hair once I clip it, all right?" Sara nodded, and Richard opened the blades of the scissors. The metal looked hard and cruel next to my daughter's soft skin, and I cried out, suddenly certain he was going to harm her.

Instead, he snipped a section of Sara's hair. Sara held the shorn locks tight in her fist. "Good girl." Richard set the scissors on the floor and pulled a zip lock baggie from another pocket in his jacket. "Drop that in here," he instructed her, and Sara carefully placed the hair inside. "Just so." Richard grinned at her and slid the bag closed. "Easy-peasy. Hop down. Sophie's turn."

Seeing Sara's bravery erased any hesitation Sophie might've had. She jumped up on Richard's knee and held out her curls for him to cut. She wasn't even frightened by the flies, which had now settled on Richard's head and shoulders, crawling in his ears and mouth. One settled on the handle of the scissors and then flitted over to land on Sophie's upheld wrist as Richard snipped her hair.

He sealed her hair into a second baggie and kissed the top of her head, to applaud her for a job well done. "Why don't you and your sister go play in your room? I'd like a word with your mother. I'll come get you in a bit, and then I'll take you to see the dolls." Sophie nodded and took Sara's hand, leading her out of my line of sight. "Good girls," he called to them. "Yes, take the dog with you. Now, close the door and don't come out until I say." The bedroom door clicked as it closed. Then it was just him and me.

Richard eyed me for a moment. "Ah, Tawny. It seems I gave you too much GHB. You're about to fall on the floor. Mustn't have that." He set down the scissors to ease me off my chair, cradling my neck as he laid me on the floor.

"G…h…?" I asked, struggling to form the letters.

"Just a little something the doctor gave my father for his bouts with narcolepsy. Pity he took too much. I warned him about the dangers of mixing his prescription with alcohol—I told him again and again—but when did that old drunk ever listen to me? Respiratory failure, and he blamed me for it." He shook his head, and the fly tracing a course along his eyebrow flitted off. "I could see it in his eyes. Course, I'm not the one who snuck him the booze. I made sure they canned his nurse for that." Another fly trailed the line of his jaw, and he scratched at his chin absently, shooing the insect away as his fingers brushed against his stubble. He didn't seem to notice the flies crawling all over him.

"I'm not saying my father didn't deserve to die, not after what he did to my mother. Did you know he killed her?" He laughed softly, his eyes filled with bitterness. "Killed her and told me she killed herself. That she left me. And I believed him, for years—until I saw him for what he was. Maybe if he'd died instead of her, things would be different. I'd be different." He shrugged. "What can you do? If wishes were horses, beggars would ride." He bent over me, lifting my head to free my hair, spreading it out on the floor. "But we were talking about you, weren't we?"

He retrieved a third baggie from his jacket pocket and reached over for the scissors. I cringed, or at least I thought I did—it was hard to make my body obey my will. My limbs felt heavy, unwieldy. I tried again to speak. "Why? Why…doing this?"

He stared at me as if surprised, and then ran his fingers through my hair, combing out the tangles in the curls so he could make the cut. "Because I love you. You and your daughters. I thought you and

I had a connection. I felt it that first moment you walked into my shop." He cocked his head, looking down at me. "Didn't you?"

I couldn't pull my thoughts together to answer. He chuckled, dismissing me as I opened and closed my mouth like a fish, no words forming.

"It's all right. I don't expect an answer." He selected a length of my hair and cut it, and then laid the scissors aside to place the hair in the bag. As he sealed it shut, he gave me a sad look. "It wasn't meant to be, I guess. Not when you had a happy handyman around. I didn't expect your marriage to last, not with all that fighting going on between you and the hubby." He laughed to himself. "Frankly, I'm surprised you stuck it out as long as you did, with all the nasty things Mark said to you. Not to mention his affair. But I didn't think you'd move on so quickly. I thought I'd at least have time to help you pick up the pieces."

How could he know about Mark and me fighting? I couldn't remember ever telling him about that. I was missing something critical here, but I couldn't think straight, and I couldn't form the questions I wanted to ask.

"It doesn't matter," Richard said, more to himself than me. "I now see you're like everyone else. You'd never be able to understand me, to appreciate the beauty of what I do." He gave me a shy smile. "I realized what my work was missing. I've put so much effort into the artistry of these dolls, I forgot about family. They need someone to look after them—a mother. And though I might fault you for many things, I could never fault you for that." He stroked my cheek. "I wish my own mother had been as gentle and loving as you."

I stared up at him, trying to understand what he was saying, and then I realized I couldn't. Not because I was drugged, but because he'd clearly lost his mind. There was no logic to his madness. I opened my mouth, trying to object, to say something to stop him from doing whatever it was he had planned. I couldn't do a thing.

Richard leaned over and placed his mouth on mine, kissing me. Then he moved on top of me, straddled my hips, placed his large hands around my throat, and began to squeeze. All I could see was his face. Dark spots formed in front of my eyes and the light faded as the sound of the buzzing grew louder, drowning out everything else. Flies crawled on me, over my face, inching toward my eyes. They crawled on my hands, limp by my sides. I willed my hands to obey, to reach up and push Richard off me, but I couldn't move. I just laid there while he squeezed the life out of me.

Then there was a thump that carried over the buzzing of the flies, and Richard's head snapped forward as something hit him from behind. His grip on my neck loosened, and the black spots faded from my eyes. There was another thump, and his full weight was on top of me as something hit him again.

Hands pulled him off me, rolling Richard to the floor. Air flooded my lungs without his hands strangling me or his weight smothering me. I managed to turn my head to the side, fighting the urge to vomit as my vision slowly cleared. There was a man sitting on Richard's chest, punching him in the face—Nicholas Stroud. Beside him was my baseball bat. That explained the thumping noise. Stroud used it to knock Richard out.

Then Richard raised his hands, wrapping them around Stroud's neck. If Richard had been rendered unconscious by Stroud's blows with the bat, he wasn't now. Stroud was older and scrawny compared to Richard Olheiser. He was no match for Richard's size and strength. Stroud's face grew red, and he began to spasm as his oxygen was cut off. I felt cold knowing I'd soon feel Richard's hands around my own neck again. Lying there in horror watching Stroud die wouldn't save me. Nothing would save me if I couldn't get my limbs to work again.

What would happen to my little girls once I was gone? Richard had said something about taking them to see his dolls. I had a feeling that was an empty promise. I wondered if Richard made a similar promise to Tara Chambers, right before he'd cut her hair and murdered her and her mother. *Move Tawny*, I told myself. *You've got to move.*

A cool, small hand touched my cheek, and a girl knelt beside me. Her face was shadowed, backlit from the overhead light, but long, light brown hair hung over one shoulder. Sara? *No, Sara, go back to your room. Hide.* I blinked, and it wasn't my daughter leaning over me. It was a girl I'd only seen in a photograph—Tara.

She gave me a sad smile and faded from sight. A grunt was followed by a tremor through the floorboards as Richard pushed Nick Stroud's body away, letting it fall with a thud. With some effort, he rolled onto his knees.

"Troublesome old goat," he said, panting as he caught his breath. He laughed, looking down at me. "Thought I killed him before, but I guess I was wrong. He'll stay dead now though, don't you worry about that. Just like his sister. She stayed dead, once I held her under long enough." He moved on top of me again and placed his hands around my throat. "And now, my dear Tawny, it's time for you to join them."

Pressure and pain collided as he cut off my air, but my vision stayed clear. With his hands locking my neck in place, I couldn't turn my head, but Tara was visible out of the corner of my eye, watching us. Her touch, cool against my skin, was like a stream of icy water, trickling from my cheek, down my neck and shoulder to my arm, my nerves prickling with pins and needles, like they'd been asleep. I reached for her, silently begging her to help me, and then my fingers closed around something—something hard and cold and unforgiving. Richard's scissors.

I focused my mind, willing my arm to rise. A shock of cold startled me as Tara seized my hand, both of her small hands grasping mine, guiding my aim. Summoning all the strength I had, I thrust the scissors into the soft flesh of Richard's throat, opening a gaping wound.

Surprised, he let go of my neck, rocking back to place his hands over the gash in his throat. Blood seeped through his fingers at first, and then flowed freely. As I regained control over my body, I shoved him off me, and he slumped sideways to the floor, hands still clutching his own neck. It did him no good. He bled out on my hardwood floor.

**

I never saw Tara again. After she helped me deal with Richard, she was gone, vanishing like the flies that plagued me for so long.

I didn't want to touch Richard's body, but I had to, long enough to get my phone back. It was tucked inside a jacket pocket, close to his now still heart. I used it to call 911 and then hung up, not bothering to stay on the line with the dispatcher. Then I called Jesse and asked him to come over. I didn't explain much because it hurt to talk and my voice was weak. I managed to tell him it was an emergency, and the police were on their way.

After that, I crawled over to Sophie's room, not trusting my legs to hold me up. I felt so dizzy, I could only move a few feet at a time before having to rest and breathe. When I opened the door and made it into the room, I collapsed on the floor.

My daughters huddled under the bed with the dog. "It's over," I said. "He can't hurt us anymore." Sara and Sophie crawled out to join me under the window, propped up against the wall. We held onto each other and cried. That was how Jesse found us, right before the cops arrived.

Chapter Twenty-three

I t was Detective Ramirez who figured out how Richard knew so much about my divorce. Scouring his house for evidence, she found a rag doll with dark stains on its dress. The one I happened to throw away not once, but twice. Jesse swore he placed the doll in the dumpster at the park, but Richard must've been watching, salvaging it after Jesse drove off.

I'd often had a feeling of being watched in our house, and attributed the feeling to the ghost sharing our home. I believe Tara communicated with my daughter, but now I know someone else was watching us. When Angela Ramirez found the doll, it lay open on the work table in Richard's basement, in the process of being equipped with a pinhole camera.

On a hunch, she came over to meet with me. Jesse was there too—he hadn't left since he found Stroud's body, Richard lying in a pool of blood, and me and the girls huddled in Sophie's room. Angela asked if we had other dolls in our house, perhaps some Richard had given us. I told her we did, and showed her the two Lolly Dollies we'd purchased from the Confection Cottage.

The detective laid one of the dolls on my kitchen table, took out her pocketknife, and slit the seam in its cheek. "Sure enough," she said, pulling a wire from behind the doll's button eyes. She held up the tiny camera, powered by a battery so small we never would've detected it, had we not opened up the doll's face and retrieved the camera from the nest of cotton stuffing inside. "With visual and audio capabilities, if it's like the other one we found." She shook her head, eyeing me. "He'd been watching you for a long time."

I shuddered at the thought of Richard Olheiser seeing and hearing everything we did. Funny how he'd accused Nicholas Stroud of being a pervert, peeping in our windows, but he was the real deviant. I remembered all those nights I'd had nightmares about someone standing over my bed, watching me. What if those moments hadn't been dreams? I pointed to the battery. "How long does that last?"

"Probably a day or two at most," Angela said. "Why?"

"Because he had to come back to change the batteries. Which means he was the one who kept breaking into the house, not Stroud," I said. I wrapped my arms around myself, thinking about that night I'd gone down to the basement and found footprints everywhere.

"That explains the boots," Angela said. Jesse raised his eyebrows in question. "We found a second pair of boots in Olheiser's house," she explained. "They were the same size as the ones we found in Stroud's house, and they had the exact same treads. When I say exact, I mean *exact*. Even the wear patterns on the boots were the same—he must've doctored one of the pairs before planting them at Stroud's to frame him. Diabolical."

"Richard was a perfectionist. Extremely detail-focused," I said, thinking about the way he was so methodical about every detail in his life—the fairy dolls, making candy. "Stroud *was* telling the truth. He was innocent, and because of me, everyone thinks he was a monster. Because of me, he's dead." I felt pummeled by guilt. I put my hands over my eyes, trying, without success, to hold back tears.

Jesse wrapped his arms around me. "Maybe Stroud didn't kill anyone, but he still punched you. He wasn't a saint, and anyone who saw what he did to you knew that."

I wiped my face and looked up at Jesse. "He was angry, and rightly so. If I hadn't said all those things about him—accusing him of breaking in, killing Ashley and Tara…"

Jesse shook his head. "He had no right to hit you."

"Jesse's right," Angela said quietly. "Even if Stroud was innocent on all other accounts, he did assault you, and clearly, he had bad intentions the night he broke in."

"Richard stopped Stroud, but he had worse intentions," Jesse said.

I shivered in Jesse's arms, remembering how close I'd come to dying, imagining what could've happened to my daughters if I had. The thought of that man's hands on my girls—I couldn't stand it.

But Richard was dead. I'd made sure of that. I felt grim satisfaction in knowing he could never hurt anyone again, but that didn't eclipse my humiliation at the idea that he'd been spying on me.

How could I have been so blind to what he really was? Because he was charming. Richard charmed everyone—me, my daughters, even my dog. I always thought Dune would protect me if someone meant to hurt me, and she did, against Nicholas Stroud. But not Richard, because she thought she knew him, just like I did. He'd broken into our house enough that he was a familiar presence. He probably bribed her with some kind of homemade doggy treat. "I still don't understand why he wanted to kill us. He said it was because he loved us."

"I don't think Richard Olheiser understood what love was," Angela said.

"Of course not. He was evil," Jesse said.

"He was, but that's not exactly what I meant," Angela said to him. She looked at me. "As far as I can glean from his history, he never dated anyone. His mother died when he was young, and he lived with an alcoholic father. Clearly, he wanted a relationship, based on the things he said to you, but I don't think he was capable of having one. I think he was sexually frustrated, perhaps even impotent. I believe that frustration led him to want to kill you."

"But what about the little girls he killed? Are you saying he killed them for the same reason?" I asked.

"We may never know," Angela said. She consulted her notebook. "He kept a journal filled with cryptic notes, some of them about the girls. He seemed to have his own ideology, justifying killing the girls to preserve their purity. He was obsessed with the concept of purity. We know that none of the victims identified so far were over the age of twelve. Except for Ashley Chambers, but I suspect he killed her to get to Tara."

"You were able to identify victims other than Tara?" Jesse asked.

"We've been looking at missing persons cases, matching the hair on the fairy dolls in Richard's store display with evidence from those cases," Angela said. "We matched Tara's DNA to the hair on one of the fairies and the blood stains on the rag doll in his basement."

"Blood stains?" I asked. I felt like I was going to be sick, thinking about getting rid of evidence that might've connected Richard to the murders sooner, if I hadn't insisted on throwing it out. I looked at Jesse. He appeared as nauseated as I felt, the color drained from his face.

The old doll I'd hated so much really had been Tara's. It had been with her at the end. I didn't feel freaked out by the doll anymore, just sad. I wish I couldn't imagine the horror of the last moments of Ashley and Tara's lives, but I could, all too well. And if Tara hadn't helped me…but I couldn't talk about that, not to Detective Ramirez. The only person I'd told was Jesse.

"Yes. We suspected he had slit Tara's wrists, but it was hard to tell because her body was in such bad shape. All we had to go on was damage to her bones from the force of something sharp. Probably a knife, or the scissors he used to cut her hair. Now we know for sure he cut her," Angela replied, oblivious to my internal conflict. "To answer your question, Jesse, the identities of three victims are still unknown, but I'm confident we'll find answers if we broaden our search to include cases from the rest of Oregon and neighboring states."

I stared at her—she sounded clinical, like she was speaking at a press conference. I couldn't tell if that was her personality or a detached demeanor acquired from years of dealing with tragic cases. It'd be tough to stay professional—to not let the heartbreak get to you. I wouldn't want her job.

"But you figured out who some of them were," Jesse said.

Angela nodded. "We did. One of the girls was Mindy Newberry, a local child taken from her home ten years ago. A couple of hikers found her body dumped near Tillamook Head. The mom's boyfriend was arrested in that case but never charged. The other was an unsolved case from 1963. MaryAnn Stroud, who happened to be—"

I cut her off. "Nicholas Stroud's sister. I did a little research when I thought Stroud was stalking me, remember?"

Angela nodded. "I remember."

I gave her a grim smile. "I really thought Stroud was the one who'd killed her, but now I realize Richard had colored my perception of him. I wonder if Stroud ever suspected Richard?"

Jesse shrugged. "We'll never know."

"What we do know is Richard started young," Angela said. "He was in his teens when he killed MaryAnn."

"Given his age, it's astounding there aren't more victims," I said, doing the math. "Six girls in over fifty years."

"Six that we know of," Angela said. "There could be more."

**

I thought about selling the house. Neither the girls nor I could stomach the thought of staying upstairs in our bedrooms, so we'd taken to sleeping in the living room. It was Jesse who convinced me to stay the course, to refinance and finish the repairs so I could open the bed and breakfast. He didn't want me to throw away that dream because some sicko tried to hurt me and my daughters.

Mark was sympathetic enough to help us get a two-bedroom apartment, so we didn't have stay at the house anymore. He didn't come the night Richard attacked me, and honestly, I didn't want him there, even though Jesse called him and told him what happened. He has been there for us financially though, and we agreed to share custody of our daughters.

I don't know what will happen between Jesse and me. We've been taking it slow. Once my divorce was finalized, six months after I found out about Mark's affair, my new relationship was out in the open. Keri hasn't bothered us again—she seems to have finally moved on with her life. I saw her once, walking down the street. I'm sure she recognized my car, but all she did was flip me off. That's hardly intimidating considering all I've been through.

Jesse and I have talked about moving in together, but after mistakes in our past relationships, we're both hesitant to jump in too quickly. For now, he has his place, and the girls and I have ours. I've been helping him build his business, and he helps with the bed and breakfast. We share meals together, and we spend a lot of time at the beach. He's in love with me and my daughters, and we've fallen in love with him, too.

Jesse was right about the house. No one wants to buy a murder house, but plenty of people want to stay in one. We've been booked solid with Seaside tourists and would be ghost-hunters since we opened in June of last year, a mere three months after Richard attacked me. It's morbid, the thought of showcasing the terrible things that happened in that house for the sake of publicity. I certainly haven't advertised it that way, but word gets around, and we live in a small town.

Everyone knows what happened in our house, how a homeless woman and her daughter were killed there and buried in the basement. How my daughters and I almost met the same fate. I guess if there is a silver lining, it's that the horror we lived through is now providing the means for me to care for my family. Still, I can't help but feel like a pariah sometimes.

I don't like to talk about it, but it's been over a year since the attack, and I owe it to Tara to tell her story, to honor her for saving me and my girls. All those times strange things happened in the house, Sara seeing her, the doll ending up in odd places, even the flies and other weird sights and sounds in the basement—I feel certain that was Tara, trying to warn us.

I'm not worried about being haunted by Richard Olheiser though. He's gone for good. Maybe someday I'll be able to forgive him, and find the strength to move back into our house—but not yet.

For now, I have too many nightmares. I can't forget his hands around my throat, or his blood spilling on the floor.

ACKNOWLEDGMENTS

My deepest gratitude to the entire team at Filles Vertes Publishing for the countless hours you spent on Pitcher Plant. My thanks especially to Myra Fiacco for the opportunity to publish with Filles Vertes and for your hard work and encouragement. I'm thrilled to work with you. Thank you to C.L. Rose and the editing team—your insight and suggestions made this book stronger.

My thanks to fellow authors Deb Vanasse, Kate Dyer-Seeley, and Marian McMahon Stanley for your friendship and encouragement, and my gratitude to a number of local writers who provided help in promoting my work or provided feedback on the novel (especially Diana Kirk, Mary Kemhus, Kay Kemhus, Gloria Linkey, Honey Perkel, Brian Ratty, and Paula Judith Johnson). Thank you to Karen Emmerling of Beach Books and Lisa Reid of Lucy's Books, who have hosted me and championed my work for many years. I'm so lucky to belong to a wonderful literary community and I truly appreciate the comradery and support.

Thanks so much to all the friends and family who offered me encouragement as I was writing this book, particularly my parents, Rick and Beverly Eskue, and my aunt, Susan Crabtree, who have all helped more than they know in cheering me on. My thanks especially to Chris, for the many sacrifices you make to give me time to write and for your continual love and support. And finally, thank you to my two beautiful boys, with whom I share a love of reading and underwater adventures. Thanks for joining me to dive with sharks.

Melissa Eskue Ousley is an award-winning author living on the Oregon coast with her family, a neurotic dog, and a piranha. Her debut novel, *Sign of the Throne*, won a 2014 Readers' Favorite International Book Award and a 2014 Eric Hoffer Book Award. Her third book, *The Sower Comes*, won a 2016 Eric Hoffer Book Award. *Sunset Empire*, a fantasy set in Astoria, Oregon, debuted in the bestselling *Secrets and Shadows* young adult boxed set. Her short stories have been included in *Rain Magazine* and *The North Coast Squid*. When she's not writing, she can be found walking along the beach, poking dead things with a stick.